PRAISE FOR THE TRENCH

"... a bold new entry into the Skulldiggery series. It is harder, more violent, and dives deeper into the mystery that has been a common thread throughout, while still introducing fresh characters and new villains. I can't say enough about how well the book is written. The metaphors, the action, finally getting to the meat of the saga, while still combining and explaining elements that have begun in the rest of the series. This felt so satisfying as a series reader... the tragedy of World War I from the first-person view...so many lines that are both poetic and heartbreaking ... such beautiful prose. He illustrates... in such a tangible way (you feel) completely immersed in the story."

  - Kelly McDonough @review_cat86

"If The Devil's Rejects and Creepshow were thrown in a blender you'd get the mind of DM Gritzmacher. With each book of this series you become more and more consumed... As the series grows the Easter Eggs are stocked and The Trench is a full-on Egg Hunt! ...The Trench is just brutal! The gore is absolutely supreme and I am so here for it! ... leaves you fiending for the next book!"

  - Caffeinatedbabbles.com Book Blog

PRAISE FOR THE SHROUD

"The chilling details are both horrifying and gratifying, delivered in a way that feels entirely fresh and new to the horror genre. Gritzmacher again has seamlessly transported this reader through time and place, completely engrossed and covered in goosebumps."
  - Brenda-Brendasbookstack

"... Gritzmacher effortlessly weaves multiple timelines... a fantastic historical horror novel... exquisite world building and diverse characters... like reading a horror version of an Indiana Jones movie..."
  - Lauren-Booksnbeers13

"The Skulldiggery series is phenomenal... overwhelmingly dark, eerie, and atmospheric... gives you goosebumps, has the hair on the back of your neck standing straight up... It's easily become one of my favorite series, and D.M. Gritzmacher has become a favorite author of mine."
  - River Gardner-Horror Author

PRAISE FOR THE LINGERING

"DM Gritzmacher is such a brilliant writer. His ability to infuse historical facts into his stories and make them his own so smoothly while still making it a solid page turner is flawless."
   - Horror Haus Books

"Part National Treasure, part Stand by Me... academic puzzle-solving and coming-of-age adventure. Fast paced, believable likable characters, engaging dialogue, and a gotdamn horrifying monster..."
   - Christine-Amazon

"...being reintroduced to the characters of Secrist and Stander was like meeting up for drinks with old friends. ...strong Stephen King vibes... It really was everything I love in a horror book..."
   - Tersie-Goodreads

PRAISE FOR THE QUARRY

"This book is absolutely amazing, heart wrenching and is very emotional at times. It was very well written and holds your attention the entire time."

- Erin S.-Goodreads

"...an extraordinarily disturbing story emanating from a dark sub terranean maze... From old wives tales to a very real unimaginable evil...

...combines gods, monsters and myths... an advanced level of scariness..."

- Mike Rankin-Horror Bookworm Reviews

"If The Descent was a book, it would be this."

- Gavin-Amazon

"Dark and terrifying. I loved every minute of the book and felt so many emotions while reading."

- Brandy-Goodreads

PRAISE FOR THE RELICT

"...a stunning read... keeps the reader wanting more and more... beautifully written... If you read the Agent Pendergast series by Preston and Child you will love this."

   - Rhonda-Goodreads

"...powerful occult thriller... a gripping blend of horror, thriller, and investigative mystery..."

   - D. Donovan-Senior Reviewer-Midwest Book Review

"Mixing Norse mythology/history with Native American folklore was brilliant. Everything was done respectfully... This is definitely a mystery, horror, thriller and I highly recommend reading this!"

   - Erin, Amazon

"This book was quite the page turner, very well written, a bit creepy and a bit gory and I kept trying to guess what was going to happen at the end! I'll definitely continue on with this series..."

   - Christina-Amazon

THE TRENCH
SKULLDIGGERY BOOK 5

DM GRITZMACHER

PIQUED PUBLISHING

First edition 2024

Library of Congress Control Number: 2024918070

The Trench Print- 979-8-9914556-0-2

The Trench EPUB- 979-8-9866387-9-9

Gritzmonster.com

CONTENT WARNING

The Trench contains graphic depictions of violence, sexual assault, and gore that may not be suitable for some readers.

TRENCH

Trench-1: A long narrow ditch embanked with its own soil and used for concealment and protection in warfare. 1b: Trenches: a place or situation in which people do very difficult work. 1c: Trenching: Long, thin excavations with heavy machinery to determine a site's stratigraphy and to help target areas for hand excavation. 2: A long, steep-sided valley on the ocean floor.

PROLOGUE
FRANCE, 1918

"BANG!!"

A gunshot shattered the silence of the night like a clap of thunder. The pistol cracking loudly before being hastily dropped. The triggered echoes that followed immediately drowned in a sea of anguished wails as the barrel of the revolver smoked listlessly on the damp ground. The ever-present smell of gunpowder growing thick once more within the tightly packed earthen walls where a small faction of soldiers congregated. Though the man who fired the shot – and those huddled around him in support – barely noticed the acrid scent.

"Welcome, my brother. Welcome to the single bastion of sanity left in this ravaged land. I'm so pleased you have chosen to join us." A man in an ill-fitted but highly decorated uniform shouts to be heard above the bloody infantryman's painful cries. "Like the rest of your new family, you have been freed. Free of the shackles that otherwise kept you chained in this Hell. Though I do hope you'll stay here with me and your new brothers."

The pimply-faced soldier who fired the shot looked up from his knees. A grateful and rapturous look plain in eyes swimming with agonized tears. His weeping mixed with the thick blood pouring from the self-inflicted gunshot wound in a red swirl that pooled between his legs. After a few moments, sure hands helped pull him to his feet once more. A piece of torn linen quickly pressed to the bullet wound in the young man's flesh. Though it was far from clean, the soiled cloth helped staunch the crimson cascade and offered some protection from the myriad of contagions the small cluster of men battled daily.

"Rest now, my brother." The uniformed man gestured to a small pile of ratty blankets lying within a nearby dugout, a shallow cavern tunneled directly into the side of the gashed earth where the men were gathered. Framed by thick timbers and sporting dirt walls, floor, and ceiling, it was previously reserved for only the commanding officer's use. But the CO had bartered away the underground location to the uniformed man before he'd been killed. Since then, the location had been primarily used to help them hide, and house the group's diminishing supplies. Though the small mound of scratchy woven cloth the uniformed man pointed at teemed with scabies and lice, the newly injured soldier gratefully lunged for the threadbare comfort it provided. The bite of the night air growing steadily harsher as winter marched ever closer. Inside the little shelter was one of the few dry spots in the earthen ditch he now called home.

The man in uniform squatted beside his new charge. He brushed several squirming parasites away from the top of the blanket before pulling it up to the chin of the young French soldier he now commanded. He gingerly tugged at the linen covering the man's fresh wound, inspecting the damage done by the bullet with a look of satisfaction. He replaced the blood-soaked piece of cloth with a drier, though equally unsanitary one, and dabbed at the gaping hole where the young soldier's nose had been. Before standing, he yanked down the handkerchief that covered the bottom half of his own face, exposing the decayed flesh of his own failing features. Between his eyes, the septum so rotted it barely divided what was left of his two nostrils.

The ruined, skull-like face smiled reassuringly. "The Bible teaches us God made man in his own image. Today, you, like your brothers before you, have severed that claim. Spiting the very face of God. Turning your back on the one responsible for allowing this Hell on earth to flourish.

No God can claim you as their own child. Now, as a man, you can pick your own destiny and path. Help create a new world with us. Find a God worthy of you..."

As the uniformed man regained his feet, he spoke softly to those nearby. "Let him rest for the remainder of the night. We'll need him tomorrow to help replenish our dwindling wood supply." The skeletal faces around him nodded solemnly. Each member of the tiny circle hanging on the uniformed man's every word. Slowly, each of the soldiers covered their equally scarred features one by one. When they were done, only the haunted eyes of the small group of French soldiers could be seen. The bottom of their mutilated faces swaddled in bloodstained cloth.

CHAPTER ONE
PRESENT DAY

THOMAS R. SECRIST TRUDGED wearily up the concrete steps. By the time he reached for the door handle, he knew, as expected, he was in for one very long Saturday night. The music inside the establishment reaching his ears before he'd even cracked the door with *In This Corner* stenciled across the front of it.

"Tommy!" A booming voice immediately rang out from behind the polished wooden bar inside the tavern. The bombastic greeting competing with a soulful Bob Seger as the singer/songwriter pined for more *"Old Time Rock & Roll"* as the tune thumped loudly from the bar's sound system. The long-haired bartender behind the counter flipped a clean Guinness glass once in the air before deftly sliding it under the tap. "About time your sorry ass finally made it," hollered the barkeep as the glass filled. "I was worried you wouldn't get here in time to grab a seat." Tom Secrist pulled out one of the few remaining empty barstools in the crowded establishment and sat heavily onto the padded cushion. By the time his elbows touched down, a coaster labeled "Round One" was slapped between them. Followed close behind by the now full Guiness glass capped with beige-colored foam.

"Go ahead," the bartender, Russell Stander, leaned in close while winking conspiratorially. "Compliment me on the perfect head you always get in here. I know that's why you 'come' so often..." He straightened and did air quotes around the word *come* before sweeping a hand once over his thick grey hair, a wry grin barely visible under his bushy white mustache.

"I don't know about that. But it sure as hell isn't for your good looks or fashion sense." Secrist lifted the full glass while gesturing at the faded jeans and black Alice Cooper shirt Stander sported. Secrist shook his head back and forth slowly as he took a long drink from his beer before dropping the glass back onto the counter and wiping at the foam covering his salt-and-pepper mustache. "Why do I suspect the suitcase for your trip over to France is already packed with more of the same?"

"Because you are, well, *were,* before you retired, a great detective." Stander turned and grabbed at an over-sized bottle of bourbon sitting along the back wall of the bar. He poured the whiskey into two separate shot glasses and placed both on the counter between himself and Secrist. Crowding them onto a new coaster with "Round Two" printed on it.

"The way you dress is elementary, my dear Watson," Secrist implies, channeling the sleuth Sherlock Holmes, one of his favorite fictional characters. "As in, you always dress like an elementary-aged school kid who just saw his first rock concert the night before."

"Iron Maiden and Quiet Riot, Piece of Mind tour in 1983." Stander nodded once before downing one of the two shots in front of him. "That was my first real..."

"I'll be giving you a piece of my mind if you don't move your butt." Behind Stander, a younger woman with wide hips and Polynesian ancestry had taken his place fixing drinks behind the bar. After Stander refilled his shot glass, she nudged him out of her way with the poke of one elbow while grabbing for the bottle of bourbon he'd left sitting beside him.

"Since you are flying out on Monday, aren't you supposed to be out mingling and enjoying yourself tonight? Like, on the other side of the bar?" Smiling, Stander held his hands up in submission and began to make his way out from behind the counter as she splashed the amber colored liquor on top of ice cubes in a short glass. "And out of my way," she finished with a knowing smile, her eyes flashing over to Secrist.

Secrist smiled and nodded back at her, "Hi, Hannah."

"How are you doing tonight, Tommy?" Hannah, the newly promoted manager of the *In This Corner* tavern Stander owned, grappled with various bottles lining the back wall of the bar. Above her head hung a large sign that read "The Sweet Science" blanketed on either side by a full-sized sword and a large shadowbox holding a blown-up color photo of four boys and a well-used, old-fashioned slingshot. The sword, so polished that it practically glowed under the overhead spotlights above, contrasted sharply with the worn and weathered old slingshot. The rest of the bar was decorated in old boxing memorabilia befitting of the tavern's namesake. Dotting the walls were vintage fight posters, framed photos of long retired boxers, cracked leather boxing gloves, and a matching set of faded boxing trunks and robe. In the buzz of the background clatter, Stander, a former prizefighter himself, sang loudly along with the overhead music in between chatting with some of the tavern's regular customers.

"Call me a relict, call me what you will
Say I'm old-fashioned, say I'm over the hill
Today's music ain't got the same soul
I like that old time rock 'n' roll"

Hannah turned towards Secrist as she mixed a series of drinks. "You still staying here in boring old Marquette, Michigan while Stander goes digging around in France? Going to be my emergency back-up or whatever?"

"Yup, I'm just a phone call away if you need me." Secrist lifted his beer once more before adding, "Not that you will. You got this, Hannah. No sweat!" She reached under the bar and pulled out a circular serving tray; the four drinks she'd mixed quickly placed on top.

"Thanks," Hannah flashed a timid smile. "But I am glad you'll be around," she added before hoisting the tray of drinks up in the air. "What are you going to do to entertain yourself while our boss is out pretending to be an archeologist? Any big plans?"

"Me? You mean besides dog sitting Frazier again while he's gone? Nah, not really. But watching Stander take care of all his dad's affairs after he passed – may Dr. Timothy Stander rest in peace – reminded me I still have boxes of crap my dad left me that I've never gotten around to going through. And he died over twenty years ago!" Secrist paused as he took a sip from his beer. "Well, adopted dad. I never actually knew my birth parents..." Secrist smiled wanly as he took a longer drink. "Anyway, I had tossed them all in the attic and just pretended the boxes would disappear. I'm pretty sure they didn't."

"Joy," Hannah said sarcastically. "But hey, maybe you'll find he left you something valuable in one of those boxes. Or find something you'd forgotten about. Life is full of surprises." Hannah, with tray in hand, made her way back down the bar just as Stander reappeared. He was dragging the only remaining barstool without a butt sitting in it from the opposite end of the tavern. He squeezed the tall chair between Secrist and the corner of the bar, crowding the bustling counter.

"I've been meaning to ask you," Secrist began. "Did you ever hear anything more about what happened while we were down in Illinois last month? Maybe from that little town Almore's chief of police or whatever he was?"

"No. Why would I? That was the whole reason we left and came back home so quickly afterwards. To avoid getting dragged into any of that small-town gossip and drama." Stander laid his thick arms across the top of the bar, his full sleeves of colorful tattoos shining brightly under the pendant lights directly above. "If we had stayed working in my great aunt's old mansion like I'd originally planned, it would have only been a matter of time before someone came snooping around asking more questions. Maybe what we found down in that hidden labyrinth under the house had something to do with the accident. But, maybe not…" Stander looked down contemplatively at the full shot glasses sitting on the countertop. Likely just to avoid the eyes of his best friend and career law enforcement officer, Tom Secrist.

"Yeah, right." Secrist let Stander off the hook as he took another swig from his beer. "I'm sure the monster the local guy said he saw 'accidently' tear apart that married couple was completely different than the one we woke up in your aunt's old home." Secrist laid the tone of his sarcasm on thick.

"Who knows what he really saw? Besides, the policeman I talked with that day said it was a car explosion that killed the two of them. But, with all the past history my Great Aunt Madeleine had with that little town, I just thought it was better if we made ourselves scarce." Stander tipped back his drink, savoring the smokey taste as he swished half the whiskey around once in his mouth before swallowing. "After all, ever since someone, namely me, returned to Relict Mansion after it sat abandoned for so long, four people from Almore have now either disappeared or been killed. I'm not going to sit around the place and wait for the villagers to storm the grounds with torches and pitchforks looking for a scapegoat. This is real life, not some ridiculous horror movie where the characters do implausibly stupid things that keeps them in constant peril. I'm the writer of my own script, not some dumbass author without a fucking clue…" Stander downed the bottom half of his drink.

"Speaking of dumbasses without a clue," Secrist skewered Stander with a gaze that left no doubt he was talking about the bar owner. "Are you really taking Chris overseas with you? Do you think that is wise? How long has he been out of rehab now?"

Stander began to nod his head up and down as he replied. "He actually just got out the other day. He asked to stay in the treatment center a little longer, and the team of doctors and counselors onsite thought it would be a good idea. Since money is not really an issue anymore with that family trust I inherited when my dad died, we went ahead and had him stay a couple extra weeks."

"Yeah, but what if he relapses while you are in France? How are you going to take care of a meth addict in a country where you don't even speak the language?" Though Chris had been a childhood friend of Stander's, Secrist had no such ties with the man. Stander had recently rescued Chris from a bad situation in the backwoods community of Almore where access to homegrown and homemade drugs was rampant.

"What other options are there? I can't let him go back to living where he was. Are you going to watch over him while I'm…?" Secrist, with a mouthful of beer, immediately began shaking his head no. "Exactly," finished Stander. "Plus, I know you haven't seen him since he went in, but Chris has come a long way already. He's put on some weight, we got his teeth fixed, and he's a lot different than the messed-up guy you were first introduced to. Who knows? Maybe he can help us figure out all this weird-ass stuff going on lately. Turns out, he's kind of an electronics and computer whiz."

"If you say so. I just hope you know what you're getting yourself into." Secrist had dealt with enough desperate addicts during his law enforcement career to have his doubts. He showed Stander the concern on his face before letting it soften. "Does Lucas know you are bringing company? You know, I think I might even be a little jealous. After all, Chris is going to see this site over in France and meet Lucas in person before I do."

"I doubt that. You said yourself you think whatever Lucas and his little team of trusted archeologists are uncovering is a waste of my time."

"I didn't exactly say that. I just think you need to…"

"What are you two arguing about now?" Hannah swept away the empty glasses in front of both men. Replacing them with another shot of whiskey for Stander and a couple of fresh beers set on top of coasters labeled "Round Three" before continuing. "You two are like some old married couple. Bitching about the other one all the time. Do you ever agree on anything?"

In unison, both replied at the same time. "Music."

Hannah did a slight double-take. Though she'd worked with Stander for more than five years, and had been introduced to Secrist her first day on the job, she'd rarely, if ever, heard the two men agree on anything. Much less answer in stereo. "Wh... what?" She managed to stammer out, shock plain on her features. "The last thing you two *ever* agree on is music. I hear you arguing all the time about what's playing from the jukebox and sound system in here. Or what Stander listens to when you guys go anywhere together in his Jeep. What music do you two agree on?"

"Bob Seger," said Secrist immediately. Stander looked across at him briefly before they both lifted and clinked their beer glasses together. "I can't even remember a time before I loved his music," he added.

Stander looked up at Hannah whose jaw hung slightly open in shock. "And you've heard me put his song, *"Roll Me Away,"* on repeat... uh... a few times before, huh?" The sentence, as all three of them knew, an understatement of epic proportions. "And I'm pretty sure his song *"We've Got Tonight"* helped me get laid after closing time in here more than once." A blissful and far-away look now clouding his blue eyes and a slight smile on his lips.

"Of all the fucked-up answers I would have..." Hannah started to say before stopping herself. "Fishing. Fishing I would have expected and would have been a normal answer. But, Bob Seger? Really?"

"*'Fire Lake*'?" All that Secrist had to say as he turned towards Stander.

"*'Fire Lake' it* is," replied Stander as he stood and made his way back around the bar where the tavern's sound system was housed.

"...Who wants to wear those gypsy leathers

All the way to

Fire Lake"

Secrist held up his previously untouched shot of bourbon as Stander returned to his seat alongside him. In turn, Stander lifted his own glass of "firewater" in salute. "Here's to safe travels back over to France," said Secrist as both men drank. "I hope it doesn't turn out to be a waste of your time."

"Hard to say, Tommy. The archeologists excavating inside the quarry discovered some sort of anomaly. They are telling Lucas it was likely buried sometime in the 19th or 20th century, and not related to their work." Stander set his shot glass down and took a sip of his beer.

"Big deal. Aren't archeologists paid to unearth buried shit and tell you what it is? Why do you have to drop everything and jump on a plane? Can't Lucas just handle it?" Secrist shifted on his stool before lifting his own glass mug and taking two quick swallows. "Afterall, you are paying him to uncover whatever it is buried on the land adjacent to that old Roman quarry. Can't he just walk over with a shovel?"

"We're trying to keep what Lucas and his little team are working on secret until we know exactly what he found. Since the anomaly is buried inside the quarry itself – land I donated to the University – I think they want me present when they unearth it. Based on the shape revealed by the scans, they think it may be a large crate or chest of some kind. So, they are probably just covering their own asses in case it has value. Or if they break it trying to get it out." Stander shrugged; he didn't really mind flying back. It gave him a good excuse to check up on the progress Lucas was making.

"Well," started Secrist, "that sounds interesting. Let me know as soon as you find out something. I'll be anxious to hear what it turns out to be."

Stander grunted his agreement. "Fine. In return then, Tommy, just help keep an eye on the place while I'm gone like we talked about." He gestured all around him at the bar and its patrons. "Here, my apartment above, and what I have locked up below us in the gym. Inside the old bank vault."

"You mean that weird glowing rock we found in that cave and the corroded sword Liz secretly shipped to you instead of the University of Michigan like she was supposed too? The one discovered in the very same cavern up on Mt. Arvon?" Secrist, his voice low, looked up at the steel weapon hanging above the bar. "Don't you think it's time you locked up *that* sword your Great Aunt Madeleine left you when she passed? It's way too much of a coincidence that both of those swords have nearly identical symbols etched into the metal of their blades. And I don't like coincidences."

"Way ahead of you, Tommy. I commissioned some artist down in Detroit to make me an aluminum copy." Stander pointed up at the shiny weapon above their heads. "That is a fake. The real one is already stored alongside the other one down in the vault. I also threw that covering or shroud, whatever it was, that we found at my great aunt's old place down there for safekeeping. As well as that golf ball-sized rock Chris held onto all these years. Just to be on the safe side. When I showed Lucas a picture of that little carved stone, he thought it might be a match for what he is unearthing in France. The size, shape, and weird coloring seems the same as a few other decorative pieces he has found buried near where they are digging."

"Good. I feel better knowing all of that is locked up and out of sight." Secrist finished off the last of his bourbon with a slight grimace. "Funny how, out of all the rundown buildings here in downtown Marquette, you ended up getting such a great deal on this one. The original old Marquette County Savings Bank built back in the 19th century with its very own steel-reinforced concrete vault right in the basement."

"I know! And I'd made them such a lowball offer I didn't think I'd even hear back from the realtor. But good thing I did. This location has turned out to be ideal. Remember when I tried to get a demolition crew in here to take apart the vault and haul it away? They didn't even want to tackle the project. Said it was too big and thick for them and their equipment to handle." Stander lifted his beer and took a long drink. "Wimps."

"Their loss was your gain. Having all that locked up underground behind such thick walls of concrete and steel must help you sleep better at night."

"You know what they say: only a mad dog sleeps undisturbed." Stander smirked as he took another drink from his glass. "And I sure ain't up all night barking at the moon…"

CHAPTER TWO

Tom Secrist pushed at the recessed entryway that allowed access into his home's attic. The rectangular piece of framed wood gave easily, gravity all that held it in place. He pulled himself through the small attic entrance while balanced precariously near the top of an eight-foot ladder. Grumbling and groaning his regrets at the task as he pulled himself inside. The tight opening, dicey footing, and dark hole he disappeared into – all reminders of why he always avoided climbing into the stuffy, cramped space in the first place.

Standing, the top of his salt and pepper colored hair brushed against the beams and wood joints at his head. The climb up the ladder depositing him in the middle of the unfinished attic where the home's roof was at its highest point. The air in the cramped space was stale. A hint of cloying rot wafting through the rafters that made him frown. Secrist reached over and pulled at a frayed piece of string that turned on the only light in the tight quarters; a single naked bulb. The dust-covered lightbulb sprang to life reassuringly, exposing layers of thick insulation that covered much of the ceiling above him and all but about twenty five percent of the floor. Secrist stepped gingerly onto the pieces of plywood laid across the attic joists at his feet. His destination – the stacked pile of boxes and trunk just a few yards from the opening.

One by one, Secrist lifted and moved each cardboard carton without peering inside. Carefully maneuvering the medium-sized boxes over to the claustrophobic attic's entrance where he could reach them from the top of the ladder below. He wanted to haul each down from the attic before beginning the painstaking process of determining what to keep and what to toss or give away. Though he hadn't packed the boxes himself, he'd rummaged through several briefly when he'd first retrieved his dad's belongings after his death.

His adopted father, Howard Davis, a long-time police officer and detective as well as a veteran of the Second World War, had died peacefully of natural causes back in 2000. The boxes, as well as his old footlocker from the war, had all been prepared and labeled well before that. His dad's neatly printed handwriting, though faded with age, still visible on all but one of the storage containers. Most of the cardboard boxes, Secrist already knew, were filled with photos and mementos of Secrist from when he was growing up. As well as personal items from his father and adopted mother, Gale, who'd died of complications from diabetes when he'd been just five years old. Secrist had only the briefest memories of the sweet and gentle woman. Most of them, unfortunately, of her in a cold and harsh hospital room when her condition worsened near the end of her life.

Secrist hated hospitals.

Howard Davis had later moved himself and his adopted son to Michigan after Gale's untimely death. Telling Secrist much later that he'd found he could no longer stay living in her hometown of Rock Island, Illinois. Too many ghosts, he'd said cryptically. So, instead, father and son lived together in Ann Arbor, where his dad took a job working for the University of Michigan Police Department until his retirement. Secrist remained with him until he'd graduated from the University of Michigan with a degree from their Criminal Justice Program. Following his adopted father's footsteps into a law enforcement career of his own before retiring early himself. Stander asking for Secrist's help researching his own family history and offering a salary he would have been a fool to turn down.

Secrist slid aside the last cardboard box and looked down at the battered footlocker in front of him. He recognized the green rectangular trunk from his childhood. It held, he was always told, all of his adopted father's belongings from his time serving overseas in the United States military. Though his dad had opened it a time or two for various reasons – showing a few items of interest to Secrist over the years – the majority of the contents inside were a mystery. The footlocker always padlocked securely and, as a child, Secrist had been forbidden to ever open it. After so much time, he'd nearly forgotten all about the chest. But, upon gazing down at it again, all of Secrist's childhood musings about what it held came roaring back. Absurdly, as he reached in the front pocket of his jeans for the keys, Secrist felt the pangs of his childhood wonderment.

He opened it.

Inside was a long wood tray stretched across the top with two handles on either end. It was only about four inches deep and filled with yellowing envelopes of different sizes. Secrist pawed through the packets, occasionally sliding out what was inside. Most held a myriad of official looking forms and letters. Orders to report, certifications of training, letters of promotion, citations of awards and medals, all now so faded they could barely be read.

Under the envelopes were a number of black and white photos of different planes with various sized crews standing proudly in front of them. One photo was bigger than the others and gave Secrist pause. He recognized his adopted dad standing alongside nine other men all dressed sharply in matching uniforms. Flipping over the picture he saw the name Howard Davis written in black ink along with several other names. Obviously, the other members of the flight crew. Though many of the names had disappeared over time as the ink had faded, he could still make out a few of them. There was a Charles with a "Chuck" written boldly over whatever his last name was. An Andy something or other and someone with the last name of Finn. But the other names were all illegible and now lost to time.

He lifted out the tray and set it to one side. Underneath, Secrist found several U.S Army Air Force uniforms all folded neatly that he took out and set aside. When he reached the bottom of the wood-lined trunk he found a battered shoebox with a number of awards and medals inside along with more conventional sized black and white photos. He started to pull out the small stacks of pictures when he discovered, underneath the photos, a smallish book buried inside with a badly deteriorating blue cover. Attached to the cover was a small handwritten note in his adopted father's neat script. It read:

"'Thomas – You came into my life under the queerest of circumstances and at a time long after I'd given up any hope of ever having a son. I feel lucky to have been entrusted with your upbringing, and I am so proud of the life you have built for yourself and the man you have become. I'd like to think I played at least a small part in that success. Please never doubt that I have always loved you just as much as if you'd been my own flesh and blood. I hope you still believe that after reading this.

"As you already know, that fateful night I was the one who shot and killed your birth father just before he was able to harm you. Unfortunately, again, as you already are aware, I was too late to save your birth mother from the madness that overtook him. This diary was placed in my hands by your mother as she died in my arms. I did enough research into her family to authenticate that the man who wrote this was your birthmother's father – your grandfather. I believe this book is an account of his personal experiences during the First World War. Initially, I told myself I'd pass it on to you once you were older. But after reading a few random pages, I grew afraid. May God forgive me for not honoring your mother's last dying request. May God forgive me for not burning this entire book right now. May God be with you, my dearest son.'"

The message ending with the word "'Love'" and his sloping signature.

For long minutes Secrist pondered the aged book in his hands. Randomly thumbing a few pages and rereading the penned letter attached several more times. Intrigued by this unexpected discovery, he finally tucked the note down into one of his pockets and began carefully inspecting the cover and binding. Though aged and severely weathered, the hard-pressed cardboard and spine still held the pages inside firmly. It was old and crumbling on two corners; the front jacket and first several pages were stuck together from when they'd clearly gotten wet at some point. He flipped past them without reading. Noting that the tight, simply printed handwriting filled each page from top to bottom before eventually snapping the diary shut and laying it on the closed lid of the chest.

Secrist busied himself with the task of lugging each of the cardboard boxes down the ladder. But every time his head crested the attic entrance to grab another box, his eyes were drawn to the diary. His curiosity growing with each descent and ascent. By the time he'd stacked the last of the storage containers neatly against the wall under the attic entrance, his mind was made up. The boxes and what they held could wait. His exploration of the diary's contents could not. After closing up the attic and tucking the ladder back inside the second-floor hallway closet, Secrist made his way downstairs to the ground level.

Secrist's home was a two-story, three-bedroom house at the end of a quiet cul-de-sac in a nondescript area of Marquette, known as Trowbridge Park. It was a modest house that he and his wife had built when they'd first moved to town back in the 1990s. Most of the interior was painted white and trimmed in brown with matching doors. Much of the décor had become slightly outdated with the passage of time, but Secrist didn't mind. Once his wife had passed, Secrist decided he never really wanted to live anywhere else. Or really change much of anything about the home. Though she had been gone near fifteen years now, somehow her presence still lingered here. He couldn't imagine ever leaving, or living, anywhere else.

"What do you think, Frazier? You going to let me squeeze in beside you?" Frazier, Stander's brown and white, pit bull-boxer mix, looked up at Secrist with eyes that conveyed the dog's annoyance with the request. "Come on, now. Move your butt over." Frazier pushed himself up on his paws and begrudgingly made his way slowly to the opposite end of the grey couch before dramatically sighing as he flopped back down on his side. Secrist took his place, sitting down in his usual spot directly across from the living room's television. He reached over and patted the four-legged companion on his backside.

"You know, I wouldn't have to disturb you if you'd quit laying in my seat," he said with a smile before flipping on the lamp beside him. "Now, let's see what kind of guy my grandpa was. And what part he played in the First World War..."

CHAPTER THREE

THE OLD DIARY WAS small, and the simple, hard-pressed cardboard cover unimaginative and nondescript. It was only about five inches across and seven inches long, but it was bursting with crowded writing that filled each page. Thomas Secrist opened the inch or so thick book cautiously. Carefully skipping past the warped and fragile pages at the very beginning of the battered tome. The binding of the journal creaked and cracked slightly as he gingerly widened the book until the lamp beside him lit up the dark and stained passages within. He began reading midsentence at the top of what he guessed was maybe the seventh- or eighth-page in. Thinking to himself that, if he read anything compelling, he could always go back later and try to separate the yellowed, water-logged pages at the very front.

He was pleased to find the writing inside, though printed in what could pass as a grade schooler's careful block style, was easy to read. He was not pleased, however, to find the content inside was so difficult to read. The disturbing beginning like a gut-punch he never saw coming...

...severed arm came off when I tried to help him. The warmth of the soldier's blood coating my own, already filthy, hand. In the chaos of the surging battle raging all around us, I don't think anyone saw me but the man whose twitching limb I still held. The hot meal I'd been so grateful to receive just hours before all came out in a rush. Hot bile covering the limb before splashing down and coating the boots of the one I'd stopped to help. When the awful retching finally retreated, my stomach having nothing left to give, I began to apologize to the injured soldier at my feet.

My words fell on dead ears.

Another thunderous explosion separated me from his empty stare and my own two feet. I was flung backwards and showered with a troubling warmth as a mix of dirt and rock fell all around me. My head ringing and practically deaf from the nearby detonation, I could barely see and used a balled-up fist to wipe at my eyes. When it came back bloody, I grew concerned until I noticed the soldier who had unwittingly lent me his hand was now gone. I still held his amputated appendage and found it had been joined by a combination of steaming parts mixed with my own clinging vomit. My sickness and much of his innards covering my face and chest.

I had no time to care.

A German soldier suddenly vaulted into the pit alongside me. He cast a hurried look my way with eyes wide in terror. But he must have assumed the gore dripping off me was my own blood and guts, dismissing me as a threat. Motionless, I waited until he turned. The blooming violence and firefight around us capturing his attention. I could hear the crack of guns and the rumble of the earth under my back where I lie. The German crawled forward and poked his head out of the circle of mud that surrounded us. The pit, a leftover from a shell fired in some earlier skirmish here on the frontlines of this world-wide war. My hand found the leather-sheathed knife at my waist as I slowly crept towards the unsuspecting German. Without my rifle – still half-buried in the muck at my elbow – I knew my only chance was to surprise him.

Adrenaline surged inside me as I crawled across dirt sodden in years of blood and tears. The dragging motion slowly stripping me of the visceral camouflage and replacing it with a combination of sticky clay and mud. High above our position, I could hear the struggle of sputtering airplane engines competing with the constant barrage of ground-level gunfire and endless cannon detonations. I hoped the German would hear the aerial battles and look to the torn French skies above our heads. It would make slitting his throat that much easier.

A shrill scream to my left was pinched off almost as soon as it started. Immediately to my right, the repetitive pop of a small caliber pistol came and went. Somewhere just ahead of our position was mirthless laughter interrupted periodically by sobs of agony. I'm pretty sure it was the same voice.

The voice of madness.

Still undetected, I was mere feet away when the German soldier dared another look out of the hole we shared. I heard the dull plunk of metal striking metal at the same time the man was flung backwards. At my feet he landed, a perfectly circular bloodless hole in his forehead. I heard the clatter of his helmet as it skidded across the barrel of my rifle still sticking out of the mud behind me. I put the knife back in its leather scabbard with a trembling hand. It felt like I'd just dodged a bullet. Unlike the dead Hun, or Kraut, as the English soldiers so disdainfully referred to our common German foe, lying dead in the wet dirt.

I scampered back to my rifle and pulled it from the soft ground. With skittish eyes I hurriedly wiped the worst of the mud off my gun. I was still in no man's land with hundreds of yards between my current position and where command said I needed to be. The high ground required to take out the German officers I'd been ordered to eliminate. But just as I began to collect my wits and get my bearings once again, three more German infantrymen suddenly jumped into the giant mudpuddle.

Everything after happened so fast that I fear my writing of this tale may be incomplete. But I know it was blind luck that I shot the first one. I squeezed the trigger of the rifle in my hand out of sheer surprise when they appeared. Miraculously, the errant shot hit the first invader in his stomach and he went down immediately, clutching at his guts with wide eyes. When I went to raise my gun to fire upon the next German, the third one jumped so far into the mud pit that he landed right beside me. Upsetting my aim and sending the bullet whizzing harmlessly in the air. Instinctively, I lashed out with the end of my rifle, spearing the long jumper through his throat with the bayonet affixed to the end. The German soldier dropped his weapon and put strong hands on my weapon. Both of us wrestling momentarily before the cascade of blood from his neck eventually weakened the man. When I pulled the blade back to try and run him through a second time, the retreat of my bayonet all but severed his head from his body. He pitched onto his side and gurgled for several long minutes. But I had no time to enjoy the sound of his death throes.

The last German soldier repeatedly fired his gun at me but each wild shot went astray. The soft thud of the bullets punching holes in the mud walls behind me. Triumphantly, I started to fire back. Only to realize that in the earlier melee, I'd forgotten to reload my weapon. The two shots fired moments before the last of the five rounds my trusty Springfield rifle held in each magazine.

The empty clicks reverberated like nails being driven into my coffin.

My eyes met the German's and I saw the shock of not being riddled with bullets reflected back. Though I swear it wasn't until after it was all over that I realized it, the eyes were that of a boy. I lunged and ran my bayonet through him multiple times until I saw those eyes dim and begin to fade. As he convulsed under my weight, his helmet fell away revealing a boy swimming within a man's uniform. He didn't look a day over 14, but I had no time to repent for what felt like murder. There was a hand at my back fumbling for the knife at my belt.

I turned and swung my blood-tipped rifle like a baseball bat. It clipped the German soldier I'd gut-shot earlier high on his head. He spun and wobbled like a marionette strung up by an unhinged puppeteer. I went after him and finished the job. Bludgeoning him with the butt of my rifle until the grey and pink softness in his head oozed from the wide cracks as I opened in his skull.

When I was done, my chest heaved and I swear as I write this hours later, I raved like a madman. Though with the roar of war still pounding away all around me, I doubt any neighboring soldiers paid any mind. When I at last regained some control over my fraying senses, I felt drawn to the young German soldier I'd impaled just moments earlier. I scrabbled at his belongings without knowing why. Without knowing why my eyes burned with hot tears. Without knowing what I was looking for...

Until I found it.

In an inner pocket was a single black and white photo. Scrawled on the back is some faded German writing that I am unable to read but the picture on the front was clear. It was a boy kneeling beside a dog. I couldn't tell what kind of dog it was because the dog was jumping up at the boy with obvious unbridled joy. The boy was light haired and grinning ear to ear as well. The moment captured one of true bliss. Just a boy and his dog. I don't know why, but I took the photo. I'm sure the picture won't last through this awful war. Nothing resembling humanity ever does. But I kept it just the same. Took the single possession of the German soldier I'd bayonetted until he moved no more.

The boy.

I'm not ashamed to admit I collected my helmet on quivering legs. Around me laid the bodies of the four German soldiers, one of them face down in the puddle at my feet. I watched the stained water turn slowly darker as I shakily reloaded my rifle. The last of his blood flowing out and fouling the muddy hole. Above my head and all around me the battle raged on. Shells screaming across the sky before punching huge craters in the battlefield, bullets whizzing from every side. In the rare moments when the artillery slowed or paused, the howling of the injured and dying rose in a cacophony of desperation like the roar of the sea before being snuffed out once more. The sounds of the resuming bombardment either overpowering their cries, or cruelly silencing them once and for all.

I steeled myself briefly against what was to come. My destination – a small stand of leafless trees on one of the elevated knolls of the battlefield – still hundreds of yards away. I reached in my coat and tugged at the inside pocket until I could feel the softness of the bundled hawk feathers I always carry. I asked for a blessing and called out for my tribe's ancestors to help show me the way. I pressed one delicate feather between my thumb and forefinger and rubbed gently as I beseeched my forefathers for their protection. The hawk, as my people well know, has a powerful connection to the divine. Even a single brown and white feather from a mature hawk can tip the balances in our favor. Far outweighing the heaviness of evil no matter where it hides.

Even in a world-wide war.

I took off running. The dying foliage and stunted trees of the small rise my only focus. Darting and dipping as I ran, hurdling the scattered dead of the frontline, zig-zagging across the jagged edges of the trenches I sprinted along the top of. Astonished eyes peering out from grimy faces under battered helmets my only companions. I got within a hundred yards of my destination before the bullets began pitting my path with regularity. My brazen sprint catching the attention, and ire, of the enemy we fought. Somewhere to my left, through the grainy and smoke-filled battlefield, I saw a riderless officer's horse hurtling towards me at full gallop. I skidded to a stop to avoid a collision with the panicked beast, sure this horse had just ended any hope I had of reaching the meager cover I raced for.

Seemingly out of nowhere, a whistling shell detonated and obliterated the wild-eyed steed. The explosion and crater left behind directly in my path. It seems likely, sitting here now in reflection as I write, that the unhitched horse saved my life in its desperation to escape the raging battle. But I had no time to contemplate the reason or even be thankful as more firepower soon began to rain down around me. Somehow, I avoided the deluge and was able to eventually take cover within the stark stretch of broken and clipped trees where I'd been ordered. Hunkering down behind what was left of the battered timber in a low-lying ditch.

Patiently, I stayed perfectly still until the attention I'd drawn with my desperate dash waned. Hidden within a cluster of bark-less trees, dead where they stood. Tucked inside the protective folds of the earth.

As I waited to be completely forgotten by the Germans, I checked and cleaned my rifle. As my squad's designated marksman, or sniper as the United States army had recently begun to call us, I was used to working alone and silently. I loathe the ebb and flow of battles where you had to expect the unexpected and rely on others. But staying silent and still, coiled and deadly as a rattlesnake lying in wait, suits me just fine. I spent my entire childhood learning the skills of the hunter. By age ten I already knew I could handle a long-barreled rifle better than most men. The only difference now was the quarry here in France.

And being paid to kill.

I took my time setting up my shot. The rifle I had been supplied with was a beauty. The Springfield, model number 1903 equipped with the Warner & Swazey 'Telescopic Musket Sight' as it was called. The scope, they said, offered six times the magnification of the human eye. I don't know for sure about that. But the rifle and scope they gave me is a far cry from the outdated hunting rifles I learned to shoot with on the reservation back home on the plains of Oklahoma. Using this new rifle, I practically never miss a target no matter how far away. A fact my superiors are more than happy to exploit.

My two shots were a little less than an hour apart. Using the telescope from my slightly elevated position made it easy to identify the officers I was ordered to assassinate. The first bullet split the head of a German officer foolishly still wearing his stripes on the front line. The panicked scrambling that followed, and blind return fire from the other Hun soldiers near him, lasted maybe twenty minutes before dying back down. Less than thirty minutes later the other officer, now wearing a jacket without stripes, began to relax. His actions returning to normal until I put my next bullet in his chest. The little command post again erupting in blind return fire that never reached my position. Eventually, as the battle soothed with the approach of nightfall, I made my way swiftly and silently back to camp.

Writing this in dying light as I wait for sleep to come.

CHAPTER FOUR

Secrist slowly lowered the smallish book, lost in his thoughts. There were several passages within the pages he'd just read that had left him confused. He wanted to learn more about the man who had written the diary. Was the writer truly a blood relation? His grandfather! And if so, what was Secrist to make of the reference to growing up on a reservation in Oklahoma? And alluding to 'his tribe.' Did that mean he, Thomas R. Secrist, had some Native American blood in him? A smile slowly spread across his features. Even the possibility touched and delighted him.

The cell phone beside him suddenly came to life, buzzing like an angry bee.

"Hi, Russ!" he answered cheerily after glancing down first to see who was calling. "You make it over to France without any problems? No delays or bad weather?" Frazier raised his head and cocked it to one side as if he knew it was Stander on the other end of the call.

"Hey ya, Tommy. Yeah, made it over without a hitch. I'm just waiting for my luggage right now." Stander paused briefly before continuing. In the background, Secrist could hear an unintelligible voice squawking loudly in French over what he assumed was the airport's intercom system "How is Frazier settling in? Oh! I think I forgot to give you his dental treats when I dropped him off. Can you grab him some the next... Fuck! There goes one of my bags! I'll call you back later, Tommy. Give Frazier some love for me. Bye!"

When the call ended, Secrist carried the newly discovered diary into his kitchen. Using a combination of steam, a razor-sharp steak knife, patience, and likely luck, he was able to carefully pry apart the waterlogged pages at the beginning of the book without tearing. He opened it wide and laid the spine of the diary down on his wooden kitchen table. Intending to let each of the pages lay flat and dry one by one before reading any more. But under the bright lights of the green ceiling fan twirling passively above his head, he couldn't help himself as he looked down at the first page. He began reading once more. Soon he was resettled on the couch beside Frazier with his nose reburied in the journal. This time starting on the first page.

There is no one here I know. But the British soldiers who I have traveled with for the last week, on the whole, have treated me well. I am currently marching towards the western front with an English Regiment made up of more than 30 officers and over 1,000 mostly battle-hardened men. I have been warned to never write down exact numbers, places, or even dates within these pages. Or share my specific orders with anyone. So, I'll just write here that, for the first time after two long years of fighting in France, I believe the end of this senseless war may finally be at hand. I am honored to be chosen as the potential catalyst for this. I only hope I am up to the task and can make my people proud.

The area of France we are trekking across is largely unspoiled by the awful fighting that lies ahead. I pick at single wildflowers absentmindedly as I march. Enjoying the vibrant colors and scents until they slowly droop, wither and die in my hands. The rolling meadows of yellow flowers and fields of crops much like the homeland of my tribe, the Anishinaabe of the Great Lakes region. Though I have never seen our ancestral lands with my own eyes, the oral tradition we maintain on the reservation in Oklahoma where I was born and raised, is strong. The elders speaking often of lush hills, valleys, of unspoiled streams, and clear lakes of blue. Their memories of a time when the green of the land meant more than the green of money.

A time now long gone.

The similarly displaced people who live in this idyllic land, though most don't speak English, are kind and generous. Allowing our Regiment to raid their fields of carrots and turnips as we pass by and bartering loaves of bread, bottles of wine, and other homegrown foods with many of us. Much like the British I now march alongside, I see some of the French people who dot this vast land looking closely at me. With only one full-blooded Anishinaabe parent, I am often mistaken as one who was born in other countries. My black hair, darkened complexion, and way of speaking often confusing to those around me. In this land, I am regularly mistaken for an Italian, a Mexican, or one born in Brazil or Cuba. I no longer bother to correct the many wrong assumptions, saying I am simply a citizen of this world. A popular answer when speaking with other soldiers in this war. This first ever world-wide war.

The sounds of distant battle have been gradually growing louder the closer we get to the western front. The intensifying booms thudding like thunder as the blue skies above us gradually darken grey with warring soot and ash. A few of the newest infantrymen cheering with delight when errant shells in the distance kick blackened dirt into the air. The inexperienced fools unaware of the horror that awaits them just miles ahead.

Today, we marched from the crack of dawn until late in the afternoon when we were ordered to board a simple train on rails that seemed to materialize out of nowhere. The narrow tracks the small, petrol-fueled locomotive ran across unceremoniously beginning where our day-long trek ended. Though the size of the entire railway operation seemed better suited for children, every soldier gladly squeezed themselves onto the exposed wooden benches that lined the tiny railcars. The chance to rest our aching feet and knotting leg muscles, a treat none would pass up.

Woodbine fags, and cheaper, army-issued cigarettes some infantrymen call "gaspers" because of their harshness, were passed back and forth among the men as the tiny train began rolling. The winding railcars speckled with tiny orange embers growing bright in the gathering dusk with every inhale. The longer we rode, the less chatter was heard as we rocked back and forth shoulder-to-shoulder along the tracks. The talking dissipating just like the exhaled smoke before finally disappearing completely the same as the windblown ashes themselves. Many of the Englishmen I traveled with grew somber and sullen once we began to pick up speed. Unlike myself, who until my recent orders had fought only alongside fellow American servicemen, the men from Britian were accustomed to this mode of transportation and knew the front lines were now very near. This "light railway" as it was called, they explained, was used to accelerate the transfer of troops, rations, artillery, and other supplies directly to the western front. And to haul the dying and worst of the wounded back again. The wood of the railcars under us stained in their pain and agony.

As the tiny train eventually slowed to a grinding halt, so too did the last of the boastful banter of those who'd never been to the frontlines before. We filed out one by one, each of us crowding onto a small strip of unspoiled land just beyond the edge of where the trenches began. The border between the warring we will join in the morning and the peace of the French countryside – a strip of green grass that gave way to trampled mud.

A clear divider of the damned.

The camp we arrived at was still far enough behind the ongoing fighting to feel relatively comfortable and safe. Massive canvas tents with flapping sides housed munitions and officers in equal favor. Long, rectangular wooden and metal troughs used for all kinds of washing were positioned in big L and T shapes on the highest rises of land, and ropes of all different lengths and widths stretched from any pole sticking far off the ground. The seemingly endless crisscrossing lines filled with drying garments of varying sizes. Blackened metal barrels, cut in half and converted into crude stoves, sat inside small fires of dancing flames. At the far end of the camp, downwind, long thick tree trunks shaped into crude beams were propped a few feet in the air and filled with bare-bottomed asses as white as snow. Soldiers, regardless of rank, sitting elbow to elbow as they defecated in unison. Like in nearly every camp I've been stationed at since the war began, paper is at a premium and nearly an unattainable luxury. The men reduced to wiping themselves with their own hand when they were done before hollering loudly so the next man in line could hurriedly take his place.

This camp as organized and clean as any I'd yet seen in this war.

As gracefully as possible, I hurried away from the pack of soldiers I'd been traveling with. Anxious to find the solitude this daily journal writing affords me. I walked swiftly to a cluster of tree stumps long missing their trunks and swaying branches. Sitting on the ground with my back to the fighting that I know waits for my return in the morning as I scribble this entry. Am I scared to plunge myself back into the fires of war? Naturally, I am. But fear itself is much like a fire. If you can control it, the flames or fears sparking the night with unknown shadows can be your most trusted ally. Should you lose control of either, however, you'll find both can burn you alive. When the flames of my fear begin to rise, I remember the hawk feathers pressed in the pocket above my heart and find comfort. Fear is not an emotion associated with hawks. They show none! The fierce birds have no qualms attacking prey bigger than themselves. Or taking on a poisonous snake armed with a lethal bite. Fear should never dictate your life. You must rise above and claim your peace. Only then can one truly soar.

The hot meal served tonight felt like a luxury. The warmth of the steaming stew coating my insides and filling me with a feeling I'd rarely felt since arriving on this foreign land. Contentment. As always, I ate alone. Putting my back against the trunk of a tree and looking out across a gently sloping valley as I finished the last of my food. Furiously writing these few passages before the natural light of the day deserts this torn land completely once again. Though winter is gradually making its upcoming arrival felt more and more with each passing day, the breeze this evening is warm and comforting. Around me, the soldiers I now fight alongside slowly fade into sleep. Time for me to join them.

After we woke and ate (hardtack biscuit again with a bit of unrecognizable meat), it was our turn to join the rotation in the trenches. The English Regiment I'd marched back to the front lines with replacing a departing group of haggard, hollow-eyed soldiers grateful for the brief reprieve. The weary men eyeing us silently as they lined the skinny rails of the diminutive train waiting to usher them out of this Hell. When asked by one skittish soldier about to enter the front lines for his first time what to expect, only one Captain bothered to even reply. Saying simply, "Fear can keep you alive out there. Just don't let the jimjams and jitters you're feeling now eat you alive. Expect that anything is likely. And absolutely nothing is certain."

Prophetic, to say the least.

We marched down a slight knoll towards the front lines. Trampling the last of the green grass until it faded to yellows and browns before finally disappearing underfoot completely. The rise of the hill we came down gave each of us a full view of the etched maze below that awaited our arrival. Long dark lines of deep ditches – jagged scars marring the landscape – dug deep enough for water and mud to pool and collect in the lowest spots. The trenches constructed in what's called a traverse system to minimize damage from the Germans' constant bombardment of shellfire. The alternating straight and angled lines, coupled with sporadic U-turns and occasional sandbag mounds, breaking up the damage should an enemy shell land inside the earthen ditch. The zig-zag pattern not allowing enemy fire to spread in a straight line through the trench and cause more damage. Or more death.

Stunted trees, gave way to mud as we filed into the gradually deepening trench. The mud that had previously only been underfoot, suddenly leapt higher and surrounded us on both sides like rolling waves before slowly being replaced by sandbags. The sandbags held in place by wooden posts cut in varying sizes.

The trenches we filed into this morning were a secondary line of ditches that led us towards the frontlines like hallways made of dirt. The long passages all looking very much lived in. Homemade signs pointing to London, New York, and Paris tried to add levity to the desperate toils of the fighting men living inside the crude cavity. A coat left hanging here, a mess tin abandoned with what might have been tea still inside over there, and a bed of sandbags with four snoring men sprawled across. The exhausted soldiers completely oblivious and unconcerned with the newcomers marching past them. Bits of planking with crude lettering directed men to where the waterpoints could be found, and communication wires were strewn everywhere it seemed. Most hanging limply from bits of nails and metal pounded into wooden poles and boards. Threadbare blankets covered cave-like dugouts where the wounded waited to be extracted from the fighting. Their moans and agonized wails adding to the ever-increasing sounds of battle just ahead of us. Black smoke darkened the skies above, and the "ping-ping" of German snipers riddling the area with their bullets grew more constant and kept us on edge. My heart pounded in my chest and the roar of my own blood filled my ears. We were nearly there.

No man's land.

Another fifty yards of marching and the stench of death hit us like an open palmed slap to the face. The unexpected shock not enough to stop you, but absolutely woke your every sense. It is a stink you never forget. Permeating your clothes, your hair, and even your food. The taste of rot never leaving you until you either add to it by leaving this world or leave the front lines completely. In between, you just suffer.

Myself and three other designated marksmen were quickly gathered and shown a crude, hastily drawn topographic map of the battlefield just ahead. We were ordered to take a small rise of battered undergrowth that overlooked a strategic post where German officers had been spotted. Command spread the four of us snipers out in different places along the trench in hopes that one of us would be able to reach the spot when the order was finally given. I huddled beside unknown men with pupils blown out with fright. Somewhere above me, on the frontline we were destined to join, a single scream rang out. The tortured sound of a crooked nail being levered out of unforgiving wood. An Englishman with red hair I'd never seen before kept sawing his arm back and forth across his teary eyes. Another stood ramrod straight sobbing as shells streamed above our position a mere three or four feet higher than his exposed head. The accompanying explosions shook the ground and rattled our teeth.

Soon after being positioned, we were given the "up and over" command and all individual sounds were lost to me. Across the top of the trench, we surged like rats escaping flooding waters. Our faces screaming masks as we darted straight into the hungry maw of the raging beast of war.

As a cascade of bullets whizzed all around, I dove into the second crater I came across when the unmistakable whistle of an incoming shell seemed to zero in on my position. I landed on my chest inside the old shell hole and covered my head with both hands. Once the dirt from the accompanying explosion stopped pelting me, I stole a peek at my surroundings and found I was not alone in the crater. An Englishman, half buried under rock and dirt, beseeched me with desperate eyes wide in terror. I crawled forward on my stomach before gaining my knees, careful to keep my head low. I reached out but his severed arm came off when I tried to help him. The warmth of the soldier's blood coating my own, already filthy, hand. In the chaos of the surging battle raging all around us, I don't think anyone saw me but the man whose twitching limb I still held. The hot meal I'd been so grateful to receive just hours before all came out in a rush. The hot bile covering the limb before splashing down and coating the boots of the one I'd stopped to help. When the awful retching finally retreated, my stomach having nothing left to give, I began to apologize to the injured soldier at my feet.

My words fell on dead ears.

Secrist, having just turned over a new page in the diary, paused his reading. The last several sentences at the top of the newest page were words he'd read earlier. He was now seven pages in, and back to the spot where he'd first started reading the smallish tome. He skimmed back over the text he'd previously read. The content inside left him wanting more, the majority of the personal journal still ahead.

Secrist placed the book beside him contemplatively. As he stood, Frazier gained his feet as well before jumping off the couch they shared. The medium-sized dog went through a series of stretches before trotting over to the backdoor and sitting on his haunches. Expectantly.

"About that time, huh, Frazier?" Secrist glanced at his kitchen clock before walking over and opening the door. Frazier hurried outside as if late for an important appointment. With a completely fenced backyard, Secrist shut the door behind him without any concern. He knew Frazier would return to the back porch when he was ready to come back inside. Secrist's house being the dog's second home.

Walking past the kitchen sink, Secrist pulled open the door on his refrigerator and grabbed a bottle of Guiness from inside. Popping off the cap and tossing it before returning to the living room. He thought briefly of turning on the television and watching the local 5:00 news. But as he reached for the remote, the tattered, open-paged journal seemed to call for him. The written words of a grandfather he never knew beckoning him to learn more and recapturing his attention. The remote control never touched as the first few words all but leapt from the next page and grabbed him by the throat. Throttling him with disturbing text until his breath grew hitched and his eyes bulged in disbelief.

CHAPTER FIVE

Today I communed with the dead. Treading miles across what could pass for the soft underbelly of a vast graveyard. The sights I witnessed firsthand seared into me like a rancher's fiery brand. Torching my spirit and burning my eyes with the worst of this world. This world of war.

Just after the morning meal was served, I was introduced to my guide. The lone soldier tasked with getting me safely through the vast maze of trenches that stretched out over the miles ahead. Without an experienced and knowledgeable chaperone, one who had previously traversed and was familiar with the labyrinth of channels, curves, and dead-ends, I could never hope to reach the land beyond.

Where my orders take me.

Much to my surprise, the guide turned out to be a Scottish American who was obviously aware of the clandestine briefings I'd been a part of days earlier. Though he wore no symbols of authority on his uniform, it was clear the highest commanders of the English regiment I'd marched back to the front lines with over the last week respected him immensely. And his role in all this. Whatever it is.

Pulling a lit cigarette from his mouth, he introduced himself as Robert Kirk and addressed me not just by my rank or even by my given Americanized name, Thomas Starr. But by the name given to me by my tribe back home, Anong, which means "star" in our native tongue. I'd rarely been called anything that wasn't derogatory, or at best, rank based, by the Americans I'd fought alongside previously in this awful war. To hear my birth name spoken without a hint of pandering or disdain by Kirk, as he asked me to call him, immediately put me at ease. His treatment of me as an equal, the truest measure of his leadership, and perhaps why I followed him blindly back into Hell.

Before leaving on my mission, I was loaded down with essentials. Extra munitions for my sniper rifle, dried and canned foodstuffs, a fresh kit of field dressings complete with an unopened bottle of iodine, and more water. As always, my only clothes were the ones I'd now worn for well over two weeks straight. Their last washing, just like my last bathing, a distant memory I didn't expect duplicated anytime soon. I hid this journal, a most selfish possession I know, rolled up inside the trench coat I'd need later when the icy winds began to grow colder. Though my pack was heavy, it was a comforting burden. I know to be more concerned when it begins to lighten. Nothing inside not of a great value to the undertaking ahead.

By comparison, Kirk, his olive-green wool uniform a match for my own, carried only weapons and ammunition. A Browning Automatic Rifle slung over his shoulder, and a pistol and knife lashed to one side. His short-cropped brown hair was tucked under his dough-boy, or "dishpan" helmet as we call it, and he peered out from under the metal brim with steady and confident brown eyes. His square jaw bristled with several days' growth that flattered his handsome features. When he spoke, his tone was measured and sure. Once we felt we had all that was needed, we filed out of the supply tent and began our hike back towards the battlefield where I'd fought the day before.

Kirk's step was decisive and quick, smoke from a dangling cigarette leaving a visible trail I could easily follow. The soldiers ahead of him spreading to let us pass, hushed murmurs on their lips. The endless stares only stopping when Kirk took a sharp left down an abandoned earthen channel heading away from the fighting I'd taken part in the day before. After a few hundred yards, Kirk took a new channel with a gradual curve that dipped low; the top of the ditch soaring several feet above our heads. We splashed across water-filled puddles. Kirk in the lead as I trailed behind with my head on a swivel.

Silently and alone − the shadows inside swallowing us − we entered the trench.

We matched strides as we pushed ahead, moving at a quick clip through the battle-scarred land. All around us, dirt-brown fields raped and ravaged by the machinations of war. Though fighting still raged nearby, the sounds grew muted the farther we traveled. Still, we dared not say a word. Uncertain if the enemy lingered near, or how close the different turns and twists of the trench might bring us to trigger happy combatants on either side of this conflict.

After hours of walking the nearly empty sandbagged and dirt-lined channels, we hit a dead-end. The abrupt conclusion of the trench was clearly expected by Kirk; his indifference helping me feel better about what was to come next. We both took turns poking our heads out of the ditch. Our field glasses pressed to our straining eyes as we searched for any sign of enemy combatants. When our path forward appeared clear, Kirk began to speak in low tones. The words our first exchanged since leaving the relative safety of the basecamp now miles behind us.

"The next leg of this journey takes us out of our walled shelter, Anong." He said this while gesturing at the walls that hid us. "Both sides have recently pulled back from this area, but there is no guarantee how long that will last. So, don't take too much comfort in the empty land ahead. There could still be snipers within range of our location." I nodded without speaking. After two years of fighting in this awful place, I'd learned the less said the better. "Stay low and follow my footsteps. Don't stray from the path I take you. The ground we'll be traveling across is no longer solid. Try to avoid the craters if you can; they are often deeper than they look. We need to reach the duckboards to make it safely to the fields of barbed wire about a half mile ahead of us. Understand?"

Once again, I simply nodded. Duckboards are slats of wood laid down to provide safe footing in camps, the bottoms of swampy trenches and, as was likely the case ahead of us, on war-torn battle grounds where shells, vehicles, and bombings had compromised the integrity of the land. The boards were also often extremely slippery and hazardous in their own way.

There are no easy pathways in war.

"One more thing," Kirk reached over and squeezed my shoulder. His hand warm, strong, and comforting. The opposite of my knees in that moment as I looked into his eyes. "We pushed the enemy back from this area only a day earlier. This is the most direct route for you to get where you need to be." He nodded at me solemnly, both of us aware of the end goal. "Our men were merciless in clearing all this for you. We may see things that…" Kirk wavered briefly before growing focused once again. "Just stick to the boards. No matter what you see or hear, stick to the boards. You understand me?" I nodded distractedly, anxious to get moving again. Kirk reached for my shoulder a second time, the tenderness and comfort gone as he buried his fingers in the meat. "That is an order, Anong."

We hurtled up and over then, Kirk in the lead and running. We were instantly enveloped in the stench of death and decay that swirled all around the eerily silent battleground. By the time we hit the duckboards, my boots had begun sinking so low in the mud of the squalid, torn field that they were filled with an icy chill that began to numb my toes. The uneven ground of the desolate land swampy and churned.

We slowed to a trot as the soles of our boots clattered noisily along the wood now under our rushed steps. In the distance, our next destination along the hellish pathway, was a tangled spiderweb of gnarled barbwire. I caught only glimpses of the twisted and rusted barriers as we hurried forward, no clear path discernible. With no bullets or enemy firepower raining down on us, my eyes began to scan the barren wasteland.

No man's land.

The duckboards stretched across mud sewn with the dead. Torn mules and ruined horses teemed with scurrying rats of impressive size working together to strip the last of the remaining flesh from the abandoned beasts. The rats' gnashing yellow teeth only pausing when we drew near, their long pink tails slithering inside the splayed cavities and disappearing until we'd passed. All around us, on both sides of the wooden path, giant shell holes pocked the razed earth. Scattered about us bits of metal and blown-apart munitions. Hollow cannon barrels, hit by enemy fire, were stuck upside down on the battleground like monuments to failure. Circular tires off long-gone wagons and other vehicles were scattered about like black checkers wiped off a gameboard in frustration by the loser.

By the time the first of the human remains began to turn up, I could no longer tear my eyes from the dark land. Arms here, legs there. Gleaming skulls peeled of skin. It was like walking through the underside of a graveyard; one that didn't use coffins. Stagnant pools of water with bobbing limbs, and other bits and pieces, all in various stages of decomposition. Endless bodies of young soldiers, pale and punctured, drowning in a marshy graveyard. Mottled skin and oozing gore dripping from their fatal wounds, sightless eyes fading of color like the moon losing its luster in an early morning sky. The brave men reduced to gruesome ghouls dripping in rot.

Yet, it wasn't until the cries began that the last veneer of civilization was swept away. As we neared the confusion of wired barbs, desperate and choked wails began to ring out. Without a thought, I turned toward the calls, my feet leaving the relative safety of the duckboards for the first time since arriving at this upside-down garden of dead. I barely took two hurried steps off the wood track before sinking nearly to my waist. My backpack and rifle just missing being encased in the suffocating mud as my feet kicked desperately underneath for a solid foothold of some kind.

I could hear Kirk swearing behind me, but my focus remained on the desperate sobs and pleas of the soldier who'd miraculously survived the earlier battle, the bitter cold, and what had to be an endless night of terror. When I finally identified where the voice was coming from, I locked eyes with the grateful man and we shared the briefest of smiles. An instant later, over my shoulder came one lone, loud clap as Kirk pulled the trigger of his weapon. The bullet shattered the soldier's face I'd leapt to save. The shot echoing across the field and sending a flurry of ravens screeching as they climbed the sky above our heads. Their cries somehow both accusatory and taunting at the same time.

By the time Kirk extracted me from the marshy mix of the dead – chastising my foolishness the entire while – we identified a second choked cry coming in the distance from our right. Kirk merely pointed without needing to explain as he lit a new smoke for himself. His pistol and Browning rifle unable to strike a target that far away. Even if we could spare the time without jeopardizing my mission, there was simply no way to safely rescue someone from the deadly combination of displaced earth, mud, and brackish water of the bog-like battlefield. I cleaned the worst of the dirt from me, much of it sliding off in wide globs of sticky mud, before kneeling on one knee. The scavenging birds of black took to flight once more as my single shot rang out. Their caws the last of the cries we heard on that ravaged wasteland.

Kirk and I began silently walking once more.

At the edge of the barbed wire, on our side, we were greeted by a pile of bodies shuddering with life. The vermin infesting the mound spearing us with their beady eyes and emitting grunts and growls before begrudgingly running from the buffet.

"Looks like our guys made a barricade of the dead to protect themselves," Kirk said somberly. The practice, though hard to square with normal human behavior, was a well-used tactic – likely ever since projectiles were first introduced by warring men. The gruesome stack appeared to be three or four bodies high, but with so much missing from the unknown soldiers, it was hard to say what really made the entirety of the shield.

We leaned against our fallen comrades and took stock of our position as we shared water from Kirk's canteen. As my guide periodically watched for any movement across the stretch of tangled wires with his field glasses, I took the opportunity to wash more of the drying mud from my uniform. Pulling off my boots to wipe them and my feet as best I could before replacing my ruined socks with a pair of dry ones. I'd seen enough "trench feet" to know that water was often the most insidious of all enemies. Waterlogged and poorly fitted footwear left unattended or untreated, often allowed gangrene to set in and costing men toes. Or worse...

"See where I am pointing?" Kirk directing me to a narrow, barely visible path cut through the web of rusty barbs just ahead of us. "That is our exit out of this place. Once we get out of those tangles, we'll follow the remainder of that wire fence west where it ends just outside a small French village untouched by this conflict." Kirk squatted and showed me a portion of map. "See this?" His finger smudging a circled dot. "Once you get around that little farming community, you will only have one more fighting field to cross before reaching your destination." Kirk refolded the map and then handed it over to me. "We'll talk more about that when the time comes. Ready?"

"Yes, sir." I surprised myself by speaking for the first time since we'd left basecamp. Though I can (obviously) read and write very well in English, I have mostly taught myself both skills. When I am forced to talk, I hate the sounds I make when speaking. My native tongue seems crowded with marbles that draws attention to my jumbled dialect and making it seem I am no sharper than one. Since signing up to serve in this war, I've found my mispronunciation of words I've never actually heard spoken aloud on the reservation often gets me laughed at and teased. While on the other hand, my actions, primarily on the battlefields we cross, bring me praise and reward. Since talking is an artificial thing – all language just a series of made-up grunts and exclamations – I let my actions speak for me. After all, movement is much nearer to man's true nature. Much like the soaring of a hawk... And as one of a very few Native Americans fighting in this foreign land, I always seem outnumbered and without the dialogue or the chance to defend myself. If silence truly was golden, as they say, my riches would be immeasurable.

On hands and knees, I slithered after Kirk as he attacked the initial wall of barbs with his wire cutters. Carefully bending the stabbing steel shards out of his way before advancing. We slowly worked our way past the freshly clipped ends and soon were tunneling into an opening that Kirk cut right through the very heart of the bales of wire. We trudged over long forgotten bodies all but ground right into the battered earth. My knees and bare hands landing on jellylike limbs that split under my weight. Pieces of torn flesh sticking between my fingers, and whatever spilled out oozing under my fingernails. The suffocating decay of the fallen soldiers inescapable as we crawled over an endless sea of the dead for what felt like hours.

At our heads and on either side of us hung the unfortunates who'd become hopelessly tangled in the strewn mesh. Ravaged torsos and abbreviated legs, likely from men caught in cannon fire and shell blasts on the battlefield, were scattered everywhere along the barrier. A clustered group of five full-bodied men, their flesh now blackened by rot, looked as if they'd run blindly into the unforgiving fence before becoming hopelessly entangled. The soldiers had clearly struggled mightily to extricate themselves from the clutching barbs. Their hands were missing fingers and had been sliced to ribbons by the desperate struggle. The stretched skin of their faces twisted in silent screams, and much of their bodies crisscrossed with violent tears and wounds. The disturbing poses a silent pantomime of their last anguished moments of life.

When Kirk finally spilled out the other side, he turned and reached down to help me with a face ashen and white. A moment passed between us, and though I may be simply flattering myself, it seemed the shared experience, horrid as it was, somehow bonded us. In the far distance, back in the direction where our hellish journey had begun, we could hear shelling had resumed. Yet where we stood, now on the German side of the frontline, only an unnerving silence greeted our arrival. Nothing stirred as the last of the daylight began to bleed into the night.

Without comment, Kirk dropped his eyes and began walking along a fence that led away from the massive thicket of barbs we'd emerged from. The footing was solid as long as we didn't stray far from the taut barrier, and we stayed silent and low as we carefully made our way along the fence line. Slowly but surely, the wall of wire grew less jumbled until we found ourselves trotting along the edge of a single border. A simple fence in a meadow held in place by thick limbs cut from trees, likely put in place years before by farmers and not soldiers.

When we spied the remains of a burned out building with two sides of a partial stone wall still standing, we decided to rest for the night. Enclosing the top of the corner with a few long shards of broken planks to create a simple lean-to shelter and occupying the crook of the bend to shield the light from our tiny fire as we rested and ate. A few meaningful glances were exchanged but few words were spoken between us. After walking untold miles within a depressing landscape of death and decay, what needed to be said?

We huddled under our trench coats. Using them like blankets as the tiny fire crackled and spit sparks before eventually collapsing in a fit of wispy smoke. Not daring to relight it and tempt fate, instead we drew close to help fight the dipping temperatures. It worked as the close proximity soon filled me with a comfort and warmth I'd rarely experienced since arriving on these foreign shores. I felt my heart soften on the inside while on the outside, between my legs, something stirred. When Kirk finally reached around for me, I felt the twin urgency of his need at my back. We laid together – our limbs entangled and our flesh becoming one – each of us likely using the other. Taking turns. Neither of us minding or commenting in the golden silence. When sleep finally came for me, my rest was peaceful and easy.

CHAPTER SIX

Secrist slowly set the diary down and rose to his feet. He arched his back once and rolled his head back and forth before deciding he should probably check on Frazier. He sniffed loudly a few times with a growing frown; something rotten in the air. The sickly smell from the attic, perhaps, still clinging to his clothes and hair. Or had thoroughly permeated the boxes that he'd brought down after being stored in the stuffy space for so long.

Secrist grabbed the dog's leash and headed out his backdoor where he found Frazier lying contently in the evening sun on his stained wood porch. Sprawled comfortably inside the last slice of warm rays before they left the Michigan sky to the emerging stars. "You doing okay out here, buddy? About ready to take a little walk around the neighborhood with me?" Frazier lifted his head and seemed to smile before breaking out in a faint pant. Secrist kneeled and began scratching the dog's belly before Frazier eventually rolled over and pushed himself up. Shaking once before allowing the leash to be attached to his collar.

As Frazier led him along their usual route, Secrist ran the contents of what he'd read so far in the journal back and forth through his head. The read was shocking to say the least. The same-sex coupling really hadn't phased him. He'd known and been friends with numerous gay men and women over the years. People are just people, after all. He certainly wasn't uncomfortable hearing his grandfather favoring a man's company over a woman's. Although, he thought to himself, it did call into question whether the writer was actually related to him or not. Had his grandfather fathered *children with women after the war? Or was the woman who died in Secrist's adopted father's arms mistaken about the diary's author? Surely, he reasoned, she must have read the book. She'd used her very last breath to ensure it got into her son's hands!*

By the time Secrist's house was back in sight, he found himself impatient to begin reading again. Quickly filling Frazier's food dish and water bowl before throwing a frozen pizza in the oven for himself. While Frazier ate and Secrist waited for the sausage and pepperoni pie to bake, he cracked open the book once more. This time sitting at his kitchen table as he began reading again.

The morning was lonely, desolate, and cold. The weather wasn't much better...

When I woke, Kirk had rebuilt and moved our tiny fire to the opposite side of the wall from the previous night. Away from me. The wind had changed, he explained, and he was concerned somebody might see the smoke before we were ready to move. He'd already eaten his ration and soon left me to eat alone. Saying he wanted to scout ahead a bit before we began moving once again. I'd barely been awake a full minute before he disappeared into the mist of the chilly morning, saying he would return shortly so we could get an early start. Hardly meeting my eye before lighting up a cigarette and stepping away.

I have always found the differences between men and women to be blurry and confusing. I can be drawn to either and enjoy my time equally with both. The human spirit deep inside far more attractive and important to me than whether the spirit came into our world as a man or a woman. Even the confused grappling of the night is, for me anyway, often indistinguishable between the two. The heated urgency not really any different and the selfish culmination always the same. But as similar as the groping in the darkness can be, the time after – often a morning just like today – is where the real differences show.

Most men, even among my own tribe back on the reservation, are much like Kirk this morning. Silent, unsure, brooding with thoughts they keep to themselves. While, on the other hand, the women I've spent the night with are talkative and confident. Often clamoring to discuss what had happened and all the possible reasons why. Dissecting the fleeting moment as if some hidden meaning was buried within. Both can be infuriating and intoxicating in equal parts. Just like the physical differences.

No right or wrong. Just different.

I hurriedly ate and repacked my gear. By the time Kirk returned, I was also anxious to get moving again. Few words were spoken as the new day's hike began. I followed a couple steps behind my guide, both of us hugging the wire fence we'd followed out of the battlefield the day before. The early morning mist reduced to ghostly wisps rolling around our knees and ankles before dissipating completely as the sun began its day-long struggle to make a meaningful appearance.

We marched nearly the entirety of the morning before finally cresting the top of a hill with a sweeping view of the valley below. In the far distance, we could see a farming community of thirty or so houses. We stopped then and snacked hurriedly, both of us using our field glasses to periodically spy on the village and ensure we remained unobserved.

"You'll circle around this ridge until you reach that rocky peak," Kirk pointed and gestured as he spoke. "From there you'll be able see the next battleground. Once you get past that, the city where you are headed is due west on the other side of the forest." I nodded silently; my features a mask of indifference. "Once you reach the city limits, just follow the river to your destination. Like they told you in the briefing, you can't miss it."

I nodded once more. My eyes avoiding Kirk's face as I prepared to leave. When I turned to go, I felt Kirk's hand land on my shoulder and he gently pulled me near, "Anong," he began. "I need to tell you something before we part ways." I looked over at Kirk then. Inside, my frayed feeling lurching from one extreme to the other. A moment earlier I was ready to turn on my heel, doubting I'd ever let myself even think of this man again, and feeling no remorse at that decision. But now my heart surged inside my chest and I felt joy pulling my lips into a bashful smile. I stepped to Kirk expectantly, basking in the glow of his ruggedly good-looking face.

"Do you believe in God?" I remember I blinked slowly once before confusion reshaped the entirety of my features. "Or whatever your people pray to?" I felt my insides collapse then, just like a house built out of a deck of playing cards. My roiling emotions falling as flat as a card game's discard pile. Unneeded, unwanted, and no longer in contention for the win. My foolish gamble blown once more; the queen of hearts ensuring my loss was complete. I quickly looked away, unwilling to let the victor see how hard I took the defeat.

"My... my people?" Once again, I felt reduced to the color of my skin, the place I'd been born, and the trappings of a society still stuck in the past. Even Kirk couldn't see me for who I was. Only seeing what I was in *his* world. I felt my face blush with rage. The potential satire of my reddening skin rising to the surface not lost on me. Somehow, I replied in a measured tone. Each word clipped and carefully enunciated.

"Of course, sir. *My people*, as you say it, pray and revere many deities just like *your people*. But deep down we all know that, no matter where we were born or what we were taught, there is but one true God we all pray to. The one we all call out for when we are truly in need. Whether it is on our knees, standing with arms raised, bowing on a rug, facing a certain direction, or doing a combination of any of these only at certain times. There is but one."

When I finished, my chest was heaving. Without recognizing the irony in that moment, I said a simple prayer to Mother Earth. She from whom *my people* were sprung, and she whom is in charge of the four orders of the earth. The soil, the plants, the animals, and the people. The brief unspoken words and focus clearing my heart of the broken pieces this man had chipped away.

"Well, I don't know about all that." Kirk shifted uncomfortably on his feet, his face soft and his eyes kind once more. Like they'd been the previous night. "But whatever you believe, you cling to that, you hear me, Anong? Because where you are going next, that empty battlefield is a dead-zone. A blight on this land where only the worst of man resides. Neither side in this war claiming – or even wanting the territory you'll be passing through anymore."

Kirk reached out, wrapping me in an awkward hug and kissing me hard once on my lips. Before I knew what had happened, he had taken two steps back, his wonderful face shadowed in authority again. "Take this," he said, pressing his pistol in my hand. "Keep it loaded and hidden somewhere on your person. Down there," he gestured where my path would take me next, "God will never show up. There is nothing of God's grace in those trenches. Only madness."

I should have left then, or better yet, left before the conversation even started. But something kept me rooted as I secreted his pistol away. Perhaps I merely longed for more of Kirk's company, but I heard my voice asking what he meant and what to watch out for. Wondering out loud what had chased the enemies of this war from the battleground I was ordered to cross.

"I've only heard whispered rumors, Anong." Kirk spoke as he busied himself with lighting up a new smoke and exhaling deeply. "But terrible things have happened down there. I know chemical warfare was used several times on that battlefield. Since then, communication has not been reestablished. Supposedly, that is true on the German side as well. By now the poisonous gas should have all dispersed, but keep your gasmask handy. And... and stay clear of the men without faces."

"Men without faces?"

"Don't let them catch you no matter what. Understand?" Kirk then turned without a goodbye. I watched the retreat of his step as he headed back the way we'd come. He never turned around once, and in minutes he'd vanished down the far side of the hill. A trail of fading smoke drifting listlessly in the air where he'd walked.

I shifted my pack and began walking towards the rocky peak he'd directed. When I reached the elevated spot, I looked down the side of a timbered hill. Just beyond lay the battlefield Kirk had so cryptically described. The land barren, bleak, and appearing lifeless. A lingering mist or whiteish smoke obscured much of the fighting field, and only the dark lines of several trenches were visible through the haze from my position. I pulled out my field glasses and searched for any sign of movement, but found none. The last of the morning's fog clinging stubbornly to the land far below me. But, I reasoned, even if there were men still stationed in that lifeless stretch of valley, it couldn't be many. All I could really make out was what looked like three twisted and towering poles. Or perhaps, I thought at the time, they were leafless and largely branchless trees sticking awkwardly out of the otherwise leveled field. With no other landmark to guide me, I headed towards the strange markers. Descending the gradual incline of the hill before entering a slim line of trees that would keep me hidden until I reached my destination.

When I emerged from the skinny stand of trees less than an hour later, I saw I'd completely misjudged the three protruding poles or trees I thought I'd glimpsed from the peak high above. Though they were wooden, and standing some fifteen feet in the air, the work was obviously manmade. It was a sign. A clear message. An unmistakable warning.

Three crucifixions.

The bodies were suspended by thick metal spikes that had been pounded through their limbs and driven deeply into the wood they hung from. Each corpse was nude and covered from head to toe in unnatural wounds. The three men had all been dead for quite some time. One, barely recognizable as human, had clearly been hanging the longest. The rot, or perhaps wild animals, had left the sagging bag of bones dangling from a single peg by the lone remaining arm. Both legs and his head nowhere to be seen. Drag marks and various paw prints visible in the mud at the base of the cross. The man directly to his left seemed to be the last one pierced and fastened. Though his eyes and nose were gone – likely lost to scavenging birds – much of his body seemed firm and largely still held its shape. The individual on the far right, however, was missing much of his skin. Though the body wasn't blackened by fire, the figure most resembled a melted candle. Layers of sagging flesh, fat, and viscera had pooled in different places along the body. Rolls of skin visible at the neck under a grinning skull, and putrid meat bunched around the waist and ankles that left large pink and red-looking swaths of angry wounds behind.

I know I stood lost in shock for long minutes, mesmerized by the hanging carnage. Trying to wrap my head around what these men – enemies in war or not – could have possibly done to deserve such a tortured end. When I finally regained a measure of composure, I realized how exposed my position was under the ominous effigies. I sprinted from the ghastly scene, scuttling into the nearest trench not even ten feet from the site of the crucifixions. Hiding without looking back at the anguished trio, the image forever imprinted on my spirit.

I hurriedly referenced my compass, ensuring my path remained westward, before I began moving once more. I wanted to abandon this land of ash and death as quickly as I could. I began making my way along the crude trench the Germans had constructed; the interior all but barren and appearing to have been recently dug. I only got another fifty feet before the earthen ditch veered right and ended. I cautiously poked my head out and scanned the area ahead of me. My rifle at the ready. I'd hoped to find another trench to stay tucked inside of as I navigated the eerie and hazy battlefield. But the low-lying fog hid most of the land.

I exited the trench, crouching low and moving quietly as I steadily crept forward along the fighting field. Sloppy mud under my heel, grey clouds overhead, and a soupy haze obscuring much of my vision. In the air hung a lingering taste that reminded me of horseradish or burned garlic. Likely remnants of the infamous mustard gas I'd been warned about. I debated internally whether to slip on my gasmask but decided to hold off. The lenses on the cumbersome headgear always hindered my vision, and it was already difficult enough to see where my steps were landing in the bog-like conditions of the battlefield. My eyes darting to the ground every few steps to see what was at my feet. Stepping around lips of big shell holes to avoid falling down inside the endless craters.

The farther I traveled, the more I began to find evidence of the deadly battles recently fought across this bleak landscape. Broken handheld weapons, burned out flamethrowers, headless helmets, and boots with bloody and charred stumps tucked inside. Mounds of spent cannon shells as thick as my thighs; their brass casings sparkling and winking obscenely any time the clouds above briefly parted. A pile of dead soldiers awaiting burials that would never come. The unmoving men's uniforms in tatters, and their rotting skin black as coal. A few had been sewn into filthy burial blankets while others had only been partially concealed under thin layers of dirt. All hastily abandoned by their comrades before the interments were completed. A smattering of digging tools lay scattered as if they'd all been dropped in a rush at the same exact time.

I stepped across puddles of reflective water that all held my haunted features. Squalid mirrors baring my spooked eyes. I walked over rounded bones drowning in the soupy black abyss like a sunken ship's ballast stones; the far-flung limbs bobbing in the bloodbath I trekked across. Undeterred and numb to the horrid conditions of the dead this war churned out daily, I kept moving forward.

It wasn't until movement caught my eye in the shifting shadows ahead of me that my heart began to hammer in my chest. I'd not seen a single person or animal since entering this dead zone. Not even a rat! Yet, something in the way of my path was coming closer. I slowly lowered myself to the cold ground and hastily looked for some nearby cover where I could conceal myself. But the barren and near lifeless land betrayed me, the mist along the ground obscuring any trenches I could quickly dive into. I pressed myself into the muck and strained for a glance at whatever was stirring in the distance.

I mistook the first one to simply be a lost German soldier. It wore the frayed remains of a uniform and limped slightly as it crested the small rise it climbed. I couldn't see the face which was masked in a dark apparatus meant to protect the eyes, nose, and throat from the threat of chemical warfare. The German gasmask had insect-like eyes and a long snout where a filter could be attached and replaced with a new one as needed. I could see no filter in place.

The one in the lead was followed close behind by a motley throng of others struggling to keep pace. Each of their steps disoriented and wobbly like a new born calf or deer. When I peered through my rifle's scope, I calmly counted seven shufflers in total before the absurdity of what I was seeing began to sink in. Despite the cold, the soldiers were only partially clothed, and I could see festering, open wounds on several of them. They each carried crude weapons of a sort that dangled limply at their sides. Splintered planks of wood and thin bars of metal carried by their ends like clubs. One of the walkers was missing an arm, and another limped along on only a partial leg. The stump, just above where the ankle should be, landing in the mud every third step.

Completely transfixed, I couldn't turn away as I watched one suddenly stop walking, bend over, and begin retching violently. The brutal cough not stopping until I watched the thing pull long strands of something black and dripping from his own mouth. I couldn't be certain, but, as the wet flesh hit the ground at his feet, I became convinced it was part of his own lung. Or, perhaps, something else equally vital and important.

When he finally quit the awful hacking, he'd pitched onto his side and stopped moving all together. A dark, chunky fluid draining slowly from his slack mouth.

The others it travelled with gradually took notice. Stepping to their fallen comrade and encircling him like kids on a playground gathering to watch a schoolyard fight. Horrified, I looked on as the things began reaching down and pawing at their companion. Thin fingers poking at the bloody strands still leaking from its black lips. As soon as one raised a gore-soaked hand to their own mouth, slurping as it cleaned each digit with a diseased looking tongue, the others converged in a rush. Moments later, like a pack of wild dogs, they tore into him. Pulling pink and red chunks slippery with hot blood off the splayed body.

I watched them feast until, one by one, each was finally sated. Staggering dully to their feet and turning away from the meat smorgasbord as if no longer confident in what they'd done. What was left at their feet wasn't wholly a man anymore. It reminded me of a chalk drawing a child might make of a person. Scribbles of red where the arms and legs should be. Splashes of color – falling well outside of the lines...

It was then the "leader" must have first seen me. The uniformed man pulled at his gasmask as if to get a better view. But when he did, much of the skin on his face came off along with it. Lengthy strands of oozing flesh stretching between his tortured features and the mask he tugged off. When he was done – the gasmask dangling from around his neck – his lipless mouth was two rows of gleaming teeth that dripped blood. His lidless eyes pinning me with a stare I know will haunt my nightmares for years to come.

A faceless man!

CHAPTER SEVEN

Secrist tugged at the stringy white cheese with his teeth. He'd pulled the pizza from the oven on time, but it had sat while he'd continued reading the hellish account of his grandfather's time in France. When he'd finally found a good stopping place, he set the book aside long enough to wolf-down his dinner. Secrist didn't want to risk staining or ruining the 100-plus-year-old diary with fingers dripping with tomato sauce and slippery grease. As he ate, he tossed an occasional piece of crust towards the attentive dog at his feet. Frazier rising slightly each time to snatch the pieces midair before snapping his jaws shut.

"Don't tell Stander about me giving you any of this, you understand?" Secrist smiled down at his four-legged dinner companion. "I'll never hear the end of it."

Outside the kitchen window, the nighttime sky slowly became a sea of black from which a giant fishhook of white dangled down in hopes it would catch an eye or two. The darkness descending and the evening evolving into the nighttime. Secrist finished eating and then cleared away the dirty dishes and utensils he'd used from both lunch and dinner. Chucking everything inside his dishwasher and turning it on. As the whir-whir-whir of the appliance began serenading him, Secrist returned to the living room and his couch. Once again having to cajole Frazier into vacating his favorite spot on the furniture before being able to sit.

With his feet propped up on a cushioned footstool, Secrist reopened the journal and began reading. Though he'd read steadily for several hours now, he was only about a fourth of the way through the diary. He pulled the tattered book close to his face. His eyes anxious to find the spot where earlier he'd left off.

Kirk had cautioned me to avoid the 'faceless' men of this haunting battlefield. At the time of the warning, I'd been unclear what he'd meant. But as I sprinted in the opposite direction of the shambling things I'd come across, I became certain what they really were.

The Wendigo.

I recognize this evil from the many stories and legends that have been handed down across generations of my bloodline. As a direct descendant of one of the earliest Wendigo slayers known by my tribe, my family has traditionally been the spring from which our tribe's Shaman are sprung. The bundle of hawk feathers I carry blessed by my own uncle, currently our tribe's Medicine Man.

As a boy growing up, my uncle often told me the story of our family's forefather who, more than a thousand years before I was born, was a powerful Shaman and the very first Wendigo slayer. My ancestor is said to have been guided by the hand of Mother Earth herself from which all my people, regardless of tribe, come. With the help of her wisdom and strength, he'd beheaded and imprisoned a powerful Wendigo spirit high atop a cursed mountain that was once the homeland of the Anishinaabe, the name of the Great Lakes tribe my people are descended from.

Someone possessed by a Wendigo spirit, as I was taught, will always appear gaunt to the point of emaciation. Sharp bones pushing out against the skin no matter how much it consumes. The skin or complexion always an ash-gray color of death. The monster, an unclean thing that without the spirit of the Wendigo inhabiting it, would have stayed interred in its grave. And while there may be subtle differences between the Wendigo of my homeland and this country's version of the walking dead, I am convinced they are one and the same.

Ghouls with an insatiable hunger for human flesh.

When I felt comfortable that I'd put enough distance between myself and the pack of undead, I scrambled down inside a crater to try and collect my wits and get my bearings. I avoided looking at the dark pool in the deepest portion of the hole as I hastily attached my bayonet to the end of my rifle. The stench rising from the putrid liquid warning me to keep my eyes to myself. The floating carcasses, toothless with mouths of black, were obviously men who'd fallen victim to the horrors of chemical warfare. Their twisted bodies rapidly decaying in the harsh environment.

"Come with me if you want to live." I nearly screeched when the young man's head crested the outer rim of the dirt basin I'd taken refuge in. Though laced in French, the words he spoke were English, and likely the only reason I was able to quell the reflex of my trigger finger in that moment. The lanky figure stretched a filthy hand out to me; his deep French accent even more apparent. "If you have a gasmask, put it on, Monsieur. Otherwise, we need to run right now. C'est urgent! They are almost upon us!" The man stretched his long arm down farther, beckoning me with a desperate shake of his hand. Instinctively, I reached for it, leaving my gasmask buried in my pack as I was helped up the side of the slippery hole.

The man nodded once before turning to lead. I noted his uniform was French but could determine little else about his rank or expertise. Though he carried himself with the confidence of a man much older, the French soldier was young and I judged him to be less than twenty years of age. He towered over me and was likely a good six-and-a-half-feet tall. He wore a filthy cloth mask stained in browns and yellows that covered the bottom half of his features like a train robbing bandit straight out of the Wild West of America. He sprinted confidently across the landscape, artfully dodging craters as he veered to the left and began running up a slight hill. Once we came down the far side of it, nestled between the hill and a narrow trench that clearly was his destination, the man turned to me.

"Sorry for the panicked rush, Monsieur. But there is a group of deranged soldiers poisoned by whatever chemicals and gas bombs the German command used on this stretch of the frontline. The Boche bastards! The madmen must have seen you because they were headed to where you were hiding." As the man spoke, the cloth of his mask was sucked in and out of his mouth. If not for the circumstances, it would be comical. "It is fortunate I came across you, no? This cursed place is not safe! We must leave!" He must have seen my stare. His next words addressing my unspoken questions.

"My gasmask was lost in earlier fighting. This," he pointed to the flapping material under his eyes, "is the next best thing. If you have some thick cloth, Monsieur, just tear it into the shape of a handkerchief and fasten it around your neck. The trick is to pee right on it and let the urine really soak in. You'll get used to the smell, and it sure beats ending up like those poor bastards back there." The Frenchman pointed back over the hill where we had just come from. "I got separated from my battalion when our Brigade fell back a few days early. I am headed east until I reach the new frontline. Where they are stationed. If you are lost, you are welcome to join me. You are American, no? I'm sure we can get you back in contact with them."

"Thank you...uh...?"

"Aloysius, Monsieur. Aloysius Leroux at your service." The young man bowed slightly, a hint of nobility in his speech and mannerisms.

"Thank you, Aloysius. But my orders take me in the opposite direction." I kept my face neutral and I spoke slowly. "I wish you safe travels, friend."

"Oh, Monsieur. If we must part ways, please watch yourself. The direction where you are headed, west, there are many dangers much different than this war we find ourselves in. Is there no other way you can go? The forest on the western edge of this battlefield is said to be dangerous and home to many wild beasts." The young soldier's concern was touching.

"I do not fear the creatures of the forest. Most, I have found, leave me in peace if I do the same. Usually scattering from the presence of man. I'll be fine." We both paused, though clearly anxious to be on his way, Aloysius seemed troubled to find out I had no intention of traveling back with him. Yet, I was likely even more anxious about the safety of the young, weaponless Frenchman who'd risked himself to ensure I was unharmed.

As we prepared to part and go our separate ways, we somberly shook hands and wished each other well. But as Aloysius turned to descend the wall of the trench, he stopped. "Oh no! They have found us!" His trembling voice a harsh whisper.

"Who? Who has found us?" I could see nothing from where I stood. Whomever was coming hidden from me inside the valleyed walls of dirt.

"The sick soldiers we were running from. The ones who were closing in on you." Aloysius turned towards me with desperate eyes. His arms raising slowly above his head in obvious surrender as three men in French uniforms that matched what Aloysius wore pulled themselves from the earthen ditch.

"But those aren't the same ones I saw..." I raised my rifle slightly though I kept the aim of the barrel unthreatening and neutral. Unsure why these soldiers, all wearing torn cloth over the bottom of their faces in the same manner as Aloysius, pointed their weapons at the young Frenchman.

"American?" As one of them spoke, his English not smooth but still easy to understand, another of the new soldiers circled behind Aloysius. His gun trained on him. I nodded my head once to confirm the question before he continued. "I see you found our deserter..."

Aloysius stepped forward, briefly erupting in loud protests before the soldier behind him lashed out. The butt of his rifle making contact with the back of Aloysius's head and driving the young Frenchman to the ground. Unconscious. Instinctively, I raised my own weapon higher. The questions I had plain on my face. But I found myself staring down the barrel of three rifles pointed back at me. "Please unhand your weapon and let me explain. This one," the man half kicked, half nudged the prostrate form, "has denied the very brotherhood this war demands of all of us." The man took a step towards me, his hand beckoning and eyes on my gun. I stood my ground. My only response, a curt shake of my head no. My rifle leveled at his chest.

"Let us be reasonable." A new voice came from out of the trench the three soldiers had just ascended. I watched two more men climb up and out, both of the newcomers wearing the same dirty cloth masks as Aloysius and the others. Dirt-creased foreheads and darting eyes all the features of their faces I could see. The man who spoke had on a uniform full of stripes, medals, and assorted pins that jangled when he moved. A long warm coat, far too big for him, was unbuttoned and hung loosely from his shoulders. "Please. We all face the same enemy here. A common foe. Brothers," the man with the decorative coat placed a hand lightly on one French soldier's gun and immediately all three were lowered to the ground, "this American deserves our respect. Let us help him. He has obviously lost his way." A pause. "Like so many of us, hmmm?" The man's voice was authoritative yet honeyed. "Please tell us, what brings you to our little outpost? Are you here to report on our actions?"

The man in the long coat asked reasonable enough questions. But something in his choice of words mixed with the garish medals and stripes he boldly wore didn't feel right. But with the five French soldiers seeming reluctant to let me pass without an explanation, and their leader pointedly questioning my arrival, I felt compelled to explain. Unsure if I didn't, how I would be treated or if they'd allow me to continue on.

"I am neither lost nor here on your behalf. I have orders to move west. There is a target I am to... to acquire." I also lowered my weapon slightly in hopes it would ease the palpable threat so heavy in the air the small group of soldiers breathed.

"Acquire? You mean kill. Assassinate." The man in the long coat appraised me with a sharp stare. Taking in my uniform, my bulging pack, and my rifle, before boring into my own eyes. "You are a sniper, yes? Heading west to the border. How interesting..."

"That is my role and my orders." Which was all I'd been warned to ever share. To avoid saying more I quickly changed the subject. "Earlier, this man," I pointed to the prostrate form of Aloysius still lying in the dark, cold mud at our feet, "saved me from a small horde of very sickened men. Victims of a chemical attack of some sort. What happened to them? What are they?"

"What do you think they are?" The man answered my question with one of his own. Giving me nothing in return.

"The Wendigo." I spoke out loud without thinking and immediately regretted it. Obviously, these soldiers born half a world away, would have no idea what I was talking about.

"I don't know what that is or means. But we call them zombies because they walk like living dead men. I myself come from French nobility and my family helped colonize an island in the Caribbean Sea named Haiti. There is a plague of sickened people – very much like what you saw here – on that island that we had to learn to live with. The locals of that land call them zombies. They say they are stuck between life and death. Slaves to a master who orders them around for their own selfish means."

"Like soldiers," again I spoke without thinking. I'd already said more than I normally ever would have among my American counterparts. What was it about that desolate killing field that had made me so uncomfortable?

"You are a soldier, no?" I could see the narrowing of the man's eyes as he spoke. "Like us, you also feel enslaved? Wouldn't it be nice to disappear for a while? Follow a path of your own choosing instead of being ordered around like a child?"

I remember for a moment I hesitated. I'd been doing what I was supposed to do all my life. Only living on land, a reservation, where I was told I could. Only being taught what I was told was important by my people's oppressors. Teased and bullied for my clumsy attempts at mimicking the ways I'd been shown by those already educated in them. Dismissed and scorned by those I lived with for even trying to fit in. All but disowned by my own people when I signed up to join the fight for a country I can never hope to own land in myself. My own family not believing I could make our country **ever** see me as anything other than a red-skinned Indian savage. No matter how many of us proud Native Americans joined this war to prove our allegiance. All of us doing so in the hope that all of the original people of our land would one day take part in what some now call "the American dream." To travel without fear, to work for fair wages, to vote for leaders, and raise children who get to live without borders or prejudices.

Though I thought all these things, I stayed silent. The unspoken questions plain in my eyes.

"You doubt what I say could be true, no? Ah, Monsieur... what if I showed you? Showed you a true brotherhood born not of blood or race, but by like-mindedness. Untroubled by those who see our value only as cannon fodder." The man spoke quickly. His words intoxicating, dripping with sweetness.

"Tell me, friend. What freedoms have any of us truly experienced since being born? As soon as we can walk, we are lined up at the start of this game called life. Told we will all get a fair turn. We are given a name and set on *go*. Lined up straight and what are we truly taught? Nothing. So, we all just do what we are told. The amount of money in our pockets, they say, is our only worth. Lying in bed at night, we even dream as we're told. And while we sleep," the leader gestured around him to include his men along with Aloysius and I, "we are sold and bought."

The leader in the long coat had a carefully practiced tempo and pace to his cadence I recognized from my youth. The kind my mother warned me against. It was the same staccato or ebb and flow used by the Christian missionaries who sometimes plagued our reservation. Preaching to us of their pale God, of his kindness and of his grace. It could be an oddly hypnotic rhythm, and many in our tribe fell for the trick. Handing over pennies they could hardly spare. Giving themselves over and some even traveling alongside the preachers as they visited different settlements across our land. None suspecting, like my mom at age 14, that the *blessing* these holy men bestowed upon them would never be seen by these righteous men when, nine months later, the *blessing* was born. Leaving broken girls, and little boys like me in their wake.

A half breed bastard son.

"Stealing our backs but leaving the shirts and asking us to be thankful. Paying us in..." The man, clearly in love with the sound of his own voice, continued his speech. Each of the four French soldiers transfixed by his words. I stole a peek down at Aloysius and found his own desperate stare already searching for my eyes. A few discrete nods and gestures exchanged while the man in the long coat droned on.

"... let me show you. But before I do, our brother's body is yet warm. Will you come see?" The leader stopped and asked me a question. But I had completely shut his voice out while trying to discreetly communicate with Aloysius. Without knowing what I was answering, I simply shook my head no. "But you must! As I said, this one must be punished for killing one of our brothers. These crucifixions and sacrifices are what gives us life! Keeps the others away. Would you really deny Mithras?"

My mind raced as I tried recall what the leader in the long coat had just been saying. It was so ridiculous I had been able to easily ignore the mad ramblings. But he had been saying something about sacrificing non-believers. That their spilled blood was helping revive some old Roman God. Mithras? That was it. The leader was going to show me the face of his God, this Mithras.

"Show me the face of your God then." I didn't realize it at the time, but I know I reached for my bundled feathers. I stroked the long, soft wing tips as the leader in the long coat reached across his face and pulled down his facial covering. "Show me," I repeated as I watched the arc of his arm and the swing of his hand as he pulled aside the mask.

His nose was gone. The soft flesh and cartilage missing as if they were made of wax and lit on fire sometime in the past. Below his nose, where skin and lips are meant to hide the savagery of our bite, was only angry red meat. A few oddly angled and crooked teeth jutting from the obscene hole. All of the skin and most of the structure of the face missing from the nose down.

It was worse than I have the words to write.

Back home on the reservation, I had seen firsthand the damage a deadly pox like syphilis can do. The split and tortured faces of the untreated matched only by the madness it is often accompanied by. It was clear the leader of this handful of French soldiers was very sick with the disease. The contagion, I knew, ran rampant across much of the fighting forces on these shores. The victims' brains often as ruptured and rotten as their skin.

How the man in the long coat had drawn and earned the trust of those rogue soldiers is still beyond me. Perhaps they were deserters like they accused Aloysius of being. Perhaps they'd not been right in the head when they first hit the battlefield. Or perhaps a different sickness, 'shell-shock' some were now calling it, had left them vulnerable and directionless. Whatever the reason, the other four followed suit. Removing their stained masks one at a time as I stood transfixed.

Five faceless men.

Each gruesome face was marred and split. A valley of torn flesh where their noses should have been. The grisly wounds each starting at the top of their upper lips before ending with a long slice that split the skin of their foreheads in two. I stared at each of the nearly identical gaps with undisguised disgust, struggling to understand what I was seeing. These wounds were weeks old at the most. Clearly not the result of syphilis like their leader. Had their noses been shot off in some bizarre sacrifice? I had a million questions on the tip of my tongue – but a gasp was all I could manage.

"Join us," said the man in the long coat. The diseased face stretching, cracking and oozing hideously. "Spite the face of God as we have. Break the shackles. Live free with us! Mithras provides. His influence is growing with every..."

At their feet, Aloysius suddenly sprang to action. He spun his body and rolled towards the four surprised soldiers while lashing out with his arms and feet. The leader instantly lost his footing in the sloppy mud of the battleground, and he lunged towards me in an effort to keep his balance. The end of my rifle, bayonet still affixed, sunk into his chest before bursting out his back along with a rush of air and a spray of red blood. My gun went off as I struggled to shake off the impaled leader. The bullet cleaving a hole in the head of the soldier just behind him. He dropped unmoving on the ground.

I felt the whiz of a bullet scream past my ear just as I was able to dislodge the blade on the end of my rifle from the chest of the struggling leader. I returned fire, three shots in quick succession riddling the chest of another of the disfigured soldiers. I watched him fall just as Aloysius overpowered the only one still moving. The crook of his long arm choking out the last breaths the man would ever take. Beside him lay the bludgeoned remains of the first soldier Aloysius had subdued. The split wood of the rifle he'd used to beat him lying broken on the ground.

"They were going to crucify me when I refused to join them. That one," Aloysius, winded and breathing hard, pointed to the wide-eyed leader struggling to turn over on the ground, "should be..." But his words went unspoken. Interrupted and shouted down by the wounded leader in the long coat.

"Mithras will find you and strike you down! You dare judge me? You believe my insides are as rotten as my face? Ha!" The man pushed himself from the ground with a loud groan, resting on all fours as he berated and cursed us with what was likely the last bit of his strength. "As we are, so shall you be. Wherever you hide, no matter how long it takes. Mithras will come for you. You hear me! When you leave this world, you'll be holding the hand of Mithras as the flesh rots and falls from your body. You'll feel every piece of flesh that dies. With this I curse you, Aloysius Leroux!"

We turned then, both of us hastening to leave the foul-faced thing spewing such poison, when the nearby trench suddenly erupted. Out of the valleyed dirt came the shambling group of monstrous German soldiers I'd run from earlier. Their focus on the bleeding and broken dead at our feet. "Run!" I screamed and pushed Aloysius the opposite way I was headed, hoping to propel him towards safety and desperate to be done with this fiendish killing field. As I scrambled once more for the timber that bordered the battlefield, I could hear the tortured last screams of the faceless man with the long coat.

I wondered if his God heard...

CHAPTER EIGHT

It was near dark before Secrist found time to reopen the old diary the following day, the journal lying untouched on the wooden end table beside his couch where he'd left it the night before. The bizarre passages and vivid description of his grandfather's time in France during the First World War had begun to seem more fiction than fact. The crucifixions, zombies, and accounts of diseased and disturbed soldiers like something out of one of those pulpy horror comics he used to enjoy as a kid. The read was entertaining for sure.

But was any of it real?

Secrist sat contemplatively on his couch. The plain blue cover of the diary in his hands as Frazier softly serenaded him with assorted grunts and snores from the opposite end of the furniture. Beside him, a sandstone coaster caught the beaded condensation running down his just-opened bottle of Guinness. He pulled his cell phone from his pocket and checked he hadn't missed any calls before lying it next to his beer. He was a little surprised he hadn't heard from Stander. Thinking to himself that, if he didn't hear from his best friend by tomorrow night, he'd try to reach him.

In the meantime, back to reading...

When I finally reached the shelter of the woods, I dove for the thick brush and hastened to make myself as small as possible. Hiding among the shadows with the bayonet end of my loaded rifle pointed at the path I'd just carved and looking out across the empty battlefield I'd run from.

My eyes and ears straining for any hint that I was being followed. As long minutes ticked slowly past, my racing breaths and pounding heart gradually began to calm. When I was certain no one was tracking me, I pushed a little deeper into the dark timber until I found a small gulley where I could shelter and rest. Hunkering down among the tall, swaying weeds and covering myself with a blanket of smallish branches before writing down the day's horrors. Once it grew dark, I picked at my rations in between snatching a few winks of sleep under the relative safety of the night. Waiting impatiently for morning to come, knowing that trying to navigate an unfamiliar forest in the dark would be foolhardy.

When the black sky finally began to grey and lighten, I rechecked my compass once more before beginning my hike. I spent the morning climbing up and down deeply rutted hills and parting the wispy mist that gathered along the low-lying dips in the forest floor. Moving steadily until I partnered for a time with a gurgling stream rushing westward the same as I. The sound of the tumbling water helping mask the sound of my footfalls as I navigated the gravelly shoreline. It seemed at nearly every bend of the stream various woodland animals were gathered and drinking. Many of them likely driven into the compacted wooded area I crossed by the surrounding fighting and proximity to the frontline. Skittish deer, hares, squirrels, and foxes all scattering at my approach. A brown and white dog darting inside a skinny canyon of dirt. A wild boar squealing loudly as it splashed across the shallow waters, and small flocks of birds throwing themselves at the branches of the surrounding trees when I drew near. The chilly air they glided across clear and untainted by the machinations of the war.

I pushed forward knowing my destination, where I was ordered, lie beyond the forest I was cutting across. If there was to be any hope of my mission being successful, I needed to be hidden and entrenched well ahead of my target's arrival. It had taken me a week of clandestine travel to reach my objective undetected. As close as I was now, I still wasn't, literally, out of the woods just yet. Once I was, I knew the most perilous part of this undertaking would begin.

Cresting a small rise, I surprised a small pack or family of wolves. The grey of their pelts coupled with the tawny fur bordering their white necks a dead giveaway as they dissolved into the surrounding timber. When I stepped to where they had been gathered – hoping to see some clear paw prints – any doubts I had faded. The scavenging pack had been feasting before dropping their meal in a panicked retreat at my arrival. What they'd left behind, now at my feet, were the torn and glistening remains of what had once been a beautiful dog. Possibly, judging from the size and markings, the very same brown and white dog I'd surprised earlier as it drank along the side of the stream. Perhaps, as the saying goes, I'd led the lamb right to the slaughter...

Much of the innards and underside of the scrawny mutt was missing. But I could still tell the dog was a she and recently, a mother. From what was left of her chest hung long pink nipples likely still producing milk. My heart hurt for her pups. They'd either already been devoured like their mother was on the way to becoming, or, if she'd left them in a den somewhere, their cries of hunger would go unanswered.

I'm not sure why the dead dog affected me as it did. I'd seen far worse in this war done to men, women, and children. Many times over. Without thinking, I pulled out the photo I'd scavenged from the boy-like German soldier I'd bayonetted to death just days earlier. When my eyes landed on the face of the smiling boy in the picture, they began to burn with tears. I could still feel the last of his shuddering breaths after I'd run him through. His eyes growing dim and sightless beneath me.

Just like this dog.

I dragged a sleeved arm across my wet face before pocketing the black and white photo. I began moving, rushing to put some space between myself and the hungry wolves. Moving steadily once again as I slowly closed in on the German border town where my orders led me.

Periodically consulting my compass as I carefully picked my way through the undergrowth of the thick forest. Thistles with prickly stems and thorns with tearing barbs desperately clutching at me as I passed, as if warning me of what is to come. Walled in on all sides by rugged timber, my eyes searched for game trails to help ease my travel. Far above my head, the topmost branches of the towering trees lightly fingered the breeze that swayed them. The sun still stubbornly refusing to brighten the day.

When the trees abruptly ended a short time later, I found myself looking out across a large homestead consisting of several dilapidated houses, multiple small sheds, and a barn. One of the homes had been partially devoured by a fire, and I could tell the surrounding fields and farmland had not recently been worked. The meadow closest to me was bordered by a crude wooden fence that held nothing inside. Any farm animals, like the family who once cultivated the land, all long gone. Casualties of the war no doubt. I started to move along the edge of the woods in hopes I could circle around the property undetected when a door on one shed suddenly flew open.

"No!" A scrawny boy with blonde hair charged from the opening. His screams piercing the silence of the abandoned farm as I flung myself to the ground to avoid being seen by him. Behind the child, barreling down on the boy like a locomotive train, came a shirtless man. He tugged off the belt at his waist as he closed the gap. The strap coming down just as he reached the skinny boy and knocking him off his feet. The boy screamed as he was harshly whipped several times by the brutish looking man. His cries melting into sobs when the man dragged him up by the scruff of his collar and threw him over his shoulder. It was only then I noticed the child wore a shirt and nothing more; his bare feet kicking wildly in the air.

The man who had chased the boy seemed to cast his eyes around the deserted fields of the farm as if to be certain the boy hadn't drawn any unwanted attention. A moment later he turned on his heel, boy still in tow, and walked back towards the open doorway both man and child had first burst through. It was being held open by a second man, and I could see a third figure lingering just behind him. When the man and boy crossed the threshold of the doorway, the door was swiftly slammed shut so hard that the latch didn't catch. As if embarrassed by what it was hiding inside, the wooden door slowly reopened. The sounds of the boy's earsplitting cries following just behind its lazy swing.

I squeezed my eyes shut and clamped both fists over my ears. Yet, though sightless and deaf by my own hands, I still saw and heard. My mind conjuring up subtle details I'd missed as the chase and beating had happened. Adding to the tragedy I tried my best to ignore and block out.

The third figure in the background of the doorway was definitely a man. Both his chin and nose long – like the snout of a wolf. His eyes dripping with hunger. The man who'd held the door was skinny as a rail, skeletal even. The slender fingers on his right-hand pawing at the 'Y' between his hips the entire time he'd watched the boy being beaten and carried back inside the shed. And the brutish man, older and thicker than the others, had pulled off a belt affixed with a large brass symbol. The unifying symbol of all the individual German states.

The Iron Cross!

I slinked backwards on my stomach until the trees at my back sheltered and hid me in their long shadows. I pretended I didn't hear the muffled sounds as I stood and turned my back to them. Though I knew which direction, I busied myself with another read of my compass. My eyes looking anywhere but at the shed as I started walking once more. But, with nothing to look at, my mind produced images to play along with the tortured soundtrack of screams still reaching my ears. My mind turning the men into wolves; their long teeth tearing and biting as they devoured what was once an innocent boy. Taking everything they wanted, and leaving a broken and bloodied wreck behind. I wondered where the boy's family was. Had his parents been killed like the brown and white dog I'd stumbled upon earlier? Was the boy like a lost puppy finally waylaid by the beasts that roamed this war-torn countryside?

As I hurried away, I thought of the government-funded and church-run Indian Boarding School I'd been forced to attend as a boy. How the teachers had done everything they could to kill the Indian inside me. Replacing my tribal name, Anong, with their white tribal name, Thomas Starr. How they would force all the native children to speak only in English and beating any of us who defied their order. One day, I simply decided I couldn't take the abuse any longer and I ran away from the school. Sneaking off the grounds and cautiously making my way into a nearby town in the desperate hope I would see a kind face. Someone who would understand and could help me. But instead, since I stuck out like a sore thumb, my naivety and desperate hopes were quickly dashed.

Boys, many years older and much, much bigger than I'd been at the time, spotted me almost as soon as I reached the outskirts of town. They pointed at my ragged clothing and dark skin. Teasing, chasing, and throwing rocks until they finally cornered me. I remember crying out to several adult men and women who passed close enough to see what was happening. But each of those *good citizens* turned a blind eye as the biggest of the boys grabbed me by my arms and dragged me down a dead-end alley. The rest of the boys surrounding and towering over me as I'd blubbered and begged them to let me go. Any light from above darkened by their menacing advance.

I've never forgotten how scared I was at that very moment. Or the pain of all the wounds they'd opened that day. How the older boys had taunted and humiliated me. The things they'd made me do to myself while, delighted by my submission, they watched and laughed. Striking me over and over if I disobeyed their twisted commands.

How they'd hurt me. One after the other.

How they'd left me. Afraid to even open my eyes.

How I'd trembled. Alone on the ground.

How I'd been soiled. My body torn.

Without realizing it – my mind's eye blind to everything but the hurt of that day – I suddenly found myself turning and advancing on the storage shed of tortured screams. The door had remained slightly ajar, and it offered a full view of the brutality as I closed the gap. The men inside were in a state of undress, and I could see the uniforms they'd pulled off and tossed aside were definitely German. The biggest of them, the one who'd chased and beaten the boy with his belt, had his back to me. His glaringly white buttocks in stark contrast to the curly black hair that covered much of his back. On either side of him, what held his attention, I could see the other two men. Their naked bodies obscene. The boy on all fours between them and suffering badly.

The brute with his back to the doorway never saw me coming. I reached around his thick neck and drew the serrated end of my knife across the front of his throat. The color red poured from his neck, and hot blood spewed from the long wound. He started to turn to see who had ended his life, but he only made it halfway before collapsing onto the dirt floor of the shed.

Sightless.

I quickly pirouetted and slammed my fist down like a hammer on top of the head of the skinny, skeletal German. Burying the sharp end of my blade up to its hilt in his skull. I remember being surprised at the ease with which I'd punctured the bone. But I had no time to contemplate if it was my rage that had made it possible or if I'd simply been lucky.

The third German soldier vaulted to his feet. His long nose making a mockery of the tiny nub barely jutting from between his legs. I aimed for the diminutive target as I swung my leg between both of his as hard as I could. I felt and heard a satisfying crunch. My heavy army boot burying itself between his exposed thighs. The man collapsed to his knees and fell into one corner, propped up by the interior walls of the cramped shelter. I pounced at him, holding him upright by his short greasy hair as I repeatedly drove my knee into the side of his head as hard as I could. The corner keeping him pinned in one place while I lashed out again and again until his dead body slid to the floor. My knee soaked and dripping.

My chest heaved and I wondered if my heart might explode in my chest, but my thoughts quickly turned to the boy. He was curled up on the dirt floor and shivering violently. His naked, bruised, and bleeding body quivering and shaking nearly uncontrollably. He uttered not a sound in response when I tried to speak with him. His eyes glassy and unseeing. He didn't fight me as I gently cleaned him. Using water from my canteen to dab at where he bled before wiping him down with the scattered garments the three German soldiers would no longer be needing. I pieced together the boy's clothes and soon had him dressed. He let me move his arms and legs as needed without resistance but never actually helped dress himself. I didn't push.

I judged the boy, blond-hair and blue-eyes, to be roughly ten-years-old. He didn't respond to any of the questions I put to him. Though, since I spoke no German, it seems likely he would not have understood them anyway. He watched unseeing as I liberated the three Germans of their meager supplies. Finding some dried fruits, wood matches, and replenishing my canteen with water before trying on each of their coats. I chose the brute's plain brown coat since it was the largest. The unremarkable garment covering my uniform completely should I be seen from a distance.

I left the boy once I finished raiding the dead men of their unneeded belongings. He didn't seem to notice as I covered the faces of each. Or when I closed the door to the shed behind me when I left. But he was dressed and safe. At least for the moment. Though the woods and farmland were not currently part of the ongoing fighting, the frontline still raged nearby. A slight change in priorities or goals by either side could envelope the entire area in the conflict.

As I walked away from the farmstead, my fingers found the photograph of the jumping dog and his young owner. I was disappointed in myself for failing to show the photo to the boy. Seeing the dog might have lifted his spirits. Perhaps he could have even translated the German writing on the back for me. I left the picture tucked where it was. Instead, rubbing the bundle of hawk feathers I kept next to my breast and calling on Mother Earth to watch over the boy and provide him with someone who cares.

Something to believe in...

CHAPTER NINE

The cell phone rang and Secrist was happy to see it was Stander calling. He'd been anxious to get an update and hear what the team working inside the quarry had discovered. Secrist gave Stander a quick update on Frazier – letting him know everything was going fine and not to worry – before asking what had been found so far.

"Nothing yet," came the uninspiring answer. "They just finished digging down to the anomaly this afternoon. They are planning to open it tomorrow. Hopefully I'll know more then."

"Do they have any idea what it might be? Does the crate, or whatever it is, have any markings on it?" Secrist had yet to see the archeology site for himself and hoped to fly over sometime soon. "How old do they think it is?"

"I wouldn't get my hopes up, Tommy. Remember what I told you before I left? Whatever it is, it was buried way after the quarry was first dug by the Romans. Hopefully we'll know for sure tomorrow, but the archeologists are pretty certain it was buried sometime in the 20th century. It's not like the big box is a fucking pirate treasure. This is France, not Florida..."

"Well, maybe it will be filled with fine wine and cheese then." Secrist chuckled a little before adding, "Would that make it the world's first-ever boxed wine?"

"You might have just hit the nail on the head."

"Oh, come on. What do you mean, Russ?" Secrist reached over and scratched Frazier behind the ear as he spoke. "If it was a vintage wine, I'm pretty sure it would be in barrels not boxes."

"Not the wine, the cheese." A brief pause. "Earlier today, Lucas spoke with a grad student of his working over in the quarry. The guy told him there is a terrible stench coming from the crate." The good humor draining from Stander's voice a little more with every word he spilled. "The guy told Lucas that it smelled like spoiled cheese." He paused a second time before finishing. "Or like something inside had died..."

It wasn't long before I realized I was being followed. The tracker keeping their distance but matching my pace if I slowed down or sped up. Having spent much of my life hunting wild game back on our reservation in Oklahoma, it was with relative ease I discovered the identity of my new admirer.

It was the boy.

I turned the tables and methodically circled back until I was able to locate him. The boy was limping, but his small frame allowed him to slip around the various downed logs, thick brush, and stands of tightly clustered trees with relative ease. He hurried along in the same direction I had been traveling. His eyes scanning the land at his feet for any sign of my path. When he reached the spot where I'd turned and began backtracking, the boy stopped.

As I watched his confusion at my trail's sudden end, I weighed the options. I could easily slip off and leave the boy. My orders, and where I was headed, didn't leave room for a partner or second party. As it was explained during my briefing, the success of this mission is contingent on my ability to secret myself away within range of the target. That was why only one sniper, me, had been deployed. Command's logic being that more than one traveler would make it hard to remain undetected and harder to explain away if we were somehow seized or caught. Discovery and capture – not an option open to me.

And that was an order.

But on the other hand, I thought to myself, traveling with a child over this last stretch of wooded forest might be the perfect cover. Any Germans – soldiers or civilians – who saw us together from a distance would assume we were both local, friendly, and possibly related. Two brothers, maybe an uncle and nephew, or perhaps even father and son. Though, should anyone draw very close, it would be obvious I was far too young to be the boy's parent. Of course, that's assuming they could look past my black hair and our starkly contrasting skin color.

It seemed obvious to me that the boy was all alone and scared. Why else would he be following me unless it was in hopes I could provide some sort of protection? But would he go along with the deception? Stay silent? After all, I am an enemy to his homeland. Could the boy be trusted?

Impulsively, I split the tall weeds and brush that hid me. No longer remaining quiet, I emerged just behind the boy and all but scared the kid right out of his skin. He didn't scream, but his face flushed a bright red color. Once he recovered from the shock, he was obviously embarrassed by the ease in which I'd snuck up on him. I just gave the boy a smile and a shrug, hoping he understood he shouldn't be ashamed I'd gotten the drop on him. I patted him lightly on the shoulder as I strolled past. My path and journey resumed once more. The boy stood unmoving as the distance between us began to increase. I suspected he was having the same doubts about me that I had about him.

Trust always in short supply when you are at war.

The blond-haired boy soon moved off the spot and trailed some twenty feet behind for much of the day. The timber we walked along allowed for relatively smooth passage. Periodically, a path materialized that headed the same direction I needed to go. The game trails and looping switchbacks a welcome sight as we pushed forward through the remainder of the afternoon. When I spied a series of three trees that had fallen almost right on top of each other sometime in the past, I decided to stop for the night and make camp underneath the impromptu shelter. The boy intuitively began helping me clear away the surrounding brush and we used some of the fallen limbs for cover.

We shared food and drink over a small fire in silence. The boy remained mute and impassive, rarely meeting my eyes and showing little interest in my clumsy attempts to bridge the communication gap between us. When I pulled out this journal and began writing my account of the day, the boy fell fast asleep. In between these passages I scribble, I watch him sleep and try to imagine what the boy's dreams are like. This child of war. Did he still dream of toys, candy, and puppy dogs' tails as they say? Does he dream of his country's victory? Or, as it had begun to seem more likely, did he understand there was little hope left for them? Perhaps already dreaming of revenge and hoping to take part in it when he grew to be a man.

I awoke hours later – the fire reduced to barely glowing embers and the sky above still black – to the sound of stifled bawling and sobs. I understood immediately where the cries were coming from. I looked over and saw the boy's alabaster, cherub-like face split by his shuddering tears. I instinctively reached for the boy. I'd spent many nights crying myself to sleep when I was young like him, and I knew how meaningful the simple touch of another could be when you feel all alone. I hugged the boy close. His spiny back and protruding ribs hard like the bony fingers of death's closing grip. Without words to comfort him, I pressed my forehead to his. Stroking his hair until the sobs slowed and died. Eventually, sleep finding us both again.

I rose hours later as the moon fell behind the barren trees that surrounded us. My movements awakening the boy as I readied a simple meal and prepared for what I expected to be the last full day of travel. My destination now only a handful of miles away. We shared the unsatisfying breakfast and, though I didn't encourage him, we both left together before the sun made its first appearance of the new day. The boy sticking very close to my side and no longer letting me out of his sight. As we trudged along, rounding hills and slipping in and out of the clustered timber, our breath visible in the chilly morning breeze, my mind began to weigh the consequences of my actions.

I still believed my chances of discreetly reaching the city for which I was headed would improve if accompanied by the child. But I knew once I arrived, we would have to part ways. Though I could easily abandon the boy at any time – and part of me wondered if doing so in these unpopulated woods might be wise – I still felt a responsibility for his well-being. A kinship even. And, if I was honest with myself, I longed for the simple pleasure of uncomplicated company. The boy saw me for my actions and not the color of my skin or uniform. With neither of us speaking the same language, I didn't even have to worry about what I said or how it came out. So, I relented and we walked side by side together across the downed logs, trickling streams, and muddy gullies of the forest.

After the first few miles, each hour greyer than the one before, a light shower of snow flurries began to swirl among the leafless trees. The dizzying flakes melting as soon as they touched down on anything solid. The boy remained silent and stoic beside me, unmoved by the magic of Mother Earth. I swatted at flakes that floated near my face as if they were hornets or bees. Being overly dramatic and silly in hopes I could make the boy smile and begin to recover some of the joy he'd once known. Though, I knew from personal experience, those injuries inside may never fully heal. Someone would always come along and rip away the scabs no matter if they were visible or not.

Some wounds never get healthy enough to scar.

When my attempts at levity failed to register on the boy's face, I switched tactics. Though I knew the German child couldn't understand me, I began talking. The forest around us devoid of eavesdroppers. I introduced myself and started talking about the weather. Gesturing to the sky and prattling on about the dropping temperature and making bold predictions of the snow soon to arrive. Slowly, I could see the expression under the blond hair and blue eyes softening. My unintelligible chatter distracting enough that the boy could tear his thoughts from the awful events of the day before. Or, for all I knew, days, weeks, or months before. This awful war, now in its fourth year, likely all the boy knows.

I kept babbling.

I spoke of nickelodeons, the five-cent temporary theatres showing moving pictures that were popping up all across America. I mimed the great Charlie Chaplain and his character The Tramp – wildly popular on both sides of the Atlantic – in hopes the boy would smile at the ridiculousness of his comedic misadventures. As time went on, without realizing it, I even began to explain where we were headed and my current orders. The boy nodding along. Blissfully unaware I was sharing the most secret of missions. Words that, if understood, could upset the carefully laid plan. The plan to assassinate Germany's leader, Kaiser Wilhelm II.

Britain had recently learned of a captured French chateau which, intelligence work had revealed, was currently in use by the Kaiser as his secret Western Front operational residence. The grand home, though technically in France, sat on land under German control. In as little as a week the RAF, Britain's Royal Air Force, would launch an air raid from a covert airfield near the frontline. The bombing biplane's target would be the French chateau, their mission to kill the leader of Germany. It is expected to fail.

Which is where I come in.

Intelligence had also uncovered the owner of the chateau to be an American woman. Some lady living in the Midwest named Madeleine something-or-other that had inherited the estate in the past from a distant French relative. None of that would have really mattered except she'd also revealed the estate included a secret underground passageway. A long subterranean corridor that had been carved out sometime in the storied past of the grand home. A hidden underground route that provided safe passage from the chateau to a nearby German village. A hidden escape route if the home was in jeopardy or came under attack. Or was bombed. The several miles long secret tunnel undercutting the border and connecting France and Germany.

My orders, I happily shared with my uncomprehending hiking companion, were to stakeout the tunnel's exit. And wait. The small German town housing the chateau's clandestine opening had been shelled without mercy for much of the last week to soften the area up and help clear my path. The aerial attack meant to scatter any lingering soldiers and drive much of the civilian population away from the immediate area. Hopefully making my clandestine arrival safe and allowing me time to secure a hiding location. Once I was entrenched, I need only to watch and wait for the RAF's planes to fly directly over the German town on their way to bomb the chateau. If after one week's time I'd still not seen the aerial attackers, the assassination attempt either failed or was called off, and I was to retreat and return to command. However, if the planes did fly, I was ordered to maintain a hidden location within range of the subterranean tunnel's exit. The secret escape route, as revealed to me during my briefing, opened up in the courtyard to a block of flats within the city limits of the town I was headed for. If the Kaiser emerged, I was to shoot him right between his eyes.

The boy and I stopped to rest and eat, when just a mile or so in the distance, the outskirts of the German town gradually became visible. The sky above the buildings thick with plumes of black smoke rising nonchalantly from the piles of rubble below. The soot choking the winter air before the grey ashes intertwined with the white snow flurries falling against our faces as we silently ate. The familiar aroma of fire and death reacquainting itself and reawakening my every sense.

With my focus returning fully to my mission, it was perhaps not a complete surprise that I didn't hear the approach of the small dog until it was practically upon us. The dog, an undecipherable mixture of black fur and white paws, burst over the edge of the slight rise where we sat. The black dog's tail a blur as it fearlessly advanced on the smiling boy. For a moment, I thought the unbridled joy I saw in the child's eyes was a sign of recognition. But when the boy spied several additional shapes moving between the trees in the distance, back where the dog had come running from, he quickly shuffled behind me. The joy in his expression and eyes wilting like flowers starved of rain.

The dog, practically a puppy and likely not yet even a year old, soon sprinted back the way it had come with both tongue and tail wagging. Clearly done investigating us and happy to return to its owner. The figures moving parallel to our position were obviously who it had run from. I pressed a finger to my lips and hoped the symbol for silence was universal as I quietly lowered myself to my belly on the cold ground. The boy mimicked my actions and noiselessly joined me on the floor of the forest. The small group of travelers unaware of our position as I slowly pointed my rifle their way.

Unknown to them or the quaking child pressed against my side, I spied on our fellow forest dwellers. Their actions brought near by the telescopic lens affixed to the barrel of my rifle. Including the dog, now panting contently at their side, the group consisted of six travelers. One by one I zeroed in on each of the figures. My finger poised on the trigger.

None of them uniformed.

Oblivious to the presence of the boy and I, for long minutes I appraised their actions. Focusing on each hiker until I was certain the group was clearly a family of some sort. Two of the figures were adults. Parents, or perhaps simply a man and a woman thrown together by the chaos of war. While the other three appeared to be children of various ages; the tallest one a girl I judged nearly the same age as the boy beside me. Where they were headed and why unclear. The dog, having already investigated us, was onto its next adventure. Trotting ahead of the supposed family with a nose to the ground and occasionally stopping to paw at branches and logs that had fallen before joyfully jumping over them in search of more intriguing finds.

When I lowered my rifle, my eyes landed on the face of the blue-eyed, blond-haired boy. I knew where I was headed would not be safe for him. Likely, it wasn't going to be safe for me either. There was nothing I could do about that; I had my orders. But I could do one more thing for the child. Give him a chance.

Without words, I gestured at the group as they closed within a hundred yards of where we hid. Initially, the boy seemed grief stricken. His eyes pooled and his features contorted in fear. I continued to pantomime as best I could. Mimicking breasts and a pregnant belly until he seemed to understand that one of the walkers was a mother before I held my hand out at different heights and pointing. Helping, I hoped, to make him see the group included children. After some additional coaxing, recognition began to spread across his features.

"Familie?" The boy whispered in German. His face lighting up when I vigorously nodded my head up and down in agreement.

"Family," I replied, smiling. Stunned and grateful the German and English word were nearly identical. I pointed to the small group and encouraged him to join them. Making crude shooing gestures with my hands and smiling. But the boy remained glued to my side. His eyes roaming from mine over to the now gradually shrinking family. The space between our hiding place and their path increasing once again. Desperate for the boy to take advantage of what fate had tossed our way, I briefly pulled out the photo of the dog and German boy-soldier I'd been carrying. I pointed to the smiling face in the picture, then at my young companion before pointing at the dwindling figures in the woods. He didn't understand until I placed a finger at each corner of his mouth and turned up the thin lips on his face. Forcing his blank expression into a crooked smile before smiling myself and gently nudging him until he stood. "Go," I kept repeating.

The boy's indecision lasted a few more moments before he began to move. He retreated a few steps before reclaiming them; worry ruining the smile I'd forced on him. I shook my head no and shooed him away again. Encouraging him to leave me. He turned and walked five or six steps away before suddenly spinning and running back. Our eyes didn't meet as he briefly wrapped his bony arms around me and I hugged him in return. "Danke," he breathed into our embrace before pulling away and sprinting after the family in the distance. When I looked down at the front of the coat I wore, I could see it was wet from the boy's tears. Though, I supposed as drops rolled off the end of my nose, they could have just as easily been mine.

I looked down at the black-and-white face of the young German in the photo. While the smiling face and the look of the two boys were vastly different, the memento had suddenly grown into something more. It was now a bridge to my time with the boy, the dog, the family, and the new life he'd raced after. I tucked the picture into the breast pocket of my uniform shirt.

Right next to my heart.

CHAPTER TEN

SECRIST LET THE NEXT *day dissolve into a starry evening before he began to grow concerned. He had expected to hear from Stander again today. Afterall, this was supposed to be the day the unknown anomaly was being pulled from the ground in France. Its century old burial ending, and whatever was housed within the mysterious crate brought to light. Stander, a lifelong loner, certainly wasn't in the habit of checking in with anyone on a regular basis. But Secrist had expressed interest in the enigmatic find the night before, and it wasn't like Stander to blow him off. Secrist's thumb briefly hovered over the buttons on his phone before, sighing, he'd repocketed it.*

"He probably just has his hands full dealing with whatever they found." Secrist spoke to Frazier as the dog meandered from the kitchen to the living room. "Probably a lot of paperwork involved." Stander's dog vaulted onto the couch and sat on his haunches beside Secrist. "It's not like I can help him with anything from here. Maybe we should give him another day or two, huh, Frazier?" Secrist pet the dog on his head before scratching him under his chin a few times. The dog's snout high in the air as he leaned against him contently. "Tell you what. When he does finally call, we'll put the call on speaker so you can hear." Secrist pulled his hand away and reached for the nearby journal lying on the side table. "I'll tell Russ I think you really miss him. That'll make him feel guilty for not calling us earlier." Frazier's eyes seemed to smile behind his soft pant.

The diary in his lap, Secrist pulled out the bookmark and laid it beside him. Opening the book to the page he'd left off. The read drawing him in deep again...

The leafless trees hid little of the town as I gradually drew closer. My hurried steps slowing as I began gingerly making my way from one stand of trees to another. I knew the close proximity of the populated area greatly increased the chances of my discovery.

Above me, the sun periodically winked from its hiding place behind the grey clouds that crowded the sky. The snow flurries had ceased, but the wind began to pick up. I moved as close to the edge of town as I dared under the intermittent sunshine that brightened the otherwise bleak landscape. My ears detected the nearby sound of gurgling water and I soon spied the smallish river I sought. The stream itself was unremarkable. But the waterway would lead me to the tenement housing, or as the multi-unit flats were sometimes now called, apartment buildings, that I sought. The one beside the secret tunnel entrance that connected this town to the French chateau where German Command administered their orders for the western front.

Keeping myself hidden along the edges of the timber bordering the town, I followed the rushing water until it split from the side of the woods. The stream cutting a jagged line right through the very heart of the German city. I dared not enter the town proper in the daylight. Instead, I hunkered down behind a row of trees that bordered a surprisingly large cemetery and waited for nightfall to come. My eyes searching for civilians and soldiers in equal order. Any German citizen a threat and danger to both myself and my mission.

As boredom relentlessly stalked me – eyelids growing heavy and chin periodically bouncing off my chest – I began to survey the nearby garden of the dead. Looking for something to occupy my mind and keep me alert until it was finally safe to move. Some of the headstones closest to my position were still upright. Though, across much of the graveyard, many had recently been disturbed and toppled. The war, the shelling, and the falling bombs didn't discriminate against the dead.

The consecrated ground was littered with the cracked and toppled markers. The war obliterating the last testament to the lives of these German citizens. Nearly all the tombstones were etched with versions of the Christian cross, and I could see the vast acreage held a multitude of sober-faced angels and other stone statues of various sizes. The symbols of faith now cracking under the strain of reality; most crooked and standing on little that could be considered solid ground. The warring politicians distorting and bending the holy symbol to their will. Their faithful followers oblivious to the grift.

No different than in times of peace.

Something else about the gravestones caught my eye and began to whisper in my ear. The dates. The carved lettering on most of the monuments had been done in German and, outside of a few simple words I'd picked up over the last couple of years, that was a script unknown to me. But many of the markers held numbers that I could recognize, and a quick calculation between the two sets of numbers provided the age of the interred. Many of the graveyard's tenants, at least the ones I could read, had died well before the war. I was shocked, based on the size of the town in front of me, how many citizens had passed over the previous years and decades. More puzzling, it seemed countless had perished early in life. Many not even reaching forty years of age! I began to wonder if there had been a plague. An outbreak that had shortened the townsfolks' lives well before this awful war had ever begun. I thought back to the faceless French soldiers I'd encountered. Their leader's hideously diseased features. Perhaps it was only a coincidence.

But I don't like coincidences.

I turned my eyes and thoughts to the city itself. The town I surveyed had been left in shambles by the earlier bombing raids. Like a dense grove of lifeless trees after a blazing forest fire, blackened brick chimneys stood stark and naked against the background of the destruction. The homes and buildings they'd once warmed now cold and reduced to piles of rubble at their base. The walls meant to keep them safe had mostly tumbled to the earth. Though some structures still stood, many were now just crumbling piles of concrete, rebar, and limestone. I'd clearly missed the worst of the citizens' misery.

Every few blocks I could see a series of cement arches holding up nothing but air. Their burden removed by the onslaught of war. Fires still burned somewhere unseen among the ruins; the black smoke streaming high into the air in various places. Family homes were missing entire walls. The blown-out sides gaping in wide-mouthed horror at what had been done to the city. Doorways yawned without doors, and glassless wood panes framed disheartening scenes out of the age-old story of man's greed. A fool's play nobody wanted to see acted out anymore. The tired scenes as subtle as a kick to the teeth.

Mankind can't win when man loses all kindness.

Though few and far between, haggard citizens of the town made sporadic appearances within the rubble. Cautiously picking their way through the splintered streets and gathering anything they deemed valuable. Most I assumed, like me, waiting for darkness to descend before moving more freely out in the open. But when nighttime was finally ushered in – accompanied by biting gusts that pricked my bare skin like needles – the dropping temperature cleared the last of the scavengers from the streets. Driving the displaced townsfolk back into whatever shelter they could find.

The black of the frigid night wrapped me in confidence as I meticulously made my way to the side of the river. The hurrying of the icy waters hid my advance as I navigated the uneven shoreline. I rushed along the side of the waterway until my objective came into view. The apartment building of flats I sought as easy to locate as Command had assured me. It had been, and three sides still were, the tallest structure in the town. It also looked like it might be among the oldest. Clearly, what was now broken into individual apartments had once been an estate. A grand home of many individual rooms from a bygone era. The style of the architecture centuries old. I ducked under what was left of a carriage or wagon that had burned in the recent past. Only the rusted metal frame remained to hide behind.

From my stomach, I counted the floors of the marred building to ensure there were five. I could see, despite the damage done by the earlier bombing, the shingled roof of a tiny structure a mere three or four feet off the ground on the eastern side of the apartments. The low-lying roof covering a handful of stairsteps that descended under the diminutive structure. The tell-tale sign something of substance had been built under the ground.

In America, we call them storm cellars and, especially in Oklahoma where I'd grown up, they generally only house canned fruits and vegetables until a storm blew in. When bad weather would hit, usually a tornado, anyone within earshot would pile into the cramped quarters and wait for the storm to pass overhead. I didn't know if this part of Germany dealt with tornados or not. But, according to the officers who'd briefed me on this mission, the low-lying roof covered an underground stairway and exit. Not a cellar. If the German leader, Kaiser Wilhelm II, escaped the assassination attempt that would soon flatten the French chateau he commanded from, it would be through there.

With my objective now reached, it was time for the next phase of my clandestine assignment. I needed to secure a position from which I could observe the comings and goings of the converted apartment building and the secret tunnel entrance poking up from the courtyard below. My eyes scoured the landscape as I weighed the advantages and disadvantages of several locations that I thought looked promising. The experience I'd gained over the years serving in this war as an assassin and sniper had sharply honed my skill at finding clever hiding spots.

A sharp screech split the hush of the darkness, and I flinched at the unexpected outburst. I recognized the avian's call just as a large bird of prey swooped down from whatever lofty perch it had launched from. Its wavering shadow passed overhead. The luminescence of the full moon doing its best to penetrate the swirling cloud cover that hid it. I watched the path the flight took as what I recognized to be a hawk landed nearby, roosting on the highest point of a collapsed building. It was far too dark for me to make out the pattern on the hawk's feathers or to be certain of identification. But it was one of the more common hawks I'd often seen soaring in the skies of France since my arrival. Likely either a Sparrowhawk or the Northern Goshawk; both plentiful in Germany and France.

It wasn't until moments later when the bird of prey lifted off, disappearing silently into the nighttime sky, that I realized the wisdom of where it had perched. Though it had rested on top of rubble, the view of the underground tunnel's exit, covered by that shingled roof, was unobstructed. Yet far enough away to be lost among the seemingly endless piles of building debris. It was perfect.

Too perfect, perhaps…

Using the cover of the shaded moon, I darted from one concealed spot to another until I hid among the wreckage of the collapsed building the hawk had drawn my attention to. Secreting myself away within the damage until I could ascertain if the site was stable and could provide me with everything I needed. I pulled out my field glasses and surveyed the surrounding area.

My objective, the low-lying rooftop the Kaiser would emerge from, now tiny in the distance, resembled a prop from a staged play. A minute representation of a full-sized building front and center in the drama it had been written into. Directly behind the "stage," the backdrop was the apartment building I'd sought. The façade of the wall facing me badly damaged by the earlier shelling and leaving behind a patchwork of partially exposed flats or apartments. Their most hidden and precious contents bared to the victors of the earlier assault. The bombs and projectiles, fired on my behalf, splaying the tiny homes open much like the dead still scattered about the area. The unclaimed bodies lumpy and misshapen like toppled scarecrows with much of their stuffing raided by scavenging animals. The unmoving figures just more props for the upcoming feature.

The converted multi-family housing unit was exposed like an open autopsy. Leaving the curious little to guess about the complex innerworkings. The colors of the walls, the cut of the curtains, the quality of the furniture within, et cetera. In one apartment, a dining room table sat upright while the four wooden chairs at its sides had all toppled. In another, I could make out a baby crib I prayed was unoccupied, and, in the next one over, I spied a bookcase overflowing with assorted-sized volumes. Each of the exposed apartments were little vignettes into the lives of everyday German citizens. It would be against this backdrop of normalcy that I would kill one of the most powerful men in the world. I had no doubt, once I set up my shot, my assassination attempt would be successful.

But for all the strengths of the nest from which my bullets would hatch, I also recognized this spot would eventually be identified when my shots started flying. Once it was, I would be targeted by those emerging from the tunnel. I would need to find a way to dig in. Lose and protect myself in the shelter of the misshapen rubble and be prepared to return fire until I was certain of my success. Cover myself in debris and shelter down inside a canyon of dirt.

A trench.

I would either be digging my own grave or the trench I carved into the earth would save me. That much seemed clear. But I suspected if dug tonight, before the dropping temperatures froze the earth under me any harder, my chances of staying undetected while I watched the skies would be greatly improved. Spending even one more day hiding in the surrounding timber, much less trying to return here unnoticed again tomorrow night, only further imperiled the mission. I would cover myself and marinate in the soil of this bloodstained land. Conceal myself right under the noses of this city's refugees and give no indication the knowledge of the secret escape route had been compromised.

Decision made, I spent the remaining hours of darkness laboring. Pulling debris from under the collapsed roof of the building and clearing out a spot where, incognito, I had a clear view of my surroundings. The surreptitious tunnel exit dead in my sights. Once I'd settled on where I would hide, I used my bayonet to scratch at the surface of the near frozen ground until the dirt below finally softened and loosened. I pulled out handful after handful until the depression was deep enough. The piles of dirt crowded around the pit and were ready to be pulled over me once I was in position.

By the time I'd finished, the sky had begun to lighten in preparation for the upcoming day. As I finish writing this entry, I've now been up for nearly 24 hours straight. The previous two days spent pulling myself, mile after mile, through wooded timber. I am drained both physically and mentally. But I have made it. Made it where I'd been ordered, secured a perch any sniper would be proud of, and feel confident I had done so undetected.

Now, I lay in wait.

I dozed fitfully, exhaustion and tension pulling at both frayed ends with equal success. When the rays of the climbing morning sun finally hit the apartment building I'd hiked miles and miles to reach, I was shocked at what was revealed. Though the immediate area was now mostly leveled, it clearly had recently been the very center of urban sprawl. An inner city littered with the remnants of small shops and other assorted businesses sandwiched between dilapidated housing centers. Whether the decline was from the last couple years of non-stop war along the border, or from a mundane and depressed local economy was unclear. But this German town was obviously home to a financially challenged people. I thought again of the overflowing graveyard and multitude of early deaths the cemetery held. Perhaps disease had ravaged the poor town long before the machines of war had descended.

The backdrop to my upcoming drama, the apartment building, soon stole all of my attention. It wasn't just the height that made it stand out. It was the ornate and distinguished design of the building itself. Centuries ago, it likely had been an impressive home. Surrounded back then, I imagined, by only the wilds of the land. On one side of the converted manor ran the river I'd followed; the remaining three sides likely once blanketed by acres of timber. The current concrete-laden streets, what I saw now, had clearly been built more recently than the grand home's original construction. The drab buildings that now crowded it springing up like colorless mushrooms sprouting from the decay of what must have once been the lands of a powerful and wealthy family. The one-time mansion had long ago been plundered of its pearls. Only the heart, the bosom of the family they once adorned, still remained.

"Good bones," I remember the old carpenter I sometimes worked with back on the reservation would say, "are the most important part of any home." The carpenter, a half-breed like me, had only one arm and liked to dispense bits of his wisdom while he worked. Usually, when I would be stuck holding something for him as he measured and cut the various building materials we used. "If it has good bones," he'd say, "almost anything you create can be brought back from the dead."

I gazed across at the ruins of the once proud mansion and the rubble-covered land that surrounded it. Reimagining how it may have appeared in its prime and wondering what tragedy had brought down the family who once called the grand manor home. Were they all interred in the nearby graveyard? What about the chateau just across the French border? The underground passageway I was to watch connected the two. Same family?

I remember wondering what skeletons might still lurk in that family's closets. If good bones could be brought back from the dead, I pondered as sleep reclaimed me, what would bad bones bring back with them from the land of the dead?

CHAPTER ELEVEN

THE TAVERN, AS USUAL, had a good crowd for a Thursday evening. Secrist was gratified to hear so many friendly greetings as he pulled a stool up to the polished counter of his favorite bar, In This Corner. It wasn't until Frazier had raced over to greet Hannah that he understood the boisterous regulars were clamoring more for the dog than him. He wryly surveyed the customers and nodded or waved at the familiar faces who frequented the joint. The bar and Hannah, like Stander and Frazier, the closest thing to family he had.

"Hi, Tommy. You come in to check up on me?" Hannah placed a full glass of Guinness on top of a Round One coaster. "Or was Frazier going through withdrawal?" The bar's manager gesturing towards the friendly canine as he happily pranced from familiar face to familiar face. Devouring all the attention as the patrons fawned over him and the occasional French fry or bite of hamburger for his trouble.

"Maybe a little of both," Secrist replied with a smile before tilting back his glass. "I haven't heard from you all week. Everything going alright? Anything you need help with?"

"No. It's all been good so far. Maybe a little on the slow side. But with Stander traveling so much this last year it almost seems normal not having him around. I even get out of here on time." Hannah winked once before dipping the glasses in her hand into the sink of sudsy water at her waist.

"Speaking of our beloved boss," Secrist began after taking another drink of his beer. "Have you heard from him today?"

Hannah kept working as they talked, her hands pumping like pistons in the multi-compartment sink. "Hmmm... let's see. He called on Tuesday, the second day he was gone. Thought he had to remind me to place the food order." Secrist chuckled at her overly dramatic eyeroll and dismissive headshake combo.

"I haven't heard from him since Tuesday either." Secrist shrugged nonchalantly, but it was for show. He didn't want to worry Hannah. She'd never admit it, but he knew, just like him, Stander felt like family. Maybe the unpredictable uncle you had to keep an eye on at social gatherings. But still...

"He was supposed to let me know what they found inside the quarry. And I can't believe he hasn't been pestering me every day single about how Frazier is doing. You know how often I dog sit for him. He always calls or texts. Worries what I'm feeding him..." Secrist didn't realize it but he was scowling.

"Geez! Let some sunshine in your soul there, Nosferatu." Hannah, done washing, was drying her hands with the apron at her hips. "You know Stander. He's more interested in burying his junk in some French MILF than unburying some French junk." Hannah, as always, easily bringing back to life the smile under Secrist's salt-and-pepper moustache. "Besides, just text him and find out. Or are you hinting you want me to?"

"No, no, no." Secrist waved his hands dismissively. "You're right. Forget I said anything." Secrist slapped on a plastic smile until Hannah seemed to buy the deception. "I'll text him later. After I finish doing some more reading..."

Darkness had descended. The falling weight of the starry black curtain smothering the sun until it relinquished the claim it had on the day. Freeing the moon to battle it out with the stubbornly persistent cloud cover. I'd missed the drama between the heavenly bodies above. Sleep lulling my own exhausted body and mind until I'd lost track of time. The tightly quartered trench where I hid burying my covert presence under the perfect camouflage of a collapsed building. The rubble from all the destroyed structures in this German town as countless as the branches of the weeping willow trees back home in Oklahoma.

Endless and growing.

Movement from one of the apartments in the distance caught my eye. I'd assumed the tenement housing was completely abandoned. Though the roof and three sides of the tall structure still stood, one entire outside wall had been so badly damaged I thought the rest of the building was likely unstable. The shelled and compromised wall exposing much of the old manor's interior. But now I could see the soft glow of several small fires and oil-fueled lanterns in several of the apartments. With nowhere else to hide or run in a war zone, the survivors likely had no choice. Taking their chances within the three remaining walls of their homes versus relocating elsewhere and abandoning all their possessions.

The previous evening, I had seen no light or movement coming from the apartment building as I'd entrenched myself under the rubble of the collapsed structure I now hid in. However, it had been much later at night when I'd finally located my destination, and the cold wind had been particularly unforgiving. It seemed likely, seeing the building was still occupied, that the tenants would have already retreated to a different interior room by the time I'd arrived onsite. Each separate flat would at least have a bedroom or two. Even the closed door of a miniscule closet afforded some privacy and comfort away from the elements.

The earlier movement of light recaptured my attention and I withdrew my field glasses from their case to get a closer look. I scanned the entirety of the damaged building and noted I could see inside six separate residences. Either partially or wholly depending on the extent of the damage to the exterior wall of the apartment. Only two of the eight dwellings facing me were still fully enclosed, the compromised building shielding those lucky tenants from the outside weather.

And my curiosity.

The topmost apartments seemed to have taken the brunt of the earlier assault. With the added magnification, I could see directly inside each. It had been the flashes of light coming from the residence on the left that first called my attention to the survivors. I could just make out the bundled form of a woman, her long black hair spilling out from a wool headscarf, as she moved between her home's rooms several times. The apartment next to hers, also on the top floor was quiet and dark. The backwall was stuffed with spines of leatherbound books, but I couldn't make out much else of the interior.

One floor down, directly below the apartment full of books, was another nearly lightless and lifeless home. Though it took me several minutes of focused concentration to figure out what I was seeing. The dwelling, I finally determined, had not been abandoned. Every couple of minutes I would catch a small circular orange light that would blaze brightly before gradually fading away. Only to make a reappearance a short time later. Someone, sitting in the dark and likely alone, smoking one cigarette after another. The brightening and fading orange orb the only clue someone was there.

The apartment beside the glowing orb, the one below the headscarf wearing woman, also appeared lifeless. The furniture I could make out covered with dust and debris. A single table was surrounded by four toppled chairs; the same view of the home's kitchen I'd seen the night before. The folks who once called it home either dead or staying away from the damaged building. Directly under that empty dwelling, was the liveliest of the homes I peered into. A family moving about freely within their humble flat. I could see a highchair loaded with a red-faced toddler being circled by slightly older children. Smiles and laughter across all of their delighted faces. A man and woman watching the children playing with looks of satisfaction on their faces. Somehow, the family finding joy within the uncomfortable confines of the war.

Nothing stirred in the remaining three apartments facing me. I couldn't see inside the two ground level units. The collapsed wall that exposed everything above lying in heaped piles along the ground. Masses of rubble obscuring my view of the two lowest dwellings. Satisfied with the company of my new neighbors, sleep and boredom soon teamed up on me. Slowly tugging on my eyelids as the activity and lights next door faded. The neighborhood noiseless and still as a tomb.

The dead of night.

I suddenly snapped awake. Befuddled and groggy. Unclear if mere moments or long hours had passed since I'd closed my eyes. A reeking smell like overripe apples left to rot in the sun wafting in the brisk air around me. With the logic of a dream, my eyes were drawn back to the apartment building and I peered once more through the field glasses in my hand. The images they held leaping at my face.

I could see the woman I'd spied earlier, the one in the topmost flat with the headscarf, staring out across the abyss of the ruined German town. At first, I thought she was still alone in her apartment. But she soon turned her back to me and seemed to gesture as if she was speaking with someone near. My eyes strained behind the lenses to find her companion, but the weak flickering of the oil lamp beside her cast more shadows than it did light. Whomever she was addressing, lingered just out of sight.

My breath, visible at my face, grew rushed the longer I watched. The woman, despite the frigid conditions, had begun to peel off layers of her clothing. When she reached behind to pull down the zipper that ran the length of the dress she wore, I dropped the field glasses from my face. Guiltily, I cast my eyes about. Embarrassed that someone might take exception to my spying, but nothing stirred nearby. I was still alone and unseen within the destruction I hid under. I looked across the empty courtyard, the deserted streets, and what was left of the pummeled town. Searching for any movement in the surrounding piles of debris and rubble. Nothing.

When I next peered through the lenses, I told myself it was only to check if any of the other apartments were burning the midnight oil, as they say. Each was dark, no movement or sign of the inhabitants inside. Soon, I found my gaze transfixed once more on the woman's apartment. It was as if I had no choice but to watch. I reached between my legs – shifting the shrinking space there. Mesmerized by the scene playing out before me.

The woman still stood in the same place. Exposing herself to the elements, my disbelieving eyes, and anyone else who might be watching. Doubtful as that was at that time of night. Somehow, the woman seemed to be unaffected by the bitter cold. Her slip puddled on the floor near her bare feet. The woman's back was still to me, and I could tell she was focused on the presumed partner hidden near the back of her apartment. Slowly, she turned and reached for a wooden chair. Affording me a full view of her nude body.

Her hair, freed from the scarf that had held it in place, was a dark and frizzy mane. An unruly thicket that bounced more than it laid. A smaller version of the black swarm covered much of her from the bellybutton on down, carpeting her sex and much of both legs. Still standing, she leaned forward against the back of the chair in her hands as if she needed it for balance, both her and the front of the chair facing me. When she leaned slightly forward, her heavy breasts swayed like two pendulums back and forth in the dim light.

The woman paused as she leaned against the back of the chair. Though the black, untamed hair covered much of her face, I could still tell the woman was older than my own mom. A bulbous nose dominated her plain features, and, when she opened her mouth, I could see she'd lost a front tooth at some point.

All of this I noted with the unconcerned detachment of a dream; eyes glued to the rings encircling the lens on my field glasses. Accepting the bizarre sequence of events as if a middle-aged woman stripping nude in plummeting temperatures was expected and normal. It wasn't until she was joined by the loiterer in the background that I understood I wasn't watching a dream.

I was participating.

The fingers that appeared at her shoulder were slender and pointed. Long enough to likely be masculine, but slim and caressing softly. A second, elongated flutter of fingers began soothing the muscles on the woman's opposite shoulder before sliding down to the crook of her elbow. At this second touch, I watched her face flush. Desire and want plain in her expression as she bent farther over the back of the chair. The two hands, still all I could see of her partner, suddenly clamped down. The clutching fingers of each sinking in her fat.

I watched ecstasy fill her expression when the lover took her from behind. I couldn't help but imagine the intensity both felt, and once more I shifted everything between my own legs. The thrill I felt watching, 'voyeurism' the French soldiers called it, squashing any guilt I had at my intrusion. I watched the violent bob of her head with every presumed thrust, her pale white skin flushing and blotchy.

It wasn't until the woman grew slack minutes later that I understood something was terribly wrong. She seemed to gradually wilt over the back of the chair, drooping lower and lower until she quit moving altogether. The slender hand at her shoulder stirred, sliding up her neck and grabbing a handful of frizzy hair before pulling the woman upright by the black strands as if she was weightless. Only then did I look away from her face and fill the lens of my field glasses with blood.

Her blood.

Dark lines crisscrossed the woman's flesh. Streams of red flowing from wounds somewhere along her backside I couldn't see. For long seconds she hung suspended by her hair, much of her weight resting against the back of the wooden chair. More crimson lines divided her pale skin.

The running blood indiscriminately creating squares and triangles on her chest and across her stomach.

My uncomprehending stare lingered, trying to make sense of what I was seeing. It was only at the last moment I caught a brief glimpse of what had killed her. A dripping bite sprouting from a dreadful mouth. I watched thin, pale lips peel back from the clenched teeth before they plummeted a final time into the soft meat of her shoulder. Moments before the black hid her completely. The woman pulled off the back of the chair from behind. Her body gradually fading from my sight and the light.

Swallowed completely by shadows.

I'm not sure how long I stared at the wavering flame of the oil lamp. But at some point, it must have run out of fuel and faded. The morning sun, the next thing I became aware of as my eyes groggily reopened. With a panicked start, I reached for the field glasses I'd spied the entire bizarre scene with. Anxious to see inside the woman's apartment now that it was daylight. But I found the binoculars back inside their carrying case and buried inside my pack. Perplexed, I began to wonder if I'd dreamed the entire episode. I didn't recall repacking my field glasses...

When I retrieved them, they showed nothing to dissuade this early morning epiphany. The woman's apartment looked exactly as it had the previous day. The oil lamp, table, and chairs, all in the same place. I could see no blood or disturbed furniture. Nor any sign of whatever I thought had attacked her. The flat was empty. Despite the realism I'd felt in the moment, I began to think the entire episode was simply a nightmare. No surprise considering all I'd witnessed over the previous days of travel. The stress of crossing over the frontlines, my covert orders, and exhaustion likely contributing to the vivid scenes.

Movement in the courtyard – the open stretch of land between myself and the converted apartment building – soon claimed my attention. There was an old man in a wheelchair struggling to navigate the craters and piles of rubble. His gnarled hands wrapped around the wide wheels on either side of the chair as he fought the treacherous terrain. My first instinct was to rush out and help the man overcome the challenge. But, of course, I knew I could not. Though still very early in the morning with few townspeople moving about, I could not risk giving away my position. The only chance of my mission being successful was to remain sedentary and still. Hidden right under the enemy's nose for as long as it took.

A few minutes later, the old man was rescued from his struggles. The same young family I'd seen living inside the apartment building crowding around him in obvious recognition. The father passed a squirming toddler to the mother with a smile before circling behind the wheelchair. There he was joined by two other children, and together they pushed the old man along. The awful scenes, or dream I'd just woken from, faded as I watched neighbor help neighbor. The simplest act of kindness often the most impactful. The family not leaving the unwalking man until he was once more back inside the apartment building. Helping him into the ground level flat to my left. Obviously, his residence.

I watched the children in turn, one after the other, reach over and hug the feeble man. The toddler, now I could see she was a little girl, reached down from her perch on her momma's hip and even kissed his wrinkled cheek. The familiarity and fondness genuine. I couldn't help but wonder after the boy I'd directed to a similar family in the forest just days earlier. I imagined him with the same kind of loving and caring people. Seeing the love of this close-knit family, even after the awful toll of this war, gave me hope. I pulled out the picture I'd been carrying and looked down at the smiling face and jumping dog captured in the image. Replacing them with the blond-haired and blue-eyed boy and black coated dog. Willing the joy expressed in the photo upon them both with a quick prayer to Mother Earth.

I shifted on to my side and made myself as comfortable as I could. Walled in by the dirt of the trench, I settled in for a long tour of watching. My eyes and ears straining for any hint of airplanes passing overhead as I update this journal. Unsure if I hoped to see the bombers on their way to destroy the neighboring French chateau or not.

In between these passages I write, I catch myself watching for any sign of movement from the woman's apartment. Equally unsure what I am hoping to see.

CHAPTER TWELVE

Secrist, feeling a bit sheepish, listened to the ringing in his ear for a second time. His phone connecting with Stander's again but, still unanswered, only going to his voicemail. He'd dialed Stander a little over an hour ago and gotten the same result. As was their habit, he hadn't left a message. Both men were usually good about quickly returning a missed call from the other. Neither really liked leaving messages or texting very much. But after a couple days of not hearing anything, his concern festering in the wake of the ongoing silence, Secrist finally broke down and left a message.

"Hey! What the hell? Call me back and let me know what's going on. What you found over there. Later..." Secrist had his feet up and was sprawled across his couch. Frazier had joined him and was nestled between his legs near his feet. Snoring and occasionally blasting Secrist with silent but deadly farts. A gas attack of the friendliest kind.

Secrist looked at his phone periodically as he distractedly flipped past a myriad of television channels. Willing it to ring when, miraculously, it finally did. Secrist lifted the phone to his ear. "About time you called. I was starting to think something had... Hey! You there?" Secrist pulled the phone from the side of his head. The call had ended. "What the," he began to say when the call from Stander came again. Once more he attempted to answer but the result was the same. The call was almost immediately dropped.

He double checked his signal was strong before he tried dialing him back. Again, after a few rings it went to Stander's voicemail, but this time he didn't leave a message. When he ended the call, his phone lit up a third time and he quickly answered.

"Tommy! Tommy! Can you hear me?" It was definitely Stander's voice, but it sounded like he was speaking at the end of a long tunnel. "I hate these shitty fucking cell phones."

"Me too. But yeah, yeah, I can hear you." A silent pause. "Can you hear me?"

"Not very well. You... to... up really bad... Fucking... wires... like... the day!" Secrist felt sure the call was about to be dropped again. He could only hear maybe every third or fourth word Stander was saying. It was likely the same on the other end. "How...and... Frazier?"

"I can't really hear you. Text me what is going on! Or call me later when you have a better signal." Silence again. "Russ! Russ! Can you... Oh, forget it!" Secrist could see he was talking to himself. The call failing once more.

A few minutes later he received a text from Stander. "Phone is fucked. Must be about to crap out on me. I can't get any kind of signal when I'm down in the quarry. Not much better out in the open over here. Sorry! But I can still text. Not much to report. Uncovered the anomaly and it was as expected. A big crate. It was sealed when the team of archeologists first pulled it from the dirt the other day. But someone must have broken into it the other night. When we went to open it, the seal was busted and the crate was mostly empty. The local university is embarrassed. Two guys have been implicated in the theft and have disappeared. BIG investigation underway. Fuckers probably pawned whatever was inside. More later. Give Frazier some love from me."

Secrist read it several times before replying. "OK. Keep me in the loop. Frazier is fine. Saw Hannah at the bar last night. Everything good here. Later."

It was the ground I felt moving first. A slight vibration that continued to rise in crescendo until I could finally hear the approach. I didn't need to see what had made the earth under me shake. It was a band of horses. I guessed anywhere from four or five to as many as ten or so. The skill to read the approach of mounted horses ingrained in me at a young age. Once upon a time, my tribe's warriors' very lives had depended upon the ability to accurately judge the numbers and distance. But anymore, with the advent of wheeled automation and recent proliferation of the automobile, the tradition was fading and rarely taught.

I never saw all the horses I felt and heard. But as I watched several uniformed soldiers suddenly appear and nonchalantly wander into my view, I knew I'd been right. A group of German forces, the men fanning out and walking slowly with their rifles slung casually across their backs, milled about the center of town smoking cigarettes and talking. Hopefully the small number I saw meant it was only a platoon temporarily passing through the pummeled city. The officers and supplies likely riding the backs of the horses I'd heard. Their travel I prayed, like the day itself, only just beginning.

This unexpected appearance was, of course, the worst scenario imaginable. If the soldiers lingered in town long, it jeopardized the entire mission. There had only been a slim hope that I could arrive safely, take the shot, and somehow recross the border and return to Command. If this German platoon of soldiers remained when the bombers attacked the nearby chateau, that hope disappeared. If I could somehow remain hidden among the rubble I'd buried myself in, I may still be able to take out the German Kaiser with a bullet. But I would have to place my next bullet between my own eyes. No way would I risk being taken alive. Especially by a wandering patrol lucky enough to blunder into the middle of an assassination attempt.

Unless...

What if these Germans had been ordered here to thwart the plan? The secrecy of my orders compromised. The carefully drawn plan now shattered and these men sent here to hunt me down. My testicles involuntarily drew up and fear filled my belly with ice. Had I somehow been betrayed? My eyes sharpened as I scooted even deeper inside the trench. I silently withdrew the small pistol Kirk had insisted I take when we parted ways. If the soldiers did discover where I lay hidden, I was confident my rifle would help take a lot of them with me. But if it came to it, Kirk's pistol would be my final escape. Swallowing a bullet preferable to capture.

The longer I observed the German soldiers, the more certain I became of two things. If they'd been ordered here to find me and disrupt the assassination attempt, the men didn't seem to be in a hurry. The only searching they did was to enrich themselves. I began to feel sorry for the townspeople who had to put up with the unexpected interlopers. Some of the unkempt soldiers bullying any villagers unfortunate enough to cross their path and forcing them to empty their pockets. While others systematically forced open doors and helped themselves to any remaining valuables and food. As I watched their selfish behavior, I became certain the Germans would lose this war. Taking out their leader, Kaiser Wilhelm II, would hasten their demise. But even if I failed, the thugs enlisted to protect their fellow countrymen also had. I became even more certain the end of the war was now just a matter of time.

My muscles soon began to ache from the stress and tension as the long hours dragged on. I couldn't relax for even a moment with a combination of soldiers and the occasional citizen passing nearby. My eyes stayed wide and my ears strained for any sign my earlier travel or current hiding place had been discovered. It was this intense focus on my surroundings that first alerted me to the presence of the dog. I could see it in the distance. A dark shape darting along the side of one street, nose to the ground, gradually working its way closer. The street it wandered down ending at the pile of rubble I'd dug myself down into.

The dog clearly wasn't very old. The canine's unbridled curiosity and playful mannerisms on display as the mutt gleefully approached. A couple of the soldiers soon took notice of the advancing pup as well. Unfortunately, turning to cut off its path and bringing both men mere yards from my hiding place. I turned to stare at the dog, my horror growing at each step forward as the dog came into focus. It had black hair and white paws. If it wasn't the same dog the boy and I had encountered in the nearby woods days earlier, it must have come from the same litter. A doppelganger, as the Germans would say. Except I knew it wasn't.

The dog, I now felt certain, was following a trail. The trail of my scent! The little dog tracing the path I had taken with nose to ground. I was filled with abject terror as I witnessed the dog pause, raise its nose and, worst of all, begin to wag its tail as it looked my way.

Happily.

I froze. My pulse rocketing and my heart hammering. Only my eyes swiveling to watch the reaction of the two nearby German soldiers. I prayed they would lose interest or suddenly be ordered away. Instead, I watched one kneel and grasp a sharp-edged chunk of broken brick roughly the size of a baseball. If the man had looked my way as he'd squatted, under the rim of the collapsed building's roof where I'd dug my trench, our eyes would have met. Mere feet separating us. Despite the cold; sweat covered my palms and made the wood finish of my rifle slippery. I cast my eyes back at the dog. It was panting and staring right at me. I must have made a face, noise, or maybe drew in a sudden breath. The black dog cocked its head once to the side before it began to bark.

At me.

The bark ended in a sharp yelp as the piece of brick the soldier had picked up hit the dog on its hindquarters. The force of the blow spinning the black dog around in a half circle as the two soldiers laughed joylessly. The dog whined and limped a few steps before a high-pitched shriek like the sound of a teakettle erupted nearby. My eyes landed on the source of the noise and found the boy. The same boy I'd rescued at the farmstead; the same boy I'd thought I'd saved; the same boy who'd joined the black dog's family. Where that family was now uncertain, but they were nowhere to be seen.

The boy's eyes streamed tears as he ran for the hurt dog. He dropped to his knees and surrounded the wounded dog with his love and both arms. Wrapping the injured pup in protection and burying his wet face in the soft black fur. When he reopened his eyes, his agonized stare found me. My dark pupils locking on his shocked blue eyes. I saw the recognition and beginning of a smile twinkle in them before the desperation of my stare quickly snuffed it out. He looked questioningly at me but all I could do was widen my eyes and rotate them to where the German soldiers still stood laughing. I gave him a quick shake of my head and hoped he would understand the brief pantomime.

The boy dropped my stare and tried to pick up the black dog, but it wiggled free from his grasp. The dog landed on its white paws and began to slowly run away. The limp gradually less pronounced the farther it retreated. The soldier who'd tossed the broken brick grabbed more chunks of the collapsed building. Launching several more errant throws the dog's way before finally giving up. The boy turned to sprint after the fleeing canine but was corralled by the second soldier. His arm snagged from behind.

The boy squealed thinly as he struggled to free himself from the grip. I cringed internally as he squirmed, a palpable desperation in the air that I understood all too well. The boy kicked and began screaming until the German clamped a soiled hand across his face, snuffing out the protests. The soldier was rat faced and beady-eyed, looking everywhere but down at the struggling kid. The boy fought for all he was worth.

Banging his shin on the corner of the collapsed roof I hid under, the German soldier nearly lost his balance and his grip on the boy before his partner joined the fray. There was a brittle edge to the second man's laughter as he wrestled with the thrashing child. His face unkind as his fat fingers held the boy firm. The rat faced man, embarrassed by his inability to control the lad, lashed out. I watched his fist strike the boy, doubling him over and knocking the wind from his lungs as the child slunk to the ground gasping.

Tortured inside, knowing even the slightest sound would mean certain death for us both, I shook with silent rage. The boy was crying with his eyes squeezed tightly shut. I was grateful I didn't have to look into them as the soldiers grabbed both his legs. They dragged him along the loose dirt. The boy's fingers leaving ten tiny trenches behind as he clawed desperately at the ground. The two men hauling him around to the backside of the crushed rubble of the building I hid under. Where they wouldn't be seen. Towing him just behind my position, mere yards from where I lay. Out of my eyesight... but not earshot.

The sounds jarring.

Words failed. None were uttered. I could hear the rustle of clothing, the rushed desperation, the cacophony of the two men taking and taking and taking. The defeated protests and endless sobbing.

Words fail me. None are sufficient. I can still hear every second and minute of the brutality. I suspect those awful sounds will haunt all my remaining years. The child being broken down.

Numb, I watched the two soldiers walk away. Casually, they joined their comrades. Smoking.

The group of fighting men had loosely clustered together near the apartment building. Either woefully ignorant or silently accepting of the two's barbaric actions. I watched as the group of soldiers attempt to break inside the two ground level apartments. The efforts unsuccessful in gaining entrance to the one on my right. But the one on my left, where the wheelchair-bound man lived, gave easily.

I aimed the long barrel of my rifle their way. Putting each German troop's head inside the circumference of my telescoping lens. Pretending to pull my trigger and killing each and every one of them with raging wet eyes. Hardly noticing as they pushed the old man out of his apartment before pulling him from his mobile seat. The men laughing as they climbed in and out of the wheeled chair one after another and taking turns riding around in it until one of the small wheels on the front broke off. Soon, like the discarded man on the ground, the soldiers abandoned the three-wheeled chair. Their attention turning to an officer on horseback clearly sent to corral the marauding men. The man riding the horse giving short commands that spurned the others into action. Within a span of minutes, the soldiers grabbing all their gear and departing. I felt the hooves pounding the ground gradually fade as the soldiers left the German city.

Silence roaring. The only citizen in sight – the broken man sitting beside his broken chair.

The boy had pulled himself along the ground. Crawling to me silently and vanishing beneath the same rubble where I hid. He had a split lip that oozed but his blue eyes, though bruised, were dry. It was my turn to cry. How could the boy even comprehend my inaction? I only hoped, despite his young age, he could understand. Understand? I'm not sure I do... Was it right to let him be taken the way he was? Was there a justification in trading his life for mine? So I could do what? Kill. If successful (a huge if). Command told me I would be saving tens of thousands of lives. Maybe even more! But was it worth it? Trading this boy's future to ensure my own? I cried and held the motionless boy.

Once again, I'd led the lamb right to the slaughter...

I'd give the boy God's grace itself if it could be found in this horrid war. Hopelessness closed in on me without mercy. What was I doing? I may have somehow avoided detection and capture this time. But what happens when the next patrol, platoon, or battalion descends on this German town? In hushed whispers I spoke. I knew the boy didn't understand me, but speaking as I tried to make him understand at least made me feel better. Maybe if I heard all my excuses, I'd even begin to believe them.

I told the boy we were going to be caught, my voice hoarse and hollow. It now seemed only a matter of time. Gesturing to the apartment building and trying to explain that I had no choice but to stay. But that he needed to leave before more soldiers returned. Eventually, he seemed to grasp my feeble attempts at communication. But his eyes frequently fell to the small pistol at my side as I spoke. He reached for it, a coldness in the stare, but I stopped him. Though I understood how vulnerable the young boy was, essentially, I was kicking him out of my hiding place anyway. The boy grew more insistent. Repeatedly reaching for the handgun Kirk had given me until I finally relented. I'd been given my very first gun at about his age. An old rifle with a split in the wood stock. I had to trust the boy could handle the weapon. Otherwise, to send him away unarmed, felt like I was handing down a death sentence.

I showed him the basics and he repeatedly mimicked my direction until I felt sure he could brandish the small gun with confidence and get a shot or two off. I also showed him if caught, as he'd just been, how to end his life if it came down to that. How to cock the weapon and where to place the end of the pistol in his mouth. The cracks in my voice filled with gravel. We practiced it, pantomiming the final solution. Mimes with frowns of black dirt. It was a lesson none should ever learn.

Or teach.

I know it was at that moment something inside me broke. Or was lost. I prayed the boy would claim it as his own; my loss. Our brokenness and dying humanity bonding us together. Two outcasts trying to be whole.

When at last the boy left – eyes dry as bone and twice as hard – I hoped I'd never see him again. I didn't want to know if giving him Kirk's gun was a mistake. I no longer wanted to know what happened to the boy anymore. I doubted his destiny was anything but bleak and his proximity seemed to only endanger myself and my mission. Seeing him reminded me of all my failures. The awful sights and sounds. Wondering what all that viciousness would do to a boy his age. What kind of man would he become?

Alone once more, my blank stare fell on the apartment building. I saw the family had returned. The husband and wife helping the crippled old man. Taking him up to their tiny home and sharing the meager belongings they had with him. The father tipping his wheelchair on end and working to replace the broken wheel in their tiny living room. Despite seeing the worst of humanity that day, their actions gave me a bit of hope for our species. Mankind. If this family could live only to help and serve others, maybe there was hope for us all. I spent the remaining hours of sunlight hoping to hear the empty sky above filled with the roar of planes. Serenely watching the day in the life of this good German family turn into the night.

CHAPTER THIRTEEN

Secrist pulled up Google on his laptop and typed "Map of Germany" with two fingers before hitting enter. His grandfather's overseas diary from the First World War was devoid of geographic references and names of towns. It was understandable he had remained vague in case of capture. But the more Secrist read, the more intrigued he became with locating the route taken. Wondering what, if any, remnants from the written account might still be standing. All the writer had given away was the close proximity of the border between France and Germany, and that it had taken days of walking from the front lines to reach his objective.

Secrist scrolled through several styles of maps before clicking on one that showed Belgium, France, and Germany in detail. He let his finger slide along the border of Germany and France. There were a good five or six unpronounceable towns in Germany that vaguely fit the story. Their size and proximity to both the border and forested areas of France marking each as a potential candidate. When Secrist next entered in a search of maps from the First World War's frontlines, it was much the same. None of the five or six possibilities obviously disqualified. But none standing out either.

Mildly disappointed, Secrist shut the screen on his computer. Thinking to himself that he'd have to ask Stander if he'd seen anything during his travels around France that might help pinpoint where the tale might have occurred. Secrist couldn't recall exactly where in France the quarry Stander owned was. But he knew it was relatively close to Germany. Maybe Lucas, Stander's French-born-and-raised archeologist would know?

Picking up the diary, Secrist thumbed the pages until he found where he'd last left off. Digging back in...

I know they call it the dead of night. But truly, darkness writhes with life. The most predatory of creatures using the cover of night to hunt and feed. The most vulnerable to run and hide. As a decorated sniper, I long ago learned to meld my orders with the obscurity nighttime can provide. Becoming one with the cover and using it to my advantage.

To hunt and hide.

When I settle in my sniper's nest – like now, waiting for the planes to appear – I become something different. Not my spirit animal, the soaring and all-seeing hawk. That part of me circles high above it all. Wise, just, and fair. All seeing and, like every creature, not questioning what I know to be right and wrong. No, instead, I become the exact opposite. I grow coldblooded, eyes unblinking, belly pressed to the dirt and with a single-minded selfishness. This is my edge and what I believe makes me such an effective sniper and killer.

My duality.

Coiled in a lair and motionless. A striking snake in the grass, a lying serpent in a garden, a stirring cock confusing gender. From what part of me did this cold-blooded killer emerge? My half that likes men or the half of me that likes women? My native blood or my white blood? Is what I've become only in service of my country? Or has this emotionless taker of lives always been part of me and just waiting for the right time to emerge? Am I a fierce warrior like Geronimo? Or a cowardly murderer like Jack the Ripper?

A taker of men or a taker of women?

I've been stuck in no man's land my whole life. This whole war I've been shuffled from one endless trench to another. Interchangeable ditches of death riddled with soiled dirt. The endless surges, the brutal carnage, and one hundred yards of chaos the men call "no man's land" is where I thrived and proved myself. I wonder if I will still be me when I'm no longer part of this collective we? I guess it doesn't really matter. Even when I leave this war, I'll still be shackled in no man's land.

A soldier, but not a voter.

After eating a small bit and discretely relieving myself – soaking up and covering my waste with loose dirt – I dozed on and off as night fell. A light drizzle coated the trees and painted the broken streets while I slept. The steady drip of collecting rainwater waking me when the drops soaked one of my pant legs where it pooled in a low spot. I shifted slightly to avoid the chilled water before raising the field glasses to my face. Looking across the deserted streets and into the apartments.

With one exception, the homes were dark. The tenants likely all asleep at such a late hour. The light I saw came from the apartment where the family lived. Inside, I couldn't see the parents or children. Only the old man stirred. I saw the generous household had cobbled together a makeshift bed for the man with the ruined legs. He was propped up and leaning against a broken piece of furniture that had once been a cushioned chair. Though the room he resided in was exposed to the elements, the man was bundled and covered with several blankets. An oil lamp burned softly near him and I could see his eyes were closed. The man well cared for after his harrowing experience earlier in the day with the troublesome troops.

Movement somewhere on the right caused me to drop my gaze. Still using the binoculars, I swept my eyes across the damaged housing units until the motion was repeated. I zeroed in on the scuttling until I recognized what had first caught my eye. It was a lanky man in dark clothing stealthily pulling himself from the bottommost flat on my right. It was the first I'd seen of this man; his apartment lifeless and dark since I'd arrived. As I looked on, the man pulled himself from a glassless window and started climbing the outside wall of the apartment building. Transfixed, I watched him navigate the barrier with little trouble. The man scaling it with the ease of a spider, skittering up the crumbling wall on spindly legs. Though I couldn't see in the dark of the night, the old manor's outside wall must have numerous cracks he could use as foot and handholds. In less than a minute, he'd reached the second floor.

Advancing on the sleeping man.

My thoughts turned to the bizarre scene I'd dismissed as a dream the night before. The woman and supposed lover. How oddly she'd behaved and the... the blood. I tore my gaze from the wallcrawler to see if anything had changed in her apartment. Or if I could see something that would confirm what I'd witnessed one way or the other. But her place was as dark as the others. I saw no sign of the woman.

When I refocused on the old man, I was stunned to see the man in black was now standing beside him. He'd likely crawled into the home the same way he'd exited his own apartment. Through an open window. I felt my pulse quicken and breath hitch. Nothing good ever happens this late at night, unless it is between two lovers. And the crippled old man hardly looked like he was expecting company. Or able to provide much affection.

Though the thing beside him resembled a man, it was more like a parody of a person. A caricature of extremes. Something not of this time – or maybe this world – throwing on a suit of flesh. Much like the Skinwalker so feared by many Native American tribes. Or, perhaps, the man had been cursed with the spirit of a Wendigo. But I tried to convince myself I was mistaken. The only monsters I'd ever actually seen were men. Perhaps he was afflicted with a disease. A strain of syphilis rotting his brain from the inside out just like the sick soldiers I'd encountered back on the frontlines.

I know I inched forward slightly in the hole I hid in. My eyes focused sharply on the newcomer as he lingered behind the sleeping old man.

The wavering yellow light of the oil lantern cast shadows that obscured much of the room. But the incandescence revealed the intruder wore no uniform and was dressed from head to toe in black. Only, it seemed, the dirt and dust from his climb marring the jacket or frock he wore. He had little or no hair, and his ears protruded from the side of his head awkwardly. His legs and arms seemed slightly out of proportion with the rest of his body. Unnaturally long, or perhaps his torso too small. Despite the obvious strength and ease with which he'd scaled the side of the wall, his appearance was awkward.

His equally hairless face was blank and emotionless. A look divested of the most human of features: age. I watched this thing advance on the old man. It stepped forward effortlessly, almost as if gliding along the floor. The face began to crack then – thin lips parting to reveal jagged canines – the mouth opening wider the closer the approach. Without a sound I screamed at the old man. Wake up! Turn around! My mind spinning every warning I knew I couldn't say without risking revealing myself. The thing hovered just over the old man's shoulder. Seeming to savor the intimacy.

Both hands snaked out. Unusually long fingers with curved and yellow nails grabbing for each shoulder. In one motion I watched the thing in black clench the old man's shoulders and violently shake him one time. The force snapping the head back and forth so viciously that I had no doubt the crippled man's neck was instantly shattered. I had no doubt because the ferocity of that single shake also splintered and tore open the flesh of the throat. The old man had been nearly decapitated in one fell swoop. Only a few sinewy strands of flesh keeping the head from completely toppling to the floor.

For the first time, I saw emotion register on that awful blank face. Glee streaming from the lively green eyes as a geyser of blood erupted from the ruined neck. The awful thing with the misshapen body and blank face latching onto the flow, stemming it with the mouth of sharpened teeth. The corpse under him shuddering as it was drained of blood. The crippled man's dead legs twitching with spasms and death throes that soon dwindled until they moved no more.

The suddenness and finality of the ambush startled me. Surprised, I inadvertently dropped my field glasses. I fumbled to raise them up again, but shattered pieces of glass tinkled to the ground rendering the binoculars useless. Disgusted with my clumsiness, I tossed them aside and quickly raised my rifle. Peering through the scope. A creature straight out of the blackest nightmares of my childhood stared right back at me. Eyes boring into mine.

The fiend seemed to grin as he bared wet teeth at me. His mouth filled with thick crimson until it dripped from the corners. His tongue, oozing and black like a long-forgotten banana rotting in the bottom of a bowl, chased the drops back into his mouth. His eyes, despite my clandestine cover and distance, never leaving mine. Somehow, this thing knew it was being watched. Coyly, almost flirtatiously, the hairless man lowered his head once again to feed. Likely draining the crippled old man of the last of his blood.

When it was all over, the creature sated, it swiftly exited the tiny apartment. Squeezing through the cracked opening in the apartment's wall; the same opening I'd used to watch the thing feed. It leapt from the second floor without concern. Landing on both feet before disappearing among the long shadows of the streets. Leaving me to ponder what it was I'd just witnessed.

Sleep evaded me the rest of the endless night. With wide eyes I watched for the horrific creatures' return, but the converted manor of separate apartments remained still and quiet. If the bloodsucking monster had once more taken refuge in the ground level apartment I'd seen him slink from, I missed it.

When the half-light that is dawn exposed the old man – the oil lamp, like the man, emptied of fuel overnight – he was slack and near colorless. His ruined neck a series of viscous pink strands barely tethered to his drooping head. Luckily, it was the grown man that woke first and discovered the gruesome scene. He appeared, understandably, shocked and horrified by the carnage. Shaken to his core. Quickly covering the tattered corpse with a ratty blanket before carrying the body of the old man downstairs. Lugging the remains outside and depositing the cadaver somewhere unseen behind the apartment building. A familiarity, purposefulness, and confidence in his actions. Almost as if it was "old hat," as they sometimes say. Though, I suppose living in a warzone, discovering and moving the dead most likely does become an everyday occurrence.

I guessed the father, now back home and hurriedly wiping up the blood that had spilled, had already seen plenty of death during this war. His focus clearly on sparing his wife and children the same fate. Waking to find the grim remains of a murdered neighbor right inside your home is a scene any father would protect his family from. Even in the midst of war. The man likely blaming the death on rebel soldiers and turning a blind eye to the potential horror just one floor away from his family. But then again, I thought to myself, if he knew of somewhere that he could escape with his family they'd already be gone. Clearly, had they any place else to stay, they wouldn't remain here with the thing that looked like a man.

No man's land.

Despite the feverish work of the father, I was nervous and anxious about what would happen next. Were authorities still in place they could contact? If so, could I possible stay undiscovered and hidden with all the additional scrutiny? But the rising sun never shined on the bustle I'd imagined. The town, the empty courtyard, and apartment building stayed quiet. After two near sleepless nights that sandwiched a stress-filled day of sadistic German troops, I found I could no longer keep my eyes open. Though I fought to keep watch for the bombing planes that would signal the beginning of the end of my mission, I lost.

I dreamt of warm bathwater. My smiling body floating and bobbing at the surface. A weightless heat that comforted and embraced me. My skin weeping greasy sweat as I drew a rag for washing across my eyes. I could hear the repetitive *plop-plop* of dripping water keeping a syncopated beat somewhere in the background. The rhythm lulling me to sleep within the dream and blocking any competing sounds. Much too soon the bath I soaked in began to cool. I let the wet rag slide casually down my face and sink in the water at my chest. The longer I stayed submerged, the colder and darker the surrounding water grew. I opened my eyes and saw my reflection in the black mirror I laid in. A disembodied head on a platter swimming in my own filth. The years of soiled fighting staining me inside and out.

Black as the bible.

A long slender arm white like alabaster split the illusion. The appendage of wiggling fingers emerging out of the dark water I'd tried to cleanse myself in. Somehow, I understood the ghostly hand had come for me. I watched it glide towards me through the water with the grace of a long-necked swan. The slow advance nothing I could run from. Paralyzed, I felt the clutching fingers at my throat just before the hand pulled me under. Dragging me into what I'd tried to wash away. This time, deeper.

I woke coughing and sputtering. The dream so real I was certain water had filled my lungs. I gasped and inhaled deeply several times before understanding I'd simply fallen asleep. The air around me ripe with a syrupy foulness I couldn't place. As I struggled to regain my faculties and see where the stench that woke me originated from, movement in the distance stole all my attention. It was near the base of the apartment building. I lifted the end of my rifle and stared through the scope, trying to locate what had caught my eye. It was the bloodsucker.

The vampire.

It stood silhouetted in the glassless blown-out window I'd first seen it emerge from the night before. When I focused on his face, the magnification filled my eye with the thing's leering sneer. Once again, the creature seemed to sense my presence despite the distance between us. As if it had waited to scale the outside wall of the apartment building until I'd awakened. But as he began to climb, once more pulling himself up the side of the building with ease, I dropped my stare from the telescoping sight. What blasphemy would I be shown this time? Why would I watch? I was powerless to help. I could do nothing without revealing my hiding place and ruining any chance of my mission's success.

I pondered the dilemma for long moments. Perhaps for a minute or two before eventually looking once again down the barrel of my rifle. The vampire hadn't moved. When I looked closer, focusing in on the monstrous thing, the morbid creature appeared to gesture my way before resuming its climb. As if it had patiently waited for me like an old friend. One who wouldn't dare let me miss what he ascended to...

The thing stopped climbing when it reached the second floor. I could see it hesitated just beyond the reach of the flickering candles that burned inside the flat. Incredibly, it seemed to wave my way again before sweeping an arm before him. Bowing slightly as he ushered my gaze into the family's apartment. Unveiling what he'd busied himself with while I'd slept.

I saw red.

Though I'd been too young at the time to understand or be aware of the butcher named Jack the Ripper, I'd later read many of the lurid reports of his ferocious attacks. The original London newspaper articles often reprinted and recirculated throughout America at different times. The anniversary of the deaths and any similar murders often the stimulant. The accompanying sketches and pictures of Jack's work all images that are not easily forgotten. The madman's work on the last victim, dissected and ripped to pieces across her own bed, was the most horrible thing I'd ever seen before joining the war.

This was far, far worse...

The interior walls, floor, and ceiling were splattered with dripping gore. The mother and father were nowhere to be seen. Only the children remained. Or should I say only the remains of the children could be seen. Somewhere in the dark the youngsters had been brutally savaged. Their little bodies splayed open. Nothing but soft piles of indistinguishable wetness. I fought back the hot bile that climbed my throat. My ears rung and my eyes welled. Rage knotting my insides tighter and tighter.

Then the father reappeared.

CHAPTER FOURTEEN

Frazier was whining. Secrist closed the diary and, puzzled, looked down at the dog's earnest face. "What's the matter, Frazier? Do you need to go outside again already?" Secrist swung his legs off the couch where he'd been reading and walked to his backdoor. He'd expected the dog to be right behind him, but Frazier hadn't moved. Frowning, Secrist let his hand drop from the unturned doorknob. "What are you doing? Do you need to go out or not?" The dog whined a few more times before turning his head to one side. Looking up the staircase to the second floor of Secrist's house.

"Something spook you? You hear a noise or something up there?" Secrist, unconcerned, walked over to the bottom of the stairs and flipped the light switch. The empty stairway and second floor hallway flooded with light from the hanging ceiling fixture. "See, buddy? Nothing up there but the stack of boxes I brought down from the attic. Go see for yourself." Secrist gestured towards the stairway and cardboard cartons with a grin.

The smile faded.

"Geez, Frazier." Grimacing, Secrist covered his nose and mouth with one hand while turning off the hallway light with the other. "You eat something that didn't agree with you? You sure you don't need to go outside?" Secrist returned to the couch and picked back up the journal he'd been reading. Stopping briefly to pet Frazier with his nose scrunched up. "Your farts could raise the dead..."

Through the scope on my rifle, I watched the father react to the carnage before him. His children, reduced to quivering heaps of unrecognizable wet flesh sullying what had once been a home. His face broke and his knees buckled. The man nearly dropping to the floor in a likely dead faint. All that saved him from falling completely was the monster that had obviously felled his children earlier. The vampire pinning him to the backwall of the apartment by his throat before my eyes could even track the movement.

The fiend looked back over his shoulder at me with a sadistic grin. Despite the piles of evidence to the contrary, I still searched my mind for a rational explanation of what I was witnessing. Longed for it. But it was clear this nightmare creature belonged with things erased, things forbidden, and things better left unsaid. I couldn't deny the pure evil radiating out of those piercing emerald eyes. Those awful, red-rimmed eyes so alive. On fire from within and burning with a lust for life.

The taking of it.

The father, still helpless, desperately scrabbled for anything hanging near him on the wall. His free hand, the one not trying to pry away the slender fingers clutching his throat, reaching for a crooked crucifix hanging beside a closet door. When at last the prize was claimed, he thrust the wood symbol at the vampire. Mere inches from that dead face with those hideously sparkling eyes.

The vampire's expression instantly dissolved. Splitting horribly and erupting obscenely. Once more the thing looked back my way. The weight of the stare heavy before the contorted face of pain gradually softened into an easy smile. One eye dramatically winked at me before a slimy tongue of rot split the bloodless lips. It stretched lewdly until the tip tickled the agonized figure of Christ obscenely. An instant later, in one fell swoop, the vampire leaned over the universal sign of Christianity and bit down. Snapping the cross in two and devouring the top half with a delightful sneer. The white man's symbol of faith, now a godless splintered shard.

The trapped man roared with rage. Finding the courage I doubt few would still have in that moment, he plunged the jagged piece of wood into the vampire's chest. Right through the heart. Impaling the undead thing with a stake made from its own blasphemous actions. For the first time since stumbling upon the slaughter of his children, I could see a wan smile on the face of the father as he was dropped to the floor. The man gasping for breath.

Behind him, I closely watched the fiend. A rare smile crossing my own chapped lips. Silently cheering on the bravery of the father. The vampire, however, seemed less than impressed with the man's efforts. Slim fingers reached for the wooden piece of the cross protruding from his chest. The creature looked down and daintily pulled it out, flicking it to one side with all of the concern of one pulling lint from clothing. Mildly annoyed.

From the floor, the man struggled to gather himself. Slowly pulling himself away from the gruesome wraith. The vampire watched his desperation with a bemused smile before casually flipping over the nearby highchair. He snapped off two legs as if they were mere toothpicks before reaching for the desperate man. Effortlessly, he lifted and pinned him against the backwall of the apartment once more. Driving the shard of one broken highchair leg into the meat of the father's shoulder before running his other shoulder through with the second splintered leg. The man was staked in place. His body held by the wood driven directly into the wall at his back. His agonized screams a chorus of pain.

The vampire toyed with the ends of the wooden posts if the man ran short of breath or seemed close to unconsciousness. A cruel grin revealing a mouthful of barbs as he playfully, one at a time, jostled the ends. A slender white finger wiggling the tops of each as the hanging man shrieked in agony. His tormentor making love to the tortured screams. The ecstasy as plain on the vampire's face as the agony was on the man.

The monster in love with the sound of new screams.

No one came to the man's aid. His desperate pleas traveling down the deserted streets before returning alone. It was then I realized I'd seen no other townspeople since the German soldiers had left the area. Had they hidden from the thugs? Or had they known this creature laid claim to the night? Regardless of the reason, I remained an audience of one as the symphony of hurt played on and on. The crescendo building with each passing moment.

The vampire abruptly shredded the clothes the man wore. The tattered cloth left in a pile at the feet of the suddenly naked man. Blood streamed from both of his shoulders. The gruesome wounds supporting all of the man's weight gradually widening and tearing. The fiend faced the father, their noses mere inches apart and his back to me. He reached around and seemed to embrace the man as his screams climbed ever higher until finally ending. I could see little, the creature's body still blocking much of my view, but I could tell the man had gone limp. I hoped his life was over as I braced for a new shower of blood.

It never came.

Transfixed, I watched as the vampire slowly worked to skin the man. His lengthy yellow nails slicing and slashing. Caping him no differently than I'd seen done by my fellow tribesmen and hunters to animals dozens of times. Just never a man. First, his head was peeled like a grapefruit. The dripping insides flopping across the chest before, methodically from head to toe, the vampire pulled all the remaining skin off. The pith underlayer of tissue much like the backside of a peel or the inside of a pumpkin. All of the man's skin pulled free in nearly one piece.

When it was done, the vampire held the hide of the father out to me. As if silently asking my opinion on the latest style or newest fashion. Casually, the man's flesh was slipped over one shoulder and then the other. The vampire soon wearing the skin like a long coat, sliding the loosest parts over his own clothing. The meatless flesh of the man's legs flopping with every step. The monster strutted to an oval mirror hanging beside an unopened closet door on the adjoining wall. Admiring himself in different poses before dropping a hand between his legs. Throwing me a shy look of reproach as his fingers explored and made a mockery of the sagging manhood that swung there. Pulling at and pretending to masturbate the man's flaccid penis. Mock indignation registering across its features when the bloodless member failed to respond to his touch.

Soon it seemed to bore of the lewd act. Or perhaps the draw of fresh blood became too great to overcome. Either way, the suit of skin was removed and casually tossed across the back of a kitchen chair. A pool of crimson growing under the formless mass. On the nearest wall, the flayed body of the man still dangled from the two wooden pegs. An ornamental splash of red in an otherwise drab apartment. The vampire drew close to the dripping mass that had once been a doting father and loving husband. Almost sensually it began licking. Lapping the thickest streams of blood right off the oozing flesh. The hideous thing treating itself no differently than a child with an ice-cream cone on a sun-filled summer day in July. His blackened tongue first swirling across the exposed skull and head. Cleaning it completely before gradually working ever lower until he was on his knees in front of the corpse. Licking from the bottom to the top and running his tongue up and down the length of the man's body. A charged eroticism in the act as the feeding became more and more frenzied.

As I watched the obscene feast, I couldn't help but wonder about the man's wife. Thankful she'd been spared these sights. It was hard to imagine anything worse for a mother than having to see what was left of her babies. Except witnessing how they'd been hurt. Each likely, I assumed, tortured much like the husband had just been.

Slowly, as if the fiend had heard my thoughts, the frantic tasting dwindled. I grew afraid at what would come next. Was it to be me? I tightened the grip on my rifle. There was no escape if it came. I'd hidden and dug myself into a spot that would be difficult to extradite myself from very quickly. The bloodsucker stood and, after turning my way with a grotesque smile, reached for the closet door beside him. It swung open slowly, revealing the contents.

Inside was the mother.

She was bound to one of the small wooden kitchen chairs. Her head held tightly in place and mouth covered with a torn piece of cloth. Eyes wild and wide open. I understood then – she had been aware of everything. Had heard the entire massacre. But worse than that, as the closet door swung all the way open, I saw it was broken in the middle. A gaping hole, at the same height her tethered head was bound to the chair, had exposed the living room to her view. She'd been forced to hear and see the mutilation of her family. Taunted with an open view of what she'd once had.

A love. A family. A life.

The terrified woman was pulled from the closet. Separated from her chair and then her life. The hideous face of the monster buried in the crook of her neck as she was yanked to her feet. The vampire's mouth coated in thick running drops as it fed. Inhaling and drinking the warmth of the mother. The bite leaving behind the grotesque grin of a clown. Dripping red edges misshapen down to the bone. It ate slowly – the woman's life that is - but her death was only another new beginning.

Once more, the wicked fiend put on a show I knew was just for me. Stealing the flesh from her bones in much the same manner the vampire had previously stripped her husband. What was left of the mother, wife, and woman discarded and ignored on the floor as the undead thing amused itself and played. Sliding on her smooth wet skin before prancing and twirling in front of the looking glass. The mirror filled with the vampire's bald head, jutting ears, and borrowed breasts. The latter sagging until the monster began lifting and squeezing the woman's bosom together. Creating cleavage that a wanton whore hunting an easy mark would be proud to sport. Apparently satisfied with its look, the vampire took a seat facing me at a simple wooden chair and table.

Leaning forward slightly, the woman's full breasts landed on top of the table in a pair. Next to them, the vampire rested his elbows on either side. He folded together all ten fingers of both hands as if in prayer before flattening them and resting his chin on top. The hideous face, shiny head, and bulging bare breasts making a trinity of the absurd that was hard to pull my eyes away from. But moments later, movement from under the table drew my eye. The fiend stirring in the seat, effeminately crossing his legs one way before shifting and recrossing. Each turn slower than the one before. The smoothness of the skinned thighs contrasting with the thatch of black hair between them. The vampire flashing the dead woman's sex at me from under the table.

Equal parts horrified, embarrassed, and sickened, I immediately dropped the scope from my eye. When I raised it next, the vampire hadn't moved. Legs spread wide and chin still resting on top of his hands. Within seconds, a slow smile broke across that awful face and, though lash-less, a flirtatious batting of the eyes followed until I looked away.

As I write this, I still remain confused by the thing's actions. This blasphemous dance of seduction it was attempting: a danse macabre. Clearly, it knew how horrid it appeared on the outside. Of that I had no doubt. Was it truly expecting to draw my favor with the parody? I have often said what's on the outside of us shouldn't matter. Gender, nationality, schooling, pigmentation, and material things important only to the shallowest of those who pollute this world. Afterall, isn't the age-old saying *it's what inside that counts?* If so, what ravenously hungering thing was operating that gaunt marionette? I raised the scope again.

The vampire had begun taking on and off the two skins of the couple. One after the other as I looked on. Each time stopping to admire itself in the hanging oval wall mirror. Changing from man to woman as if comparing what fit best. Unsure which one it felt more comfortable with. Perhaps, I thought, feeling the tug of each gender. The peel not always reflecting the ripeness of the fruit inside.

Or the rot.

It was a dueling duality I understood all too well. I was a soldier armed and skilled in killing. Yet here, as the vampire showed me, I had been reduced to nothing. Worthless and weak. A worm wallowing in dirt and my own waste. Helpless in these surroundings and unable to move, aid, or save the family. Just as I'd failed the boy... Yet my futility was a trade-off enabling me to assassinate one of the most powerful men from one of the most influential countries in the world. My actions, if successful, will have earth shattering consequences. Shifting the very axis of world power.

But before I could ponder this any further, the figure's odd behavior in my scope once more stole all my attention. He stood still, the tilt of his head and focus on the sky above where stars pierced the nighttime sky. As I looked on, he made an overly dramatic check of the time on a non-existent watch that did not circle his wrist. He mimed the action several more times. Even pulling his naked wrist up to his ear as if to verify the tick-tock before pointing to the sky excitably. Confused, I watched his lips move until I could decipher what he was saying over and over again.

"The planes. The planes. The planes..."

Once more, cutting across the distance and down my scope the vampire's eyes found mine. His flirtatious wink chilled me. A moment later I began to hear the sputtering sound of a plane engine. A minute or two passed before it was joined by several more. The dark night soon filled with the throaty growl of airplanes. The approaching roar was undeniable and, despite the horrid scenes just witnessed, I found a renewed need for the hope I was about to abandon. Hope can be a dangerous thing in war, often it ends up being the deadliest weapon of all. Preying on the most innocent.

I lowered my eye from the rifle's scope and looked up into the nighttime sky. The rumble of the engines increasing as they drew near. I searched the skies for even the smallest glint of reflection or hint of light with mothlike determination. Were these my fellow saboteurs?

My answer came when a sudden blast of the chilled air gusted around the rubble and spindly chimneys I hid amongst. Seconds later, the low-flying planes momentarily blocking the stars I gazed up at as the peal of their engines filled the German town with manmade thunder. My heart leapt up my throat. This was it! The next sound I hear should be the detonations of the bombs they drop on the French chateau where Kaiser Wilhelm II plotted with his military leaders.

But it wasn't.

I ignored the yipping until I realized it was growing louder. Annoyed, I cast my eyes down the lane from which it originated from. There I watched the rapid approach of a small figure. It was a boy kicking hard at the shadows on the street. Running for all he was worth. At his heels, the dog I'd first heard. A small dog, likely not much more than a puppy, with black hair and white paws. I didn't need to see the face of the runner careening towards me. But when I did, my heart warmed and bloomed.

Without words he came, the faithful dog interpreting for him as, still running, he mutely pointed at the sky. Jabbing a finger in the air repeatedly. The boy had understood the signal I was waiting for. Risking his life to ensure I hadn't missed it. I doubt I'll ever have children of my own. But if the roots of my family tree ever did extend deeper, I'd be proud to have a brave child like this German boy tangled up in them.

My eyes welled but I fought back the tears. The last thing I needed now was something blurring my vision. I refocused on the fragmented apartment building and waited for the explosions. When they began to detonate in the distance, just over the border and a mile or so away, my face broke into a grin. I might get a chance to play the hero! I reached for the bundle of hawk feathers and said a brief prayer to Mother Earth. Asking that my bullets fly true and help bring this awful war to a close.

I cast a hurried glance back the vampire's way. Thankful I was near done having to watch the twisted fiend. The family's apartment was unchanged. The interior still bathed in red and what was left of the tenants untouched on the floor. The suits of flesh hanging over the back of one chair. For a moment, naively, I thought the planes had scared away the thing I'd watched over the last several days. The monster nowhere to be seen. But then I realized that wraith, quite literally, likely fed off war. Perhaps always hunting near the frontlines where the chaos of battle and endless death hid his atrocities. Scurrying from skirmish to skirmish and town to town until sated or perhaps close to discovery. I imagined the fetid thing, with dawn now just an hour or so away, crawling under some new rock.

When the shriek came, I instantly recognized the anguished wail. I'd heard it far too often in the past and likely will never unhear it. I swung the barrel of my rifle just in time to see the little dog, tail tucked between its legs, scampering back down the street it had come from. Alone. I searched desperately for any sign of the boy. Briefly catching sight of his head just as it vanished inside the same first-floor apartment window that I'd first seen the vampire pull itself from. The monster, framed by the opening, stood waiting. The fiend with the mouthful of canines saluted me once when I finally located him before following after the boy. The yawning glassless window swallowing them both.

Once again, the slaughter leaped right to the lamb...

Down in the apartment building's courtyard, the door under the tiny shingled roof structure suddenly sprung open. Men in German uniforms poured out like ants running from a flooding mound. Guns in their hands and anger in their eyes.

CHAPTER FIFTEEN

Secrist entered his attic for the second time that week. Pulling himself up through the tight opening and tugging the string hanging at his face. Lighting up the cramped quarters with a tired sigh. Frazier had begun whining that evening shortly after the sun had gone down. Eventually bolting up the stairs to the second floor and pacing back and forth in the hallway until Secrist came to investigate. The dog calling Secrist's attention to a scratching and rustling sound coming from above their heads.

In the attic.

Though he hated using them, Secrist opened the package of glue traps he'd carried up the ladder with him. Intending to place several around the edges and in the corners of the attic. Sniffing the air with a frown, Secrist suspected his first guess as to the cause of the strange sounds would turn out to be proven correct. He'd been invaded in the past a time or two by mice, and the noises Frazier had first picked up on sounded like the little critters had somehow found their way inside his home again. He stood still for long moments waiting to hear it repeated. Secrist hoped the mouse was a single marauder. If he found a nest, he'd likely need more than a few sticky boards to rid his home of the tiny trespassers.

He cocked his head. The sound off to his left in the shadowy loft. When it came a second time, Secrist was able to zero in on the location. He took two steps before a flutter at his ear caused him to turn. Spinning just in time to see a swooping bat lodge itself briefly in his hair. He felt the leathery flapping of wings at his forehead and the scratching of tiny claws pricking his exposed neck. Secrist stumbled backwards cursing. Glue traps dropped as both hands went to his head. The bat freed itself and began circling around him as Secrist stumbled towards the opening at his feet. Half falling down the ladder and slamming the framed wood covering down before the flying rodent followed.

"Bats!" He bellowed as he ran his hands repeatedly over his head, hair, neck, and face until he was sure none had hitched a ride down with him. "Bats," he said less loudly but with more disgust. "What a coincidence…"

The small courtyard in front of me teemed with uniformed men. One by one, German soldiers streaming out of the underground opening under the cover of the night. My eye never left the scope that topped my sniper rifle; my finger resting confidently on the trigger. I barely blinked as I scrutinized each face that emerged. Keen to spot the telltale handlebar moustache and garish uniform of medals the German Kaiser famously sported. Both attributes marking the man I hunted and making him easily identifiable among the regular rank-and-file troops. But the mass exodus out of the clandestine channel soon dwindled and then stopped.

Kaiser Wilhelm II nowhere to be seen.

Unmoving, I barely breathed as I observed the collection of soldiers and officers. The bombing of the nearby chateau had clearly been successful. Several men had minor injuries and the excited chatter of the soldiers included plenty of gesturing. I didn't need to hear or understand what was being said to establish the aerial strike had hit the intended mark. But whether it resulted in the death of Germany's leader was unclear. I kept the barrel of my rifle pointed at the tunnel's exit as I began to count the uniformed men. I reached the number twenty before the dull thunder of an approaching engine stole my concentration. Minutes later, two large trucks both under German command pulled into the center of town. Behind them, a lone horse pulling a four-wheeled cart emblazoned with a red cross. The simple wooden ambulance wagon empty with the exception of a thickly coiled rope and a few stained canvas stretchers. The driver jumped from the cart's seat and hitched the horse and wagon to a nearby post before joining the rest of the soldiers. The carriage and beast of burden left unattended.

Once more, the quiet streets and courtyard I'd watched over the last several days were flooded with activity. One of the trucks carried only men and, upon stopping some thirty feet from my position, the soldiers were ordered out. The newcomers mingling with the earliest arrivals and clearly questioning what had occurred. Though I couldn't be sure, keeping one eye on the vacant tunnel doorway, I guessed maybe forty or fifty enemy fighters now filled the apartment building's square. I was completely encircled. Inside, I grew queasy. If the Kaiser had made an appearance right then, I had no doubt I would have ended his life. But with that many German combatants surrounding my position, it was just as certain I'd quickly join him in the afterlife.

The second truck, the cargo in the back covered by tarp, carried munitions. An authoritative voice barked orders at the men as several large wooden crates were unloaded. The two crates were both rectangular and as long as a coffin. More commands were shouted and the tops of both boxes were soon pried off. The nails screeching as they were wrenched free of the wood. One container was filled with long rifles of black metal and quickly dispersed among the Germans. The second held a large machine gun I recognized from the battlefields I'd fought across over the last several years. The rapid-fire weapon designed to sit atop a tripod and spew slugs of an impressive size. The gun and stand were hastily unloaded and, much to my dismay, assembled near the vacant doorway I watched. The muzzle pointing my way.

The officer who arrived with the trucks and oversaw the delivery of the weapons began yelling at the men once more. Confidently commanding and conferring with a small group of soldiers before the men split off in pairs. Each soldier buddied with another. In minutes, I understood the orders. My stomach tightened and the palms on each hand grew damp. They'd been told to search the surrounding area and buildings. It was now just a matter of time before I'd be discovered.

Still no sign of the Kaiser.

Anxiously, I watched the trail of each duo as they began to systematically explore. Most of the soldiers started with the city block to my left. The street wasn't residential; instead filled with various businesses, now all shuttered and empty. Most of the shops raided by the motley crew of German infantrymen just the day before. I knew it wouldn't take long for those men to thoroughly search the vacant storefronts and offices.

On my right, two men entered the apartment building. I watched as they searched the flat of the wheelchair bound man. By the time they finished, the officer who'd given the order had moved away. Engrossed in a conversation with the driver of the Red Cross wagon and the two similarly uniformed and, I guessed, ranked officers. The leaders paying little attention to the hunt.

The two searchers of the apartment building noticed their lack of focus as well. They became visibly more relaxed as they sauntered over to the entrance of the next ground floor dwelling. The one I'd first seen the vampire crawl out; the one in which the boy had vanished inside. I know my fingers found the soft feathers that I carried as I silently beseeched Mother Earth. Asking her to guide the German soldiers to the boy. I doubted the two, even with their guns, were a match for the monstrosity I'd observe callously feed on the tenants of the apartment building. But I remember thinking they might surprise the creature. Create enough of a distraction that the boy might be able to escape.

Still no sign of the Kaiser.

It took the two soldiers several tries to finally force open the door to the apartment. I braced for gunfire and prayed their bullets would fly true. But, after long minutes passed uneventfully, all I heard was more orders being shouted. The commanding officers had broken their huddle and were recalling all of the men. Something drastic happening, stress and worry tinging the barked orders with a desperation. I watched two of the leaders and wagon driver vanish back inside the doorway under the small shingled roof. Heading back, I assumed, to the German controlled section of France and the chateau across the border. All of the other soldiers hurriedly boarding the two trucks and crowding in, many having to stand. They piled into the backs of each, leaving behind the empty wooden crates they'd unpacked. The massive machine gun they'd assembled left unmanned where it sat atop the tripod stand. Barrel still pointing my way.

I watched carefully for the reemergence of the two German soldiers who had entered the vampire's lair. A drop of running sweat stinging my eyes. Nothing stirred. In mere minutes after the order was first given, the trucks had departed. Black exhaust smoke fouling the air as they rumbled away. Unaware two of their own had been left behind. The horse and wagon left waiting for the return of its driver.

Still no sign of the Kaiser.

The ensuing silence was deafening. My eyes remained focused on the door that led to the underground tunnel. Watching, waiting, and hoping to see it spring open at least one more time. Perhaps, I thought, the first wave of soldiers had been sent to secure the area. Rushing out just ahead of the German leader, rearming themselves and positioning the cannon-like machine gun just outside the entrance. Or, I wondered at the time, perhaps the rush to return was more of an all-clear. Maybe the bombs had missed the target. The soldiers ordered to return to their stations. There was just no way for me to know.

I scanned the area. My sniper rifle at the ready. Unsure if I should leave my post. But as more minutes ticked past, my concern for the mission, now possibly over, began to fade. Replaced by my worry for the boy. A good person would try to save him. What chance did he have with that thing? But, as I fantasized about a rescue, what chance did I really have? If two trained and armed German soldiers didn't even get a shot off, how could I make a difference? Besides, a loyal soldier would stay. I suffered with these conflicting thoughts and feelings. Maybe, I remember thinking, I could be a good soldier and a loyal person.

Still no sign of the Kaiser.

My eyes stayed focused on the underground opening while my ears strained to hear any sounds coming from the vampire's lair. Neither soldier emerged, and the streets around me remained quiet and deserted. Sporadic gunfire erupted in the far distance. A minor explosion somewhere unseen.

Still no sign of the Kaiser.

Tortured screams suddenly pierced the stillness of the courtyard. Shredding my concentration and clawing at my focus. Slicing it in half. Tearing into me and splitting my loyalties. For long moments I stared at the underground entrance and imagined the scene in the apartment. For long moments I stared at the apartment and imagined the Kaiser slipping past me unseen.

A maniacal cackle replaced the shrieks. It seemed to fill the air with menace before a single gunshot ended the sound.

Still no sign of the Kaiser.

I made my decision. Quietly and quickly, I secured what was left of my meager supplies. Pulling myself from the grave I'd entrenched myself in and placing everything but my rifle back down inside the shallow cavity. Camouflaging and burying what I left behind under a thin layer of dirt. I wiggled like a worm along the ground until I was finally able to wrench myself from the rubble. I took one last look from my position to ensure I was unwatched before sprinting across the courtyard. The only living creature I saw was the tethered horse. I ran for the shadowed darkness that obscured the doorway the two Germans had forced open. Arriving,

I paused once more. Still unobserved, I ducked inside the first-floor apartment, gun at the ready.

The home had been ransacked. Furniture toppled and what was left of the occupant's belongings scattered about. I doubted the tenant had much of anything of value within the four walls. But if they had, it was now long gone. Wooden drawers had been turned over and tossed. Their meager contents carpeting the floor. There was no sign of the soldiers who'd entered earlier. Or of the boy and his captor. I stepped between the various piles and ducked my head inside the single bedroom and bathroom. Each was the same. Wrecked and empty. I moved to the last doorway: the kitchen. Like the rest of the tiny one-bedroom apartment, it was lifeless and empty. A barren pantry mocked my growling stomach.

Puzzled, I inched towards the lone window in the room. I knew from my earlier observations it was the same opening the vampire had used to launch himself up the side of the building. Where had the fiend disappeared to? Where was the boy and the two Germans? Cautiously, I peeked around the edge of the glassless window frame and eyeballed the area surrounding the apartment building. I could see my previous hiding place where I'd hunkered down over the last several days. I glanced at the empty streets, the neighboring buildings, and even above my head for any sign of the wallcrawler before my eyes resettled on the tunnel entrance I'd so doggedly observed.

Still no sign of the Kaiser.

Bleeding tension and worry, I leaned against the kitchen wall. I rubbed a filthy hand across my face and over my weary eyes, body involuntarily sagging. I was exhausted. Physically, I'd barely eaten and done little over the previous days. But mentally, I'd hardly rested and only dozed fitfully. Where was the monster?

I began to doubt what I'd witnessed when a gust of wind caught the partially opened door of the pantry with bare shelves. The door creaked slightly as it widened a few more inches. The sight and sound offering me nothing I needed. But I caught an unpleasant whiff. The smell familiar like the last scenes of the dream you've just awoken from. Or a déjà vu as the French soldiers sometimes called it. An inexplicable remembrance that stays slightly beyond understanding. The scent drew me...

Though the night was still cloudless, inside the back kitchen of the tiny apartment was cloaked in darkness. Slowly I walking in to the pantry, the toe of my boot caught on a raised floorboard. Once I kneeled and inspected the bottom of the pantry, the cellar opening was fairly obvious. I grasped the recessed iron ring at its center and pulled. The stench grew. A rickety set of wooden steps presenting an option to descend.

Taking them up on their offer, down I went.

My eyes had adjusted to the night and, after some time, even the darkened gloom of the flat. When my head dipped below the apartment's floorboards – plunging myself into the basement of the old manor – I'd expected to pause once more until I could see. But the subterranean room was partially bathed in an eerie glow. The cellar appeared almost endless and ran the length of the massive building. With one exception, the walls were comprised mostly of big grey stones held together by some sort of crumbling white mortar. The wall on my right had been constructed out of massive hand-hewn beams of wood. The shaped logs ending sharply at a right angle some fifty feet ahead of me. The remainder of the basement continuing after the bend from where the strange blueish white-light radiated. When I tried to focus on the ethereal glow, a dull hum seemed to accost my senses. I turned from the source of the unexplained light and unsettling thrumming sound. I had to locate the boy.

Instead, I found the two missing soldiers.

The German men had been stripped of their uniforms and skewered. Both soldiers riding the same wooden pole like two traveling circus clowns piggybacking on a single unicycle. The men had been impaled through the anus – the implement erupting from their mouths – one man's face buried in the ass of the other. Each had been castrated. Their lifeblood caught by a foul container positioned underneath the ghastly duo; their dripping flesh slowly filling the fetid vessel with crimson. The coppery taste of their running blood mixing with the cellar's heavy stench of decay.

I tore my eyes from the gruesome scene, my gaze finally landing on the boy I sought. He stood aside from the grisly totem pole. Unmoving. His face expressionless and blank. In one hand dangled a pair of rusted metal scissors mottled with gore. I looked from the dripping shears to the ruin of the men's sex and back again. It had been the work of this innocent one. Deep inside I knew the boy had been made into a monster by my earlier inaction.

I'd led the lamb right to a slaughter.

The sweet, blond-haired boy's blue eyes were steely and hard; no longer his own. I grappled with the image of this angelic looking boy standing amidst the debauchery we'd both descended into. What had he done? Where was the vampire? Had the boy made a deal with that devil to save his own skin?

I flashed back to how the fiend had pulled the suits of skin from the savaged bodies of the family. Even the children. I refocused on the boy and marveled at the resilience he'd shown over the last several days, even as the German men's brutality shredded his innocence. It was no wonder the boy had, in turn, mutilated the bodies of these soldiers. Though, clearly, he couldn't have overpowered them and hoisted the fully grown men in the air alone. That must have been the vampire. Teamwork, a partnership.

Had the boy led me to this slaughter?

Like the slow approach of a steam-driven locomotive, it hit me. Was this beautiful one before me merely a pawn? I'd stumbled upon him just as that horrid scene back at the farmstead had begun to play out. Amazing really, come to think of it, the timing of my arrival. Afterwards,

I'd left him in the care of a good family. I thought again of the people I'd trusted to take him. The pregnant woman... Yet, the boy had been wandering the streets of this German town alone only a day or so later. And he was so quick to alert me to the planes when they'd soared over. Only the bloodthirsty vampire had been faster.

I looked over at the motionless boy. He was impossibly thin. His skin really just a threadbare covering draped across a statue of traumatized stonework. Bulging bruised veins snaking across his flesh like the painted lines of my tribe's ghost dancers. Where did his loyalties lie? Was he torn? This boy, not yet a man, perhaps stuck in no man's land the same as I. Which monster did he serve?

Who is more wrong in a world of war where nothing feels right?

I reached inside my coat. My fingers sliding past the photo until the silky feathers I sought were found. Though my actions in this foreign land may be monstrous at times, I was no monster. No matter how many sticks and stones modern society throws my way, I know I am a good person. I would not let this boy's spirit become more polluted than it already had become. Besides, I was ready to be done with this. All of this. The vampire may very well be unstoppable. But he would not take that child without a fight.

I made a quick check of my rifle and refastened the bayonet. I said one last prayer to Mother Earth with my bundle of hawk feathers in hand. When I repocketed them, I pulled out the picture of the unknown German kid and his dog. I looked for long moments at the smiling image. I could still feel the last of his shudders as I'd run him through. *Yes*, I thought to myself, *I'm done with all of this.*

I took the scissors out of the boy's hand without protest. The boy didn't react. Nor did he move when I briefly tussled his blonde hair with a smile before turning towards the unnerving blueish glow.

Time to go hunting.

CHAPTER SIXTEEN

Secrist signed the exterminator's work order before handing over his credit card for payment. The bat roosting in his attic turned out to be a common one with an uninspiring name: Big Brown Bat. A species native to Michigan and one the pest control service said they were often called to collect and release back into the wild. Secrist was surprised to learn there'd only been one flying invader found in his attic. The stench coming from the enclosed space where it had been trapped had been nearly overpowering by the time the service had been able to arrive onsite. When he'd asked the technician if a bat living by itself was normal, he'd merely shrugged. "Like people," the man had told Secrist, "bats sometimes chose to live a solitary existence. But usually, they maintain close-knit groups to help rear and protect their young."

"Protect? What would those needle-mouthed creatures fear?"

"Hawks mostly. Hawks are the most natural predator of the little monsters..."

I left the mute boy staring at his handiwork. The dead German soldiers he'd mutilated inching ever closer to the ground as gravity widened their orifices at both ends. A half-mast flagpole of misery slowly sinking to the ground.

I slipped past the horrific symbol, rifle at the ready. Pushing deeper into the basement, closing in on the eerie light with my lightest step. A throb at my temples that was more annoying than painful. I'd barely made it twenty feet before I stumbled upon the skeletal remains of a body. Looking ahead of me, it was clear this was only the beginning of the dead interred within the old manor's cellar. Heaps of unburied bodies in various stages of decomposition littered the ground I walked. The stench and putrid clusters much like the battlefields I'd haunted since arriving on these shores. The unnerving silence the only difference.

The cellar, I found as I drew closer to the strange light, was in the shape of an L. At the turn the corpses underfoot became more aged. Even the tattered remains of clothing pointed to many of the dead having arrived here decades, if not centuries, before. I began to see long barreled musket rifles, bows, arrows, swords, and spears. All manner of weapons from across a wide swath of time dating back, I imagined, to the building's original construction. This hidden basement a den of military history. Many of the weapons, I grimly noted, had never been unsheathed or fired. I looked down at my own sniper rifle with eroding faith. *No matter what happens*, I reminded myself, *I am done with all this*. I kept marching forward. A gradual incline as the bodies of dead warriors increased. The light coming from a spot just ahead of me. The intensity of the silent thrumming gradually increasing.

The mound of dead I climbed grew larger still. I began to look down with each fumbling step. The dry bones doing their best to bar me from the top before snapping under the fall of my foot. When I next glanced upwards, it was at a pyramid made of nearly fleshless bodies. It was no architectural marvel or ornate work of art. Just a pile arranged with all the thought of a dog digging at a blanket before settling in for a nap. Thrown about until it either was comfortable or provided enough cover. At the very top of the morbid hill, I found the source of the illumination that bathed the underground chamber in its blueish tinge. It was a huge slab of radiant rock.

At its center, like a heartbeat, the thrum I'd felt since entering the basement matched the waves of luminescence that poured from the squarish boulder. The blueish-light dimmed for just a moment after each wave. When it disappeared, the massive stone briefly went completely black. Shiny like coal, but smooth like glass. Black glass. A huge chunk some ten feet long and five feet wide. I want to write in this journal that the size closely matched the shape of a coffin. But I suspect that association was thrust upon me much like the disorienting, humming waves that pulsed when it became brightest. Inescapable. Just like the dead thing straddling it.

The vampire.

It smiled grotesquely at me. The hungry emerald eyes blazing lasciviously with a disturbing intensity. As it slowly stood, I could see the thing sported an erection that jutted my way. When it noticed my gaze, one slender-fingered hand rushed between its legs. I quickly averted my eyes but had trouble focusing. Dimly, I heard something inside of me screaming *shootshootshootshootshootshoot*! But the rifle grew very heavy in my hand. Each throb of fresh light from the black, glass-like stone scattering my attention like the seeds of dandelions lost in a windswept sky. The monster jumped daintily down from his perch and stepped towards me. He strode confidently down the uneven steps of the piled corpses, never once tripping over the bones as he descended.

Nearby, the wink of an eye-catching sword gave me the gift of focus. Though likely from its close proximity to the glowing black boulder – the aged blade was the nearest weapon to the throbbing rock – the slightly corroded sword seemed to radiate as well. I could see the blade was stamped with lettering I didn't recognize. The handle and hilt stood several feet in the air and the point buried. Embedded inside a fleshless skeleton, the mouth of the skull opened wide in silent agony. The sharp end, likely what had ended the life of the unknown warrior, had speared him from behind. The man impaled in the same manner as the two German soldiers had been.

Horribly.

The distraction of the sword seemed to free my mind from the molasses it had been mired in. Reminding me the boy was still near and that I had a weapon in my hand. I raised the end of my rifle and pulled the trigger in quick succession. Getting off three shots that hit nothing. The hideous bloodsucker had vanished. I had no idea where until I felt the hand at my neck and smelled death at my elbow.

I turned and faced the fiend. My mind once more muddled by the hypnotic thrum of the brightening and fading light. My strength ebbed and my legs gave out one at a time. From my knees I looked up at that face of death. Straight into those raging eyes of want. The vampire raised one hand of fluttering fingers, each armed with long yellow nails. He tugged at the fasteners of his black pants while the thumb of his opposite hand traced the oval shape of my lips before softly parting them. Dully, I noticed the filth under the thing's fingernails squirmed with life. Little white worms as thin as thread writhing animatedly. My left eye twitched as my mouth fell slack...

"Nein!"

The boy's high-pitched screech echoed across the still chamber. The sound pulling me out of the fog I'd been lost in. Sound, sight, and smell reintroducing themselves to my senses as, suddenly weak, I slumped forward. Bile filling my mouth before the vomit that churned inside me splashed onto the ground between my knees. As my retching began to fade, I watched the steam slowly rise from the puddle of my puke before looking up at my savior. The child's skinny arms stretched out before him, inside his grip the pistol I'd given him. The barrel of Kirk's gun pointed at the bald vampire in black.

Bang!

The fiend was gone. The single shot instead striking the nearby blade of the etched sword the thing had stood in front of. Like a tuning fork, the metal edge rang for long seconds. The tone pleasant like the harmonized song of a well-practiced group of talented singers.

I stood quickly. The cobwebs in my head instantly vanishing. I heard a crash and turned to see from where the commotion originated. It was the vampire lying prostrate across some of its many, long-dead victims. Though those vivid green eyes still danced maniacally, the body was frozen in a twisted state. A seizure of a sort seeming to paralyze the fiend. I gave no thought to the why as I quickly stepped to the immobilized monster. The blank expression never changed, but those dreadful eyes narrowed. I don't know if it was spite or fright I read in them, but I covered one with the barrel of my rifle and pulled the trigger with satisfaction. The boom leaving behind a vacant black tunnel as the slug exploded out of the back of its head. A second later I deposited the next bullet in the shallow chest of the vampire and kept pulling the trigger. The click of the hammer all that came out of it. I expertly expelled the spent 5 round ammunition magazine and replaced it with another before pulling back the bolt.

The vampire leapt to his feet. Both eyes raging, the hole I'd left in his head healed as if it had never appeared. In a moment, my rifle was ripped from my grip and tossed aside. In the next, I was flung across the basement like a weightless feather caught in a terrible storm. I landed on my back. The painful bite of the broken bones underneath knocking the wind out of me. I'd barely reclaimed my lost breath before the monster loomed over me. His widening mouth of sharp spikes descending when more shots suddenly rang out. One slug connecting with the fiend's arm and staying my execution. We both, monster and man, turned to see the boy repeatedly pulling the trigger on the gun I'd given him. The last of the bullets spent.

The thing dragged me absentmindedly behind as it turned and strolled towards the boy. I clutched desperately at what I was dragged across, hoping to wrap my fingers around one of the many weapons I'd seen dotting the floor of the dead. I glanced at the boy just ahead of me. I could see the invisible fingers of terror working ruthlessly inside the child's mind. Winnowing the guts of the boy until they'd become lost once more. The child soiling himself and shrinking in fear at the advance of the vampire. Part of me began to wish the boy had remained catatonic and unafraid. He'd seen enough horror and I'd seen enough death. Cackling, the monster backhanded the boy. The back of his head, behind one ear at the hairline, split open when he landed in a huff a few feet away. Blood pouring from the nasty cut.

The vampire bled the lamb to his laughter.

I struggled to find something I could use to turn back the fiend. Urgently running my hand along the ground repeatedly for a weapon. Instead, I felt only dry bones. My closed fist returning with nothing but an empty, jawless skull. The hollow eye sockets seemed to mock my impotency.

In desperation, I threw the fleshless head at the monster. But the errant, off-balance heave sent the skull sailing harmlessly past both the vampire and the bleeding boy. Landing just beyond them, near the throbbing stone before rolling back down the mound of the dead. The slow roll ending when it connected with the oddly etched sword. Bone barely kissing the steel blade.

The vampire lurched half a step before again toppling. A seizure grabbing him firmly in its grasp once more, imprisoning the monster inside itself as, on the outside, the body of the fiend seized and locked up. Struggling to my feet amid the rounded bones underfoot, I ignored my rifle this time and ran for the sword. I pulled the blade from its last victim. The odd *hum* of the steel increasing as it clanged against the hard bone from which I withdrew it. Returning to the side of the prostrate vampire, a shiver slipped down my neck as I ran the wretched thing through from behind. My desperate gamble either ending the undead life that animated this thing or my own...

Neither happened.

The screech that came out of the vampire's mouth was horrifically anguished and tortured. The agonized sound sweeter than any I'd ever heard before. The sound of real pain. No blood came from the bite of the blade, but obscenities soon began to pour from the fanged mouth. The fiend spewing them in various unrecognizable languages of which I could only guess their origin. I caught a few words in German and French before it switched to English. The recognition on my face plain as the thing continued to verbally assault me.

"...devour all of your little fucking dark skinned bastard offspring until your entire existence..." I barely heard the torrent of abuse. I'd been looked down on, spit at, cursed, and ridiculed my entire life for the color of my skin and where I was born. None of which I had any control over. What was this pasty-white, foul-mouthed, hairless creature going to call me I hadn't already heard? I ignored the vampire's warnings, threats, and insults. Focusing on the pain and wound I'd managed to inflict on the creature. Grappling with the success and trying to understand why.

The blade of the sword was embedded near its shoulder. Though I'd run him completely through, the handle of the oddly etched sword still rose a good foot or so in the air. The fiend seemed to shake with fury as it continued to berate me. But it never attempted to remove the weapon. Or try to rise from the bones it laid on. I gingerly reached out one hand towards the top of the weapon. As I did so, the vampire fell silent. His awful eyes of rage widening in fear.

I pushed and pulled on the sword slightly. The blade moving up and down in the wound with little resistance or change to the piercing look of hatred the vampire affixed me with. It was only when one of the brass buttons rimming the cuff of my coat lightly struck the metal of the weapon that the vampire's expression and demeanor visibly altered. An otherworldly screech erupting from the tormented features as the body of the vampire seized up again.

"Nein!" The boy, briefly forgotten as I'd experimented, had both hands pressed tightly to the side of his bloody head, covering his ears. Crying, he turned and began jerkily running from the scene. Slipping and falling at times, staggering as he fled. I called after him as he vanished around the corner of the basement. I started to give chase before stopping and turning back. I knew I couldn't leave the vampire here in his own stronghold. Though the mysterious sword of strange, etched symbols seemed to paralyze the monster, there was no way to tell for how long. If left alone, could it free itself in moments? Minutes? Hours or days?

I looked around the jumbled bone floor of long-dead warriors. It was clear the vampire had roosted here for a very, very long time. For the fiend to have survived across generations it clearly had a stranglehold on the village. The townspeople likely cowed; drained of resistance and unable to stop the sickness. If I left, it would likely only be a matter of time before one of its lackies would free the thing. Though silent since the sword had vibrated, the monster had made it very clear I was now its prey. Perhaps my whole family was!

I suspected once it dealt with me, it would also hunt the boy. That is if the boy could even survive the war, the "friendly" soldiers, and upcoming winter. I knew, after all I'd exposed him to and what we'd experienced together, that I had to go after the child. If I didn't, my cowardice would haunt me far longer than that undead thing squirming under the blade. I turned back towards the monster at my feet. Squatting, I placed my forefinger on the handle of the sword and looked into those awful eyes.

"You spoke English, so I know you understand me." Unmoving, the vampire watched me without protest, emerald eyes flaming hatred. "Until I can determine how best to... to dispose of you, we are going for a little walk. Just until we find my young friend. If you resist or cause problems, well..." I won't lie and write here that I didn't enjoy the thing's screams that followed. I did. I flicked my middle finger against the handle of the sword more than once. The slight waver of the blade was all it took for the vampire to comply with my every order. Still speared, I manipulated the sword by its handle until I got the shrieking wraith on its feet. Pushing gently from behind – my hand on the sword handle and making clear which way – the vampire and I shuffled like Siamese twins up and out of the basement. Soon standing in the deserted courtyard of the one-time manor and dilapidated apartment building.

I hollered for the boy with all my might. The night of black slowly turning grey as the sun approached the horizon. The only replies came from the nearby horse still hitched to his Red Cross wagon. With my rifle hanging from one shoulder by its beige canvas strap, I maneuvered the vampire over to one of the wooden crates the German soldiers earlier had emptied. "Get in," my voice not unpleasant but plain.

"I will never allow myself to be put inside a..." I didn't listen to the vampire. I didn't have to. With the flick of my wrist, I struck the sword and watched the paralyzed fiend topple face first inside the crate, the sharp end embedding itself in the wood of the crate. It was with some satisfaction I saw its forehead reverberate as it struck the corner and heard the likely break of its nose.

"Enjoy the view," I said with a smile that the undead abomination couldn't see. I hurried over and untied the horse before walking it, and the wagon it towed, over to the crate of pestilence. After a few tries I was able to leverage the large wooden box into the back of the cart. Tossing out the stretchers and sliding it alongside the coiled rope. Pushing it up to the very front of the wagon before refastening the dingy canvas covering that hid the cargo and tossing the unfastened lid of the container beside it. Once the cart was loaded, I hoisted myself onto the driver's wooden bench seat and grabbed the reins. I snapped them once and the dark brown horse began to move. I retraced the path I'd first taken into town, down the waterway and towards the cemetery. My head on a swivel as I desperately looked for the boy. The first light of the morning sun visible at the horizon.

CHAPTER SEVENTEEN

Secrist called for Frazier out his backdoor. He'd let the dog outside earlier and was surprised the porch was still vacant. The dog often found lying across the mat in front of the doorway basking in the rays of the warm sun. He shouted one more time before letting the screen swing completely shut when Frazier didn't come. Retreating with a frown to the chair he'd been sitting and reading at for the last hour. Thinking to himself he'd give his temporary four-legged roommate a bit more alone time before he'd go check on him. His yard was fenced so he really had no reason to worry. After all, nothing bad could ever happen to such a sweet and friendly dog as Frazier....

I followed the deeply rutted dirt lane west towards France and safety. Skirting the edge of the same dark timber I'd braved just days earlier. The syncopated *clop-clop* of the horse's hooves echoing through the surrounding trees. I knew almost anything could be lurking within that shadowed forest and my eyes desperately searched for any hint of danger. Above me, the emerging rays of the morning sun fought to enlighten me, but could barely penetrate a few yards into the thick woods that lined both sides of the trail. At my back, the wooden crate of ghastly cargo was hidden under the soiled canvas shroud that stretched the length of the four-wheeled wagon I was perched atop.

I'd hoped (and prayed to my hawk spirit for guidance) that my route was the same taken by the boy I hunted. Back towards where we'd parted days earlier. Where I thought I'd left him safely with the family. The young children, puppy, husband, and pregnant wife nearly the only blessing I'd seen in this godless place of death.

This no man's land.

When the boy had sprinted after them, I'd cashed in the last bit of hope I had left in me. Hoping the family was kind. Hoping they'd tend to his needs. Hoping he'd be taken in by them. It was dangerous to exhaust the last of your hope in a warzone. How could I now dare ask for any more in this awful place? The boy, I'd thought at the time, would be safe and that was all I could ever really have hoped for anyway. As the last of my hope had faded, I'd found I was left alone with what I'd done. All that I did... but much worse, all that I hadn't done. The *hope* I'd someday be able to make amends deserting me along with the damaged child.

On my right, I passed the crowded cemetery of toppled gravestones and crumbling mausoleums I'd first seen upon entering the outskirts of the German town. It was shocking to see the acres of dead bathed in the bright, morning sunshine. I could no longer recall how long it had been since I'd last seen or felt the warmth of the sun. My recent days had all seemed steeped in clouds of black despair. My own personal darkness, the savagery of my fellow man, and whatever dark God had vomited this "war to end all wars" – as the author HG Wells proclaimed it would be – out of its bowels. All this pointless brutality and violence likely lapped up by the same God, no different than a senseless dog. A spirited hound gulping man's pain down its gullet in chunks and gobs; Shakespeare's and Hugo's dog of war. Or perhaps, as I looked down to the crate at my back, a fiend or beast. The beast of Gévaudan? A thing corrupted by the spirit of a Wendigo? An undead vampire or Skinwalker stirring havoc to feed? For this was truly a land of Gods and monsters. Where man cowers from both.

I know now, as I write this account, it was then that I began to question all I was feeling and thinking. Trying to get a grip on myself and a handle on the dismal feelings crashing into me like the undulating waves of a cold ocean hiding its black undertow. Each depressing thought a barefoot step atop the brittle broken-glass edge of despair and sadness. I suppose the bleakness was understandable considering the years I'd spent fighting this brutal war. But I couldn't help wonder if the walking bag of human skin pinned inside the wooden crate beside me was somehow poisoning my thoughts. Or if I'd been corrupted by that awful pulsating rock that had hummed so ominously in the hidden cellar of the old manor. I'd felt unclean when exposed directly to the throbbing light and droning sound of the strange black stone.

I turned in my seat just in time to see the last of the long shadows from that cursed village fade from my view. Immediately, I began to feel better. More like myself. I searched for any sign of enemy combatants on the road ahead before casting my face up at the morning sun. Briefly basking in the warm rays before my new found reverie was interrupted. A muffled torrent of curses and hateful words erupting from the wooden crate just behind me. When the insults went unanswered, the ride fell silent once more. Momentarily.

"Enjoying the sunshine, Anong? Care to share a bit? Or am I destined to travel prostrate this entire journey?" Despite the change in the fiend's tactics, I remained mute. Not wanting to be drawn into conversation or engage in whatever game it was playing. After another minute or so of silence, the thing spoke to me again. "I guess that answers my question." I smiled and thought to myself, *good. Just keep quiet then until I catch up with the boy.* But the monster's taunting gravelly voice rang out again just moments later. "You **are** a top instead of a bottom." A beat of silence. "Are you looking at my posterior? Should I brace myself?"

The slurs were as simple as they were hurtful. Though it may have been a monster spewing them out, I'd heard far worse in the past out of my fellow man. I burned inside but held my tongue if not my hand. I turned and silently flicked my forefinger against the sunlit blade. A brief harmonic hum as pure and beautiful as the flutter of butterfly wings riding the breath of a newborn child's laughter echoed around me. I smiled at the melodic resonance. The smile widening to a toothy grin when I heard the vampire's ululating cry of pain that followed.

I'd, of course, heard plenty of pain before. The worst to my ear was my own and the boy's... But the otherworldly testimony to hurt I heard emanating from the crate was much, much worse. Instinctively, the sound so tortured, I reached behind and tossed aside the cloth covering the fetid beast I hauled. The vampire's body seemed to shimmer like a mirage on the horizon or a struck tuning fork. A flickering accompanying the waves of agony the monster rode. I reveled in the glorious chorus, delighting in the thing's agony.

Yes, I needed to ensure the boy was safe first. Hopefully, I'd soon catch up and find him already reunited with the family I'd left him with previously. Maybe sharing a kind word, last goodbyes, and finally discovering each other's name before I departed his life forever. But deep down I knew the monstrous cargo I towed in the bed of the wagon behind me was now my primary responsibility. I began to wonder, as the wooden wheels thumped along the uneven ground, if this thing had been the real reason I'd been summoned to this horrible land of death. Was what I hauled *my* Wendigo? Mother Earth putting me in place to discover and destroy the spirit infesting the fetid thing after centuries of poisoning these lands?

I decided that once I knew the boy was safe, I'd find some explosives and blow the undead fiend to bits on a deserted battlefield far from prying eyes. Gather and burn the blown pieces until only ashes remained... Or, if I am unable to secure the right firepower, drop the creature down the deepest, darkest hole I can find. Send it back to the hell the undead demon was birthed from. As the cart rolled on – still no sight of the boy – I fantasized all the ways I might destroy the horrid creature.

Beseeching my Wendigo slaying ancestors to share their wisdom on such things until the vampire once more intruded on my thoughts.

"I beseech you to allow my eyes to see the sun." The vampire pleading. "Let a little sunshine into my soul, as they say."

Secrist's eyes widened and he bolted to his feet. The diary falling to the floor and the cover slapping shut with a finality. Unbalanced, he ends up stumbling backwards. Finding himself falling back into the recliner he'd been seated and reading from.

Secrist bent to retrieve the journal, reopening to the page he'd been reading. He reread the last line. "Let a little sunshine into my soul..." Only days earlier, Hannah had said almost exactly the same thing to him in jest. What a bizarre coincidence.

He hated coincidences.

Secrist glanced at his phone before picking it up. A new message from Stander. Secrist clicked on it but there was no text. The message an indiscernible picture of dark images and shapes with no explanation. Frowning, he replied with a somewhat curt text. "Did you mean to send this? Or was it a butt dial? Too blurry to make it out. Resend if important. Later."

He tossed his phone aside. Thinking to himself he'd better go see what mischief Frazier was getting into. What if he had sniffed out another bat? Secrist thought of that old horror film from the 80's where the dog got bit by a bat with rabies. What was the name of it? Kolchak? No, that was the made-for-TV vampire movie that had scared the shit out of him as a kid. But it was similar sounding... Cujo! That was the one. That poor dog! Secrist made his way once more to his backdoor. "Frazier!"

"Let a little sunshine in?" I immediately regretted responding, silently cursing myself for opening my mouth. But the request made no sense. No matter how far back in time you searched, regardless of the culture, all vampire's supposedly shunned and cowered from the sun. What was I dealing with?

"Yes. Please turn me over. I beg of thee. Let my eyes see."

I didn't immediately reply. But soon my curiosity got the best of me. Perhaps I could learn something of the thing's nature. And vulnerabilities. "I've read the novel *Dracula* written by the Irish scribe *Stoker*. Before that, I'd heard tell all the legends and myths of you eternal bloodsuckers. Fiends such as you always shun the rays of the sun. Why would you seek it now?" I didn't move to turn the thing over. My rapt eyes still roaming the countryside for any sign of German soldiers as I drew nearer to the border of France.

"Oh. I see. Are you one of those? Those who believe in such nonsense?" It was tough to tell for sure, but I thought I heard the rumble of a low chuckle. "It was my ways that spawned all the little myths and legends of the so-called vampire. Since man was first spat out of the wet, bloody maw of their mothers I have haunted your existence. There is no such thing as fanciful as *Polidori's Vampyre* or a vampire named *Varney* or Count named *Dracula*. Those are all works of fiction birthed from the infantile minds of macabre authors. Could there be one feebler than a writer who pens such dreadful things? Dullards lacking imagination." The chuckle became a cackle. "There has only ever been one of what you call a vampire. But my shadow is endless and dark..."

"One? No such thing as vampires?" I knew the thing's words were all likely lies. Vanity at best. But I pressed on against my better judgment. The lane ahead and behind us vacant – still no sign of the boy. "Then tell me, if you truly were the first or only of your kind, how did you come to be?" I held out hope I'd glean some useful knowledge. Perhaps the pain from the bite of the blade would give me an advantage. "Who came before you? What demon spirit made you then?"

"Let's just say I was once kissed by the lips of Mithras. I've lusted for more ever since." His voice was muffled by the wood of the crate he spoke into, the bottom of the container.

"Mithras?" I'd never heard that name until just a handful of days ago, and now it was popping up again. Mithras had been who the disfigured and diseased soldiers said they followed. Worshipped even. It wasn't lost on me that by following after the boy, I was heading straight towards those same killing fields once again. The dead zone of faceless men Kirk had warned me to steer clear.

"Yes, Mithras. Equal even to your precious Mother Earth, Oryana, Parvati, Gaia, Pachamama, or whatever that dark-skinned bitch is calling herself now..." The last sentence barely a whisper as if the fiend feared she might hear of his blasphemy.

"Who or what is he?" Without realizing it, my fingers had involuntarily clutched for the bundle of hawk feathers at my breast.

"He? She? You of all people should know how little the curvature or shape of one's genitals matters to beings of intelligence." The vampire, or whatever it considered itself to be, paused for a moment before continuing. "I feel so helpless and submissive right now. I bet you like that. Hmmm? The things you could do... Quick! Turn me over." Another pause. "I'll show you mine if you show me yours."

For the first time since I'd run him through with the strange sword, the monster moved on its own. Though grimacing, it shifted slightly to one side. Just enough that, when I pivoted to look down into the crate, I could see most of its hideous face. And both its beautiful eyes. I quickly turned back to the reins in my hand. Ignoring the crude innuendos. "Tell me," I began again. "What did you get in exchange for a kiss from this

Mithras? An eternity of rot?" I forced a laugh I didn't feel. "Infinite loneliness forever locked in that shambling rancid mess of a body?" I dared another quick glance back.

"Or perhaps to hop across all of time in any guise I chose as I do his bidding." I could see the thing's deep green radiant eyes beaming. Sparkling and hypnotic. "Maybe spend a few lifetimes as a fetching, big-breasted blonde fuck machine feeding off the unsuspecting. Take a few long draws from their cup of life before leaving them confused and wanting more of my poison. Wanting more of me." Once again, the thing batted its lash-less eyes my way flirtatiously. Between my legs I felt an anxious rising and twitch. "Leaving them stumbling around weak and lost as I pop in and out of their lives for little nibbles and tastes. All the while keeping Mithras safe and hidden until the time is right."

I'd be lying if I wrote here that I thought what was said was ridiculous. Don't get me wrong, it was... but I could see it. I could see the feminine mannerisms it feigned. Those spellbinding, emerald green eyes inside an attractive form would certainly be alluring. Intoxicating. Who wouldn't be fooled? Especially if this thing watched its victim grow from boy to man and adjusted its appearance to match the steady march of time.

I shook my head angrily. The evil thing was likely distracting me with nonsense. Filling my head with outrageous lies like an unprincipled politician cowering from the responsibilities of his actions. It was pathetic and sad, but I had no doubt it could be effective on the weak-willed. Had the boy, who likely had limited schooling with war raging all around, fallen prey to the manipulations of this beast? I felt a new swell of pity for the child. There is no greater monster than one willing to lie to a barely educated innocent for their own selfish means. What was it the circus leading grifter P.T. Barnum famously said? *There's a sucker born every minute.*' It infuriated me to think this walking shadow of a real man thought I couldn't see through the ruse. I ignored the distraction and focused on the one single glaring, indisputable fact.

"If this Mithras is so powerful, how is it this etched sword has rendered his disciple so helpless? And why did you keep it near if it can hurt you?" I tried again to learn something I could later use to my advantage.

"Simple," came the reply from the mouth of barbs. "You should always keep your enemies close. The one who last wielded this weapon did not fully understand what he possessed. His brain overpowered by his bravery." I could hear another muffled chuckle. "It was such fun playing with the fool. And I found a perverse pleasure in seeing that cursed blade stored for so long straight up his fleshless ass. Besides, what better hiding place for something so dangerous than among a vast cache of impotent weapons and the failed warriors who wielded them? And by stashing it in my own home, I could keep an eye on it for Mithras. Hidden from those who would see this world go away."

I had more questions I could have asked. I'm sure the monster in the box was expecting more opportunities to deceive and mislead as well. But instead, I hastily pulled the wagon's covering back over the opened crate. Hiding the wretched cargo I hauled. Just ahead of me, stumbling along the side of the same dirt lane I traveled, a woman slowly staggered step by step. When she heard the approaching rumble of the Red Cross wagon I'd commandeered, she turned. Her hand leaving her bulging stomach in an attempt to flag down the horse and cart. I gasped in recognition. It was the mother of the family I'd left the boy with in the nearby forest days before. Ahead of her, down another short lane of dirt, a clapboard house stood in the middle of several fields. Her likely destination.

My heart soared! Miraculously, I'd found the family once more. But as my eyes scanned the land for any sign of the boy, the woman stumbled and fell. Landing in a huff before tumbling down the small ditch that ran alongside the dirt road just as I'd pulled even with her. I yanked on the reins until the horse stopped before grabbing my gun and jumping from my seat. When I reached the mother, I found her unresponsive. And reeking of alcohol. I quickly turned her over, gravely concerned for the unborn child she'd landed on top of. But lying on her back exposed the ruse that I had fallen for. The bulging cloth of her dress had only been hiding a pillow, not an unborn child.

The woman stirred and mumbled. Eyes closed; one hand fumbled for something in the pocket of her dress before bringing it to light. A near empty glass bottle glinting in the early morning sunshine. Shocked at the startling deception, I quickly stood and unshouldered my rifle. Though exposed on the open road, I couldn't hear or see anyone else nearby. Where was the family I'd seen the woman with? My heart sank in my chest and my throat clogged with despair. I'd been so confident I'd somehow find the boy safe with the family that, when it hit me, there likely never was a family, all I felt was sick. Mindless of the danger I was potentially putting myself in, I sprinted towards the house at the end of the small lane. My loaded rifle pointed at the front door.

I would have answers...

The house was silent and still. No trace of the boy that I could see anywhere inside or outside. Nor did I find the husband or the other children I'd seen walking in the woods that day. It was empty save a few pieces of broken furniture. A skeletal bedframe standing on three legs, a couple wooden chairs cobbled together with string, a pile of filthy straw with a threadbare blanket, a rancid bucket I didn't dare a peek inside, and one table barely big enough to fit four people around. The table, the last thing I saw before bolting from the house and hastily climbing back into the wagon. All my willpower brought to bear to avoid putting a bullet inside the skull of the unconscious woman passed out and helpless in the ditch beside the road.

Only when I knew I was a comfortable distance away did I revisit the reason for my swift departure and boiling anger. On the table had been an empty wood cup lying beside a serrated knife and a twisted fork missing several tines. The dull steel of the blade speckled with dried blood. Next to the crude cutlery was the carcass of a small animal. Really just a ribcage and few other assorted bones. All picked clean of their meat. Underneath the table, what had been deemed unpalatable by the diners, a floppy eared skull still covered in short black hair and four paws of white fur.

The family's dog.

CHAPTER EIGHTEEN

The series of texts from Stander arrived in broken pieces. Only a single word or two at a time that made no sense. A collection of disjointed messages jumbled with a confusion of seemingly random words and symbols. One text is a dark picture of a long, steel blade. Secrist let his hand fall from the knob of the backdoor. He'd go outside and find Frazier in a moment.

What is with theses messages?

Blindly, he stepped to where he kept a pen and pad of paper on his countertop, eyes never leaving the screen of his phone. Flipping back and forth between the flurry of texts still pinging his phone. Slowly, he began to jot down on the pad of paper the words he could read. "Here... us... down... there's..." Frowning over the puzzle, Secrist began to move the words around on the paper he wrote them on. Sorting and putting them in what seemed a logical order. When he was done, he sat back and read the message he'd deciphered.

"There's something down here with us," Secrist read the cryptic passage out loud. Somewhere outside, Frazier began to howl mournfully. The hair on the back of Secrist's neck rising as a parade of goosepimples marched up and down his arms. He raced for the handle of his backdoor.

Cold, numb and exhausted, I guided the horse and cart west. The vampire as silent and unmoving as the dead for much of the day. I'd now been awake for more than 24 hours straight, and my last sleep had been fitful at best. My head bobbed intime with the rhythmic rocking of the wooden wagon, and several times I caught myself blissfully nodding off. At some point I know I must have crossed back into France. Part of me had expected (and perhaps hoped?) to be accosted by German troops at the border. But as the miles and hours passed – the rise of the morning sun beginning its afternoon descent – I found the lane I travelled was largely deserted. The few weary travelers I did pass avoiding me with the same passion I avoided them.

Somewhere in the distance the familiar sounds of war resumed. The detonations I heard grew louder, and I could both feel and see the flashes of cannon strikes in the distance. I couldn't be certain, but the dead zone where I'd narrowly escaped the faceless German soldiers was likely nearby. I felt an involuntary shudder as the drifting dark smoke and blackened soot from the nearby fighting soon began marring my vision. Like a thick fog rolling in from an ageless sea, I soon found myself unable to see anything more than a few feet in any direction. I felt lost in the swirling mist. Disoriented. Even the sounds of the nearing battle seemed to fade. I tried not to think of the poisonous mustard gas the heavy fog could potentially contain, but found myself wondering over every breath of air I inhaled. With the exception of my rifle and the ammunition I carried on my person, I'd left all my supplies (including my gasmask), buried back in the trench I'd abandoned to save the boy. With nothing to protect myself, I took my mind off the danger by plotting how best to destroy the monster I hauled. I wasn't sure exactly where or how I'd do it yet, but felt certain I'd know once I found it.

Though I'd guessed I was now just scant miles from the front lines, the waves of the misty smoke gradually began to dissipate. Exposing the area of France I crossed as nearly idyllic and somehow untroubled by the nearby fighting. The harsh cold of the approaching winter coloring the rolling hills and knolls I crossed with a drab brush of browns and beiges. My troubled mind swam gratefully in the calm of the unspoiled air and fields of peacefully waving weeds I crossed. Ahead of me, I could see a tall church steeple erupting from the center of a small village of quaint homes surrounded by farms and farmland. Any crops they'd been able to grow, already harvested for the season. It was amazing to think how close the small town was to the roaring battlefields of desperate fighting. Its citizens somehow spared the atrocities so many other villages had endured during the years of conflict.

"Whoa!" Cursing, I pulled hard on the leather reins in my hands. Desperate to bring the horse and cart to a stop. Lost in my own thoughts, I'd not seen the old woman slowly walking across the rutted dirt road until it was nearly too late. The road I traveled abruptly splitting into two. I'd come to a crossroads of a sort and our paths were converging.

Though she never flinched, the horse and wagon had just missed trampling her underfoot and wheel. The horse seemed equally surprised by the hunched old woman's sudden appearance and reared up on its hindlegs. Neighing loudly with eyes wild and rolling. Under me, I felt a violent jolt and heard the groan of the wood carriage. The sudden change in direction driving one wooden wheel into a cragged rut where I heard it split. I felt the cart lean and for a moment was certain it would topple onto its side before miraculously righting itself and slamming back to the ground. Stopped dead in its tracks and tilting slightly to one side.

The tortured screech of my pinned cargo split the still air. The scream, one of agony that set my teeth on edge and raised the hairs on the back of my neck. A small flock of birds heaved themselves into the air above my head; their wings exploding as they climbed the sky. I watched them disappear over the tops of the surrounding trees and noted the afternoon sun now dipped below them. The tops of each lit brightly like the tips of burning matchsticks. Their long shadows crowding the road as if stretching to comfort the screaming banshee at my back. As the back-and-forth rocking of the cart stilled, so did the agonized wails of my cargo. A quick turn of my head confirming the ghastly thing was still pinned and hidden under the wagon's cloth covering. I swiftly jumped from my seat to calm the troubled steed. Soothing the horse with confident words spoken in low whispers and gently steadying the troubled stamping of its hooves with a firm grasp of the bridle.

As I continued comforting the spooked beast, my eyes sought out the old woman. She'd barely moved during the entire episode despite the near miss. Her white hair was stringy, long and wildly unkempt. Despite the plummeting temperatures as the sun set behind the tall trees encircling the road, she was barefoot and sleeveless. The colorless garment she wore more like a large bag she'd cut holes out of than a real dress, and it was held in place by a simple cord of frayed rope. It may have been the filtered light of the setting sun casting shadows across her features, but the frail-looking woman seemed ancient beyond measure. What I could see of her granite-like face was pockmarked. Canyons of deep wrinkles splitting what may have once been beauty, but now worn from lack of care. The few teeth left in her mouth rotted and set at odd angles. Only her eyes seemed unfazed by the ravages of time. A fiery intelligence burning deep inside each.

"You are lucky I saw you at the last moment or you'd have been crushed under..." without thought I'd begun to speak before stopping myself. The English I spoke undoubtedly just gibberish to the archaic French woman. Yet, she both understood and replied. After all the years of use, her voice creaked and cracked but was somehow still full of energy. Like a fire.

"I see the wheel of your wagon is broken." Though tinted with a strong French accent, her English was well spoken and clear. I had no doubt the shock on my face was plain as I listened with jaw agape. "You will need to unload your cargo. Allow me to help. It is the least I can do for the trouble I've caused you. If it has value, I know of a place nearby where I could allow you to store it until you can repair the cracked wheel."

To say I was caught off-guard would be an understatement. The language she spoke and directness of her thoughts belied her appearance. Despite her animated eyes, the elderly woman was tiny in stature and I doubted weighed even one hundred pounds. The thought of her helping move a full crate the size of a coffin seemed ludicrous. I told her as much in somewhat halting words. The absurdity of the conversation, and the freight I hauled, making the entire episode seem surreal in hindsight. She listened attentively before waving a hand at someone who'd stayed hidden at the side of the road.

"Perhaps this lost child could help us as well. He seems directionless at the moment and willing to labor for food and shelter." Then, before I could stop her, she reached into the back of the cart and threw aside the covering. Exposing the wretched vampire still pinned face down in the wooden container, seething and groaning in pain. "Perhaps, like me, he'd be less shocked at what you transfer than you'd expect." Splitting the brush that hid him, the kid emerged from his hiding place and let her guide him to my side. It was the boy I'd saved. The boy I'd damned.

She led the sheep I'd thought devoured.

I know I gasped and sobbed at the unexpected reveal. My face contorting as several thick tears left tracks on my cheeks; two clean lines. Dropping to my knees, I fiercely hugged the boy to my side until I was certain he was real. I could see his head wound – the deep gash behind his ear – had been crudely tended. The long cut packed with dirt to stop the bleeding. The boy stayed largely stoic and unmoving as I gave him a quick once over. Verifying his health until stepping away as the aged hag began to speak.

"It is fortunate our paths have crossed. Few would understand or have sympathy for the burden you carry." Though her wizened meaning could have many interpretations, she waved a gnarled hand at the back of the wagon to indicate she meant the monster in the box.

"If you truly understand," I looked once more at the boy by her side. Had he conveyed the horrors we'd experienced? Told her of the undead thing and the terrible weight of its influence? "Can you help me destroy this... this thing? Please don't mistake its current stillness and silence for peace. This current tranquility, I assure you, is more akin to the quiet before the storm."

"There is no destruction that is final for a fiend such as this. But I do know of a place not far from here that calls and collects ones such as these. Much like a perfect storm gaining in energy, it waits for the wind to blow favorably before releasing the tempest it conceals within the darkness. And that time grows oh so very near now..."

Before continuing, the aged hag gestured at a stand of crooked trees huddled where the meadow we looked met its end. The direction we soon headed. "You must be brave to enter. But it will safely harbor the doomed and cursed. You might say it is an eternal collector of dark souls and warriors. I believe it may be the place that has steered and beckoned you. Perhaps even the boy as well?" Her hand landed on top of his unkempt blonde hair, a pink streak highlighting the wound behind his ear. "Otherwise, to think our chance meeting at this crossroads was but coincidence strains credibility. Does it not?"

"I don't believe in coincidences." This was a lie. I do believe in them. I just don't like them. "Are you... are you a witch?" The words tickled my tongue with silliness as they fell from my lips. I tried to put what I meant in my own terms. What I truly believed. "A shaman or medicine man as my family knows healers as?"

"I have been called many, many things across the time I am cursed to walk this land." The old woman may have smiled, but her misshapen mouth blurred the gesture. "Most names, I can't deny, were deserved and not untrue. However, my name is Laurent." She bowed slightly. Though, with her hunched and crooked back her stature hardly changed. "Now, let us clear the road of your cart. An opening to the place of which I speak of is not far." She gestured at the boy and all three of us worked together to push the hobbled cart into the nearby weeds once I'd unhitched the horse.

I placed the cover back on top of the crate and used a large stone to pound the nails back into place to secure it. The thing inside unmoving and silent as if unaware. Or complicit. Above us, nearly the last of the filtered sunlight began to turn the forest around us grey. Laurent grabbed the long, thick rope the German soldiers had left behind out of the back of the wagon we deserted. "We will have use for this," was all she commented.

We stepped through the gradually darkening fauna. I wrapped the coarse rope several times around the saddle horn and secured the opposite end around the crate before following after Laurent. The horse dragging the monster in the box as I led it across a blessedly flat field of colorless weeds. Passing a series of strange ruins the likes of which I was not familiar with. An aged line of ghostly white pillars toppled near staggered square bases and flat stones that must have been part of something grand in the distant past. Laurent made no mention of the ancient granite outcroppings as we crossed over them. Ignoring the questions on my face.

The old woman directed us to a towering tree overlooking a deep hole of black. The opening into the ground a sizeable crack lined with jagged rocks. Even in the fading light of the day, the shape and look of the imposing crevice was unmistakable. The split of the earth could have been the opened mouth of a terrible beast. Each pointed stone that lined it like jagged teeth waiting to close should one dare the throat of this land. We used the strength and balance of the horse to lower the crated fiend down into this pit. The long rope reaching the depths without issue. When the wooden box touched down, I freed the horse and tied the end from the saddle around the base of the sturdy tree next to the cavern's opening. Before backtracking with the faithful animal and tethering him at the shore of a nearby river. By the time I'd returned, Laurent and the boy had already used the secured rope to descend into the pit. Unsure what was to happen next, I followed behind. Lowering myself into the empty maw of black.

As I dropped to the dirt and stone floor of the cavity – my boots kicking up dust that floated leisurely past our faces – Laurent finished lighting several crude candles. The flickering of the diminutive flames scattering our shadows as if they feared staying in one place for long. The cavern was warmer than the crisp winter air above but still cool enough that I left my coat on.

The space we'd landed in was cramped. Sharp rocks at our feet and the smell of dampness all around. I could see several squared off boulders of impressive size in one corner of the chamber. One large tunnel ahead of us that led deeper into the earth. Above our heads, the opening we'd descended funneled the last bit of dying sunlight like a spotlight of a grand theatre. The dust particles dancing in the faint lumination as they gracefully settled lower and lower.

"Is this an old mine?" I looked for rail tracks but saw none. No tools for tunneling visible. "What is this place?"

"A place most have long forgotten. A task I have labored at for longer than most could comprehend. Once these caverns were abuzz with activity. A working quarry where Romans raped the earth before..."

A desperate scream split the stillness. Laurent looked as if she'd been slapped across the face. Her lined features contorted in undisguised shock. Without finishing her answer, she spun on her heel. Moving past me before slipping behind one of the squared off boulders.

The boy and I pursued her, all of us chasing after the howling pain echoing eerily around us. Slithering along a hidden crevice more easily mistook for mere shadow. After ten feet of tight and difficult passage, the narrow channel opened into a wide room of chiseled stone. A chamber of impressive size and height with several tunnels and earthen channels leading away from it. A roaring fire in the middle lighting up the cavern. Laurent stopped before entering. All three of us still hidden in the barely visible split we'd slid down. Watching the scene around the flare of the bonfire in stunned silence.

My eyes feverishly scanned the earthen cavity. The visions they returned would have been unbelievable had I not previously witnessed this same unfolding horror mere days before. Around the blaze intoned a group of robed men seemingly enraptured by their own voices and practiced rituals. I didn't recognize any of them, but how could I. How could anyone? The men were without features. Faceless and ruined. Disfigured and scarred. Could they have been the same French soldiers I'd encountered back in no man's land? There was no way I could tell for certain but I highly doubted it. I'd seen those madmen overrun, devoured and eaten by their own. Incredibly, there were obviously more believers. More followers of that alleged God, Mithras.

The faceless men's deranged incantations were hypnotic. A chant. The reverie I slipped in and out of broken only by the desperate screams of their prisoners. A chorus of profound fear that teetered on the razor edge of madness. Two young men desperate not to join the victim of crucifixion already hoisted high above the chanting group. It was clear that man had already been dead for several days. Likely long after he'd prayed for release. I wished I hadn't recognized the dripping thing with empty eyes staring back at me from the top of the cross. But I did. It was Kirk. His body a testimony to unimaginable pain and suffering.

Only now, weeks later and secure in the military infirmary where I'd woken, do I feel safe recalling what happened next. Should anyone ever read this account I have no doubt they'd judge me a madman. And though I freely admit I can't recall much of what happened after I'd seen Kirk torn asunder and left to rot in that black pit. I swear to Mother Earth every word is true.

I wish it were not so...

Laurent seemed to vanish. Though moments before she'd been right in front of me in that cramped hidden passage, I never saw where the strange hag disappeared to. I'd slipped my rifle from my shoulder and strode out of the slim opening. I am unclear how many bullets it had taken or recall the order of my actions. But each robed man got their fill of lead. None would ever chant again or leave that pit of misery alive. Of that I can promise.

The first soldier I freed of his binds ran blindly down one of the dark corridors of the ancient quarry. Screaming out to the second one, "Go back to your momma! Tell her she was right. Her dreams..." His screams echoing as the black chasm he raced down swallowed him whole.

The second victim turned out to be a fellow American. I know that because he'd babbled endlessly as I'd continued to empty clip after clip into the twitching robes. His accent clearly from the east coast of America. Perhaps New Jersey or Boston? He was young, likely barely old enough to have signed up for service. Brown haired, long-faced, lanky, and awkward.

"This is a dream! Only a dream... This is a dream! A dream! Only a..." I'd finally reached out and grabbed him. Asking if there were any others being held elsewhere and what his name was. I remember he recoiled from my touch as if I was as much of a monster as those I'd liberated him from. He managed to croak out, "Howard, Howard Phillips..." The rest of his name cut short by a thunderous roar I could feel in my chest as much as I heard it. Drowning the rest out.

"Well, H.P.," I remember laughing for some reason as I slammed another clip into my rifle. "Good luck with believing that dream thing. This is as real as..." but the unnatural roar came again. Deeper. Louder. Closer.

The skinny young man blanched noticeably. He ran for the widest opening out of the underground room, likely betting it the safest route back to the surface.

He lost both his wager and balance as he skidded to a halt and fell to his knees.

Though the chiseled entryway he'd nearly vanished into was big enough for a full-sized locomotive to easily pass, it began to fill completely. The space crowded with writhing things both slippery and glistening. At the center of the growing mass, an ember of red radiated like the intense coal of a hot fire. Enlarging as whatever called this pit of despair home drew nearer and nearer to us. A gaggle of squirming tentacles that seemed to move independently of each other on either side. Each one reaching out to pull the squiggly mass closer. Ever closer. The red ember seeming to focus and grow larger as it pulled itself from the bowels of that cursed place.

Closer still...

One slimy tentacle, octopus-like and pocked with menacing beaked suckers, snaked out. Mere yards from the petrified young man I'd freed. The soldier, barely escaped from adolescence, stared straight into the center of the squirming thing that pulled itself up from the depths of the trench. The slithering behemoth, a mountain of madness I doubt either of us would ever forget. I had no doubt the young soldier's mind would never be the same. Perhaps already no longer his own. H.P. turned and ran. Gibberish pouring from his mouth as he disappeared down yet another dark tunnel of the ancient quarry.

I stood and stared but cannot call to mind what I'd seen. The swarm of oozing appendages, or feelers like the arms of a giant squid, all I truly recall. For the thing was without form. Or I was without the courage to see. Or without enough faith to truly believe in that horrid colossus rising from the deepest darkest pit of the quarry. But I am convinced it was featureless.

Faceless.

Mithras.

It was the boy that finally pulled me away from the writhing mass. Had he not, I believe the grasping tentacles would have claimed and dragged me into the dark depths it called home. I know the child led me down black tunnels and blind hallways that seemed endless until we suddenly reentered the room we'd first descended into. Puddles of wax barely supporting the tiny flames that still burned.

I spoke with the boy. Pulling him to me and throwing him on my back as I desperately grabbed for the rope we'd used to descend into that dark pit. Somehow finding the strength to pull both of us to the surface. Each time I looked down fearing the grasp of a wiggling tentacle and imagining that burning eye of red drawing near. But farther and farther up I climbed. The muscles of my arms burning, desperation and fear providing the motivation. As I neared the surface, the ghostly beams of the rising moon overhead lit our way.

I no longer thought of the vampire I'd imprisoned in the crate. What his fate would be and if I'd delivered him where Mother Earth had planned. If the sword pinning him inside the crate would hold and if Mithras would return for another kiss and free his disciple. Or did the blade etched in those strange symbols also hold power over that awful thing… I truly thought only of freeing the boy and I from that chasm in the earth. That pit of agony and horror.

I'm done with all of this. All. Of. It.

I know Laurent was waiting as we pulled ourselves out of the quarry. I'm sure I would have questioned her about all I'd seen deep in the bowels of the French countryside. Even now I question if the wrinkled hag was a mistress to her lover Mithras, a faithful believer or a victim the same as I. Whether she answered and I'd later forgotten or lost her words, I am uncertain. All I am sure of is that the boy and I parted ways for the last time just outside the black of the quarry.

I'd kneeled and hugged him. The blond-haired blue-eyed boy barely responding to my touch or words. My heart broke for him. The unrelenting horror that was now his life... I pulled the picture I'd carried next to my heart over the last few days. The black and white photo of the jumping dog and the smiling German boy I'd murdered on the battlefield. The one I'd been the monster in his life. I showed it to the boy without really understanding why. I guess I did it only because I'd regretted not doing so earlier. Back when I'd first tried to steer him clear of the path I was sent to walk.

The boy smiled slightly and put one finger on the image of the dog. "Der Hund." I looked up at Laurent who translated.

"He said dog. Hound." She shrugged impassively.

"Yes!" I smiled at the boy and pointed to the leaping dog. "Hund." Then pointing to myself I said, "Anong," before turning back to Laurent once more. "That means star in my people's tongue. Can you tell him my name is Anong? Star..." She nodded and translated. The boy stoic and mute.

I stood and ran a hand over his hair. Careful not to reopen the wound behind his ear. "I bet that will leave a scar you'll have forever." Unsmiling, the boy just stared. His blue eyes hard as steel. I shouldered my rifle. "Can you ask if I can know his name? Do you know his name?" Laurent shook her head no as if names were of little importance. I suppose with so many dying in that land every day I couldn't fault her indifference. She spoke to the boy again but received no reply. Again, though my heart welled with hurt and my eyes stung with tears, I couldn't blame the child for staying silent. Our time together filled only with bruises, blood, and pain.

I sighed and stepped away, back to the river where I hoped my horse was still tethered.

"Gunther." The boy spoke. I turned as he repeated himself. "Gunther."

"Gunther?"

The boy nodded curtly. "Ja." The German word for yes.

"Gunther from the quarry. I'm glad I caught that..."

CHAPTER NINETEEN
PRESENT DAY FRANCE

FOUR DAYS PRIOR

THE REPETITIVE THUMP POUNDED rhythmically in the car at their backs. Just beyond the glare beaming off the windshield a lone head of longish grey hair bobbed up and down in-time with the syncopated beat. Though Lucas and Chris had shut the doors when they'd exited the vehicle, the music coming from inside remained audible. The infectious German lyrics from the metal band *Rammstein* heard clearly by anyone within fifteen feet of the automobile.

"Du, du hast, du hast mich.
Du, du hast, du hast mich.
Du, du hast, du hast mich.
Du, du hast, du hast mich."

"So," Lucas began, "you've known Stander since you both were kids?" Though Lucas was born in France and had returned as an adult to teach at the local university, he'd spent years in America while studying and obtaining his doctorate in archeology. His flawless English held both a hint of his French upbringing and a hint of American slang. The wirerimmed glasses and neatly trimmed beard and moustache on his face in direct contrast to the frayed ponytail barely keeping the wiry black hair on his head in check. "I guess you're used to all these little idiosyncrasies of his." Smiling, he leaned against the hood and bumper of his car as he jerked a thumb back to where Stander gyrated in the front seat.

"Yeah, we go way back. The town I grew up in was just a few miles from where his Great Aunt lived." Chris, redhaired but thinning badly on the top, joined Lucas at the front of the car. Both men looking out across a field of wild yellow flowers buzzing with the politics of insects. "Rusty, that's what we all knew him by back then, would spend a lot of his summer breaks from school visiting her. We had our own little gang back then. We called ourselves a wolf pack. Me, Brian, Denny, and Rusty. We were the best of friends." Chris was smiling but the expression looked tight. As though the flesh had been yanked taut.

"Rusty, huh?" Lucas scrunched up his face. "Sorry. I just don't think I could ever get used to calling him Rusty." The archeologist turned around just in time to watch Stander pantomiming a drum fill that matched the thundering music. "Even if he does still act like a kid a lot of the time." Both he and Chris shared smiles and a few chuckles.

"I won't argue with that. Until just recently, we actually hadn't seen each other in over 30 years. He is definitely the same guy he was as a kid. But yeah, I think Stander seems more fitting of a guy in his fifties than the name Rusty does. **I** just gotta get used to calling him that." Chris paused momentarily before continuing. "How about you? You just met him last year, right? Rusty said...er... Sorry! Stander said you helped him locate the quarry where he found his mom's remains. Is that when you two became friends?"

"Sure, I guess. I mean, technically he is my boss. But we seem to get along just fine. I sure think of him as a friend." In the background, the music began to fade. "He kind of grows on you."

"Yeah. Like a fungus..." Chris laughed at his own joke as the passenger door swung open and Stander stepped out, the song he'd been listening to finished. Chris called out to him. "You finally done headbanging?"

"Man, I fucking love that song!" Stander was smiling ear to ear as he smoothed back the thick grey locks he'd tussled in exuberance. The setting sun lighting his face, thick white moustache, and the black Gojira concert shirt he wore. He tossed the keys to Lucas' car at the owner as he joined the two men. "You guys didn't have to wait. I told you I wasn't getting out of the car until that song ended. You could have gone up to your rooms without me."

Across the parking lot from where they stood, the hotel where Lucas and his small team of trusted colleagues stayed during each workweek beckoned the trio. Stander and Chris had arrived in France the previous day, Monday, and were already checked in. As the men made their way across the paved parking lot, Lucas spoke up. "I wanted to ask if you guys were up for a swim in the hotel pool in an hour or so. Our little group has gotten in the habit of gathering together most evenings after the workday ends. Jumping in the water, having a drink or two, and, I guess, just decompressing a bit." Lucas shrugged nonchalantly.

"Yeah, that sounds like a good idea. I could use a dip to wash all that cave dust off of me. Plus, that will give me time beforehand to call Tommy and update him." Chris was nodding his head in agreement as Stander reached out and opened the entrance to the hotel. All three men filing into the crowded hotel lobby.

"Great! I'll let the others know you'll be joining us." Lucas pushed the button on the lone elevator after they'd navigated past a group of bickering tourists crowding the front desk. "It was great you got to meet my team onsite earlier today. But tonight, things will be more relaxed. Hopefully, we can all get to know each other a bit better."

"That would be nice. I guess we'll see everyone a little later on, then." Chris waved as he and Stander made their way down the first-floor hallway. Both of their rooms adjacent to each other on the ground level. Behind them, the elevator "dinged" and Lucas stepped inside.

An hour later, Stander and Chris strolled into the enclosed hotel pool deck. A few pink-faced guests they didn't recognize were sweating shoulder-to-shoulder in the cramped hot tub. But Lucas and most of his team were standing and conversing in the shallow end of the nearly equally miniscule pool. Stander and Chris shed their footwear and tossed a couple towels on an unoccupied table before pulling off their shirts. Stander, though only a little over six feet tall and in his fifties, cut an imposing figure. Powerful and compact like a sparkplug, his brawny arms were filled from top to bottom with colorful tattoos and his longish grey hair fell easily across the top of his broad shoulders.

"How is the temperature?" Chris, smiling at the group of waders, walked tentatively across the wet cement that surrounded the chlorinated water. "After we checked in last night, I came down here. But I thought it was a little on the cool side and didn't get in." He grasped the rail on the steps and trod cautiously into the pool. Slowly lowering himself into the water.

Unlike Stander, Chris had no tattoos on his body. The only noticeable marks on his pale skin a jagged surgical scar by his shoulder that connected to a now healed gunshot wound pitting his chest. Permanent mementos from his last days under the spell of addiction before being whisked off to a drug treatment center by Stander.

Though Chris and Stander were of identical ages, Chris appeared older by years or even a full decade. His physical body still recovering from the damage left behind by the substance abuse he'd struggled much of his life with. By comparison, emotionally, Stander seemed more like the big brother of the odd couple. Always watching out for and protecting his childhood buddy. And although Chris may still appear sickly to many, Stander was heartened to see his friend's continued improvement. Though his pale legs and arms remained rail thin, Chris had added a good twenty pounds during his recent stay at the rehab center. With the addition of the dental bridge he'd been fitted with, even his infectious smile had come back to life.

Chris dipped one hand in the pool and began to splash handfuls of the chilly water over his shoulders, arms, and legs. Slowly acclimating himself to the change of temperature when he heard Stander bellow, "Geronimo!" Chris turned just in time to see him launch himself into the air and, midflight, tuck himself into a ball. A cannon ball.

"Awwww sssshhhhiiii...!" All Chris could get out before being sprayed with the displaced water. When Stander returned to the surface of the pool he came up to a chorus of groans. Though Chris had taken the brunt of his aqua assault, the small group clustered around Lucas were all dripping.

"You know," Lucas spoke as he wiped at his smiling face, "some of us prefer to ease into the cold water rather than being baptized."

"Yeah, well, just consider that my "icebreaker" then. And, now that I've properly introduced myself, who brought the beer?" Stander used both hands to make quotation marks in the air when he'd said icebreaker before using them to ring the water out of his thick long hair. "Wait a minute. This isn't the entire team. Weren't there a couple more?"

"We are missing Antoine and Charles, who you and Chris both met earlier today." Chris had slowly waded over to the group and now stood a little behind Lucas. Shivering.

"That's right. Charles and Antoine were the two grad students, right? Is that why they were the ones who got stuck staying all night at the quarry? Low men on the totem pole?" Stander had instantly taken a liking to both of the young men working and studying under the tutelage of Dr. Lucas Chanet.

"They won't be onsite the entire night. Just long enough to stabilize the wooden crate and finish the preparations needed so it can be safely moved and opened first thing tomorrow." Lucas shook his head wryly. "We really expected to be able to get inside that box today. But it took a lot longer digging down to it than anticipated. It was almost like something didn't want the thing unearthed." Though only Stander noticed, a shadow of concern darkened Chris' features.

"And those two were the ones who told you there was a sick fucking stench coming from the crate?" Stander asked, ignoring the worry stamped across his friend's face.

"Yes. But I suspect they'd likely just hit a small pocket of gas. Neither Charles or Antoine is very experienced working that deep underground." Lucas shrugged to show his indifference. "They're both still learning."

One by one, Stander and Chris were reintroduced and officially welcomed by the three team members flanking Lucas on either side. Jack, a colleague and peer of Lucas and also the first archeologist to join the team. He'd grown disillusioned with teaching and had jumped at the chance to work with Lucas on an active dig. Much shorter than the other three men in the pool, his head was shaved completely bald, but he sported a longish brown beard that engulfed the entire front of his neck. He'd briefly met Chris and Stander earlier in the day when Lucas gave them both a tour of the work site.

Just behind Jack were Emma and Helen. Both women had loads of experience working on various digs all across Europe. When Lucas had hired them months earlier, he'd been tickled. Gushing to Stander about their individual expertise and past accomplishments.

Helen, the oldest of the entire team, had a grandmotherly appearance that was both genuine and warm. She told Stander that Lucas was the only one who could have convinced her to put off both spending more time with her grandson and her impending retirement. During the conversation, she'd briefly left the pool just long enough to retrieve her phone. Sharing with the group a video of a young boy, her grandson Edward, running in circles while a small black dog chased and excitedly jumped up and down at his heels. Hellen had a playfulness in her speech and mannerisms that Stander immediately felt a kinship with. A bit on the heavier side, her comfort in an unflattering swimsuit, straight grey hair, and makeup-less face was as refreshing as it was real.

Emma, on the other hand, was about the same age as Lucas, likely not yet even in her forties. She seemed bashful and, at times, clearly taken aback by Stander's language and directness. Seeming to gravitate and defer to Helen despite their difference in age. She'd worn a plain blue t-shirt over her swimsuit, left her eyeglasses in place even while in the water, and her soft brown hair stayed bundled in the thick bun that sat high atop her head. Like Helen, she seemed indifferent to her appearance and shared little unless it pertained directly to her work.

The six members of the team slowly fell into casual discussions. Asking nonintrusive questions about family, work, travel, etc... over the next hour or so. The lighthearted queries and answers helping to fill in the blanks and build the emerging camaraderie they all felt. It was only after both Helen and Emma had dried off and returned to their own rooms that Chris began to pepper Lucas with more direct questions.

"I'm not sure I really understand this whole arrangement," he began. "I get that Stander first hired you to help him locate and find a way inside that ancient quarry. But why aren't you one of the archeologists working the ongoing excavations inside the actual quarry itself? I'm no history buff, but isn't what you guys found kind of a big deal? Like, a career making kind of big deal?" The four remaining men were alone beside the pool, gathered around one table. Chris, his lips tinged several different shades of blue, had his towel wrapped around his bony shoulders and was still shivering slightly.

"What you said is true enough." Lucas winced as he pulled one chair out from the table, the screech of the metal legs echoing loudly in the otherwise empty enclosure. He sat down before adding, "I just don't really care to work for the government."

"And that's another thing." Chris turned and faced Stander while, behind him, Jack pulled out an equally noisy chair and sat beside Lucas. "Why did you just give away that part of the land you inherited to the local French authorities? You were the rightful owner of what will one day be a huge museum or tourist attraction of some sort. Think of how many people would pay for the chance to see a real mass burial site from medieval times? Not to mention all the other ancient human remains." Lucas and Jack traded a knowing glance as Stander replied.

"Number one, it's not like I need the money." Stander, as Chris and Lucas were already well aware of, had recently inherited a family trust of almost unimaginable wealth, holdings, investments, and land. Most of it passed down across generations and generations until finally landing in his lap when Dr. Timothy Stander, his dad, had died. "I still don't even know what all is wrapped up in that trust. But donating some acres of French countryside isn't likely to put a dent in it." Stander nodded toward the two archeologists way. "Besides, we kept the best fucking part. Right, Lucas?"

"I certainly believe so. It absolutely is looking that way…"

"Here is another thing I don't get." Chris spoke over Lucas; his voice rising. "Why wasn't this find big news? Like, world-wide big news? An ancient Roman quarry rediscovered? A site where later the English hid the bodies of thousands of massacred French citizens? You would think the French government would be exploiting the site for all its worth!"

"You have to remember that everything you said is merely a hypothesis until proven fact. That is why both the university and the government are meticulously working hand-in-hand. Personally, having seen the evidence firsthand, I believe the quarry will turn out to be the second biggest archeological find of our lifetime. But it will be the academics application of hard science and facts that ultimately will tell the tale, as they say." Lucas replied first. His words a little speech he'd given several times before.

"I think you may also be underestimating the potential political fallout from the discovery." Jack spoke from his seat beside Lucas. "It would not surprise me to find out, as you alluded, that the powers that be are dragging their feet. Afterall, how would you like to be the English and suddenly have to contend with what happened nearly a thousand years before? Or be the French politician to announce what will sound like an accusation?" Jack shook his head slowly back and forth as he finished. "Especially in this current political environment of gaslighting and soundbites. Wars have been started for less."

Lucas quickly chimed in. Adding, "I think that's why all of the archeologists and the other assorted professionals working inside the quarry itself were required to sign a non-disclosure agreement. Government officials don't want word to get out until they've sorted all these issues. Even a single picture or post on social media could get those guys in a lot of hot water." The three men surrounding the table nodded silently, each lost in their thoughts.

"You said earlier you think the archeological dig happening inside the quarry will turn out to be the second biggest archeological find you'll ever see." Chris asked one last question as the four men began making their way out of the hotel's pool area. "What was the biggest?"

"That's easy. It will be what Stander has us working on. And right under everyone's noses!" Lucas laughed and beside him Jack grinned conspiratorially. "Our little clandestine dig is just a few hundred yards from the quarry. And I'm certain what we are uncovering is the reason ancient man ever even began digging in that area in the first place."

Chris arched a questioning eyebrow Stander's way.

"Yeah. With all the trouble we had today just getting to that fucking crate we didn't get a chance to walk you over. But once we get that wooden box opened and anything inside catalogued, I've got something amazing to show you. The mammoth monolith Lucas and the team are uncovering is... well..."

As Stander searched for the right adjective, Jack beat him to the punch. "Out of this world!"

CHAPTER TWENTY

CHRIS ZONED OUT DURING the short drive from the hotel to the dig site. His eyes enjoying the surrounding scenery as it whizzed past his backseat window. In the front seat, Lucas drove while he and Stander argued amiably about the importance of the saxophone to the early sound of rock and roll. It wasn't a discussion Chris felt any urgency to participate in.

Though he and Stander had arrived in France late Monday, and Tuesday had been shuttled back and forth across this same stretch of countryside between their hotel and the quarry, this was his first chance to take in the picturesque French landscape. Chris cracked the car window as the morning sun began to warm his side of the car. He wanted to smell what he was seeing. Taste what was in the air. He'd only recently begun to understand how his struggles with addiction had deprived him of feeling much of anything for so long. Now, he craved even the simplest of things. The breeze caressing his hair, the smell of fresh rainfall, and the kiss of warm sunshine on his cheek. Even the confident sound of his best friend's voice at his shoulder was helping resurrect his life.

He'd missed so much.

The paved road Lucas drove was brightly painted and just wide enough for two cars to pass. The lane leading them into a gently sloping valley dominated by fields of wildflowers. Chris thought the yellow blooms that crowded the meadows seemed to wave more vigorously at their approach. Urgently, as if desperate to flag them down and tell them to turn the car around and go back. Minutes later, Lucas pulled into a small parking lot layered in white rock that crunched noisily under the wheels.

With Stander and Lucas still debating as the men exited the vehicle, Chris looked more closely at the surrounding area of the quarry as the three walked a pebbled pathway. In addition to the sprawling, waist-high fields of color, a thick forest of shadowy timber walled off one side of the land that bordered the quarry. Though the radiant morning sunshine had Chris squinting, the bright light seemed to wither and fade mere feet inside those dark woods. The swaying trees deepening into a murky black ink that blotted out the day's brilliance. The seemingly endless woodland stretching in one direction as far as the eye could see.

Though they'd driven through a small village not more than a few miles from where they were, the ancient Roman quarry seemed eerily cut off from the rest of civilization. Chris shuddered involuntarily as the three men closed the gap between the parking lot and the entrance. Their destination a massive tunnel bored directly into the side of a grassy hill. The cavernous entryway big enough that a full-sized semi-truck could easily pass back and forth.

"Why the fuck are we entering here? Isn't this still the main entrance down into the quarry itself?" Stander was asking Lucas the same questions Chris was silently pondering. "Yesterday you took us in the other way. On our side of the dig. Isn't that how we are supposed to access our side of this site?"

"Normally, yes." Lucas, after signing in and fitting each with a lighted hardhat from the tiny guard shack, led them to a gated entrance. The guard service, employed only during regular work hours, restricted and monitored each person who entered and departed the active dig site. Lucas and his team had unfettered access to their side of the site and could come and go as needed. But there was only one way in and out of the quarry, and it was completely shut down and locked tight each night and weekend. "But no one has heard from Charles and Antoine since last night. They may have run into problems and had to stay way later than anticipated. But it isn't like them not to update me once they'd finished and left the site."

After passing the security checkpoint, Lucas led Stander and Chris down a narrow channel of carved rock. The last of the daylight faded behind them, darkness smothering the warmth of the sun's rays with a blanket of black. Only a single strand of electric lights illuminating their way as they ventured deeper inside the quarry. "I want to see if anyone from the university knows what happened."

After a few more sharp turns, the narrow passage deposited the three men inside a large chamber. Electric lights perched atop free-standing metal stands kept the shadows and darkness at bay. The colorless walls were of chiseled stone, and the dirt floor at their feet was littered with rocks of various sizes. Mirroring the entrance and passage they'd just walked down. The ancient underground quarry disorienting in its uniformity. Several man-sized holes of black yawned from each of the relatively squared walls as Lucas excused himself. He walked over to a small group of clustered workers and began speaking with them.

"I can't believe the size of all these tunnels and rooms. From the surface, the entrance we just came in makes it look like one big cave." Chris was wide-eyed as he took everything in. "But this is a huge maze down here. I'm all turned around. Where are we standing now compared to what Lucas was showing us yesterday?"

"Fuck if I know," answered Stander shrugging. "I think it is about a mile behind us. I guess the way we came in today was the original opening down into the quarry." Stander lowered his voice as a woman in a bulky Carhart jacket with the name Beth embroidered on it winked as she passed. She had electric cabling slung over both shoulders, wore a pair of dorky safety glasses and hid her hair under the hardhat perched atop her head. But something seemed oddly familiar to Stander as he watched her retreat down a lonely passage. "The…uh…the crate was found buried in the only carved passage that connects this," Stander gestured around him to indicate the endless labyrinth of tunnels that honeycombed the quarry, "with the giant monolith Lucas and his team are unearthing."

"You mean there is only one tunnel that leads from the quarry to where our team is working? Isn't that dangerous? What if it collapses?" Chris cast a worried glance Stander's way.

"I mean, I guess it could," Stander kept one eye on the discussion Lucas was having. He couldn't understand what was being said – the group speaking entirely in French – but Lucas had become more animated the longer the conversation continued. "But these passages have stood far longer than most things mankind ever built. And besides, the subterranean channel connecting these two archeological digs wasn't even being used until the anomaly showed up on some of the latest ground penetrating radar scans. Our team has a safe and secure entrance we use to go back and forth, and the university and government team goes in and out of the main quarry entrance. But, to be on the safe side, Lucas had a locked doorway installed at our end of the underground channel. There is no way anyone can get from the quarry to our site. Or vice-versa without Lucas and his key."

"Oh!" Chris seemed visibly relieved. "I thought the passageway was like a bottleneck everyone had to pass through to get out of here. But there is always two ways in and out? Like, if we got separated or something, I could always just follow that string of lights right back to the surface?" Chris pointed to the hanging cord they'd followed earlier.

"Pretty much. But Lucas said they do shut everything down and lock the quarry up tight on nights and weekends. If one of the workers were to stay late or get caught in the quarry, they'd have to wait until the morning, or Monday, to get back out."

"What? Why is that? Wouldn't the trapped worker just call someone to be let out?"

"Cell phones are just about worthless around here. Sometimes you can still get a little bit of a signal when you are near the surface. But for the most part, phones are just glorified timepieces."

"Great", bemoaned Chris. His anxiety ticking up a couple more notches and eyes growing wider. He wasn't surprised being so deep in the earth was proving to be unnerving for him. As kids, he and Stander had barely escaped a horrible end in a much smaller underground labyrinth. Was the ice ball forming in his stomach a reaction to what they'd experienced back then? Or was he beginning to develop claustrophobia in his old age?

"We may have a problem," Lucas had rejoined Stander and Chris. His conversation with the university officials finished. "No one has seen hide nor hair of either Charles or Antoine since they were left down here last night."

"So? Maybe they went out for drinks after?" Stander shrugged indifferently. "After staying up all night they likely needed to crash. I bet they come stumbling in all apologetically pretty soon. Probably forgot to reset their alarms or something. Don't be too hard on 'em, Lucas. Graduate students or not, they are still just college boys."

"I hope you are right." But Lucas didn't sound very hopeful nor was he smiling. "Maybe they can explain what happened to the crate."

"Uh-oh, bossman," Chris tried to add some levity, but Lucas remained stone-faced. "Did your grad students not follow your directions? Or break the crate getting it out?"

"I'm told the crate is fine and easily identifiable as one from..."

Stander blurted out, "Fuck yeah!" The *yeahyeahyeahyeah* echoing in the rock lined cavern. The clustered university workers and archeologists Lucas had been speaking with all briefly turned at the unexpected outburst. "I can't wait to see what was inside. Lead the way!" Despite earlier downplaying the possibility of the find to both Secrist and Chris, deep down he was excited by the prospect of finally eyeballing the contents of the recovered crate.

"That's the problem." Lucas began making his way down one well-lit rock passageway followed closely behind by both men. "The crate is basically empty. It is still sitting right next to the hole we dug to reach it. The university suspects Charles and Antoine of disappearing with whatever they'd found inside."

Later that afternoon, Stander, Chris, and Lucas, along with Jack, Helen and Emma, were finally left alone with the newly discovered crate. The university officials eventually satisfying themselves that there was nothing to be learned about the graduate students disappearance from the recently unearthed wooden box. The bureaucrats had insisted their security service search the quarry, take statements from everyone associated with recovering the crate, and had taken a boatload of pictures as documentation. But the exercise seemed mostly for show. Or, as Stander whispered under his breath several times, just covering their asses.

"Well," Lucas began, "there still has been no word from either Antoine or Charles. But I also don't see any proof that anything was stolen from the discovery." Frowning, he reached down and grabbed the lone item found inside the crate. "In fact, a sword like this would be of great value to the right buyer. I am certain both Antoine and Charles would have recognized that. Especially if their disappearance was motivated purely by greed." Lucas shook his head back and forth slowly as he continued speaking. "I know collectors of historic weapons are not always concerned with the item's provenance. Often willing to pay cash to make the sale virtually untraceable. But knowing both young men as I do, I just have a hard time believing either would be so callous with such potentially historic finds."

"What do you make of the crate itself?" Jack had zeroed in on the rotted box of wood where the sword was found. "The time period certainly doesn't go with the sword."

"Why do you say that? Because of the size or the saw marks?" Helen squatted beside Jack as he used a brush to remove some of the loose soil from one corner. "Is that a crack or hole in the bottom? Up near the top? Looks kind of like something took a big chunk out of the wood." Helen fingered the split. "Hmmm... maybe some groundwater seeped in at some point. The wood is really oddly discolored and stained here as well. Stagnant water might explain the smell." Helen wrinkled her nose in distaste.

"They made crates like these by the hundreds back in the day. Real commonplace all around central Europe at the turn of the century. They were used to ship and haul all sorts of different things." Jack spoke decisively. His familiarity with early 20th century finds gleaned from years of searching and digging locations from both the First and Second World Wars. "But I don't know if what the crate was originally used for is super important. The real question, in my mind, is who buried it and what was inside when they did? And why hide it down here of all places? It would have been a Herculean task to haul such a large wooden box so deep inside the quarry to begin with. Not to mention turning around and digging way down to bury it even deeper inside the earth."

Lucas turned to Stander and handed him the long sword recovered from the wooden box. "Any ideas?" Stander had stayed uncharacteristically silent once he'd laid eyes on the blade. "I don't suppose this has anything to do with your mother, does it? I know it is hard to tell in this confused network of tunnels, but you found her remains not very far from where we are standing right now. Where this was buried," Lucas pointing to the weapon.

"I am one hundred percent sure my mom had no idea this sword was here." Stander felt the weight and perfect balance of the weapon in his hand before holding it at his side to judge the length. "She came down into this fucking hellhole looking for answers about the death of her parents. Nothing more."

Stander raised the blade to his face and appraised the strange symbols stamped on it. There was no question in his mind that the sword he held in his hand was identical to the two he had stored back in Michigan. One of them bequeathed to him when his Great Aunt Madeleine had passed on, the other recovered from a cave system revered by Native Americans for more than a thousand years. "Is there a way to have this thoroughly tested?" Stander held his tongue as he handed the sword back to Lucas. "Find out exactly what those symbols mean and when it was made?"

"Absolutely. I can think of several metallurgists who can conduct all the primary testing needed. We'll keep this with the other artifacts being recovered from the monolith until everything can be properly documented." Lucas paused before turning to Emma. "Maybe you can reach out to some of the Semiotic experts you've worked with in the past? I think we need some new eyes on this symbology before we can..."

Stander, lost in his own thoughts, turned from the team of archeologists. Jack and Helen were still scrutinizing the unearthed crate from their hands and knees while Lucas and Emma started trading names of potential experts they could bring on board. Stander walked to where Chris stood alone beside the gaping hole the crate was pulled from. Though he was looking down into the opening, his eyes were closed. He was visibly startled when Stander laid a hand on his shoulder.

"Whoa!" Stander commenting on his flinch. "Sorry. Didn't mean to scare..."

"Can you smell that?" Chris gestured at the opening in the floor of the quarry's cavern where the crate had been pulled from the earth. "It freaking reeks!"

Stander leaned over the deep trench and tentatively inhaled. "Ugh! No kidding. The smell is so thick you can taste it!" With a grimace he turned his head and spit. "Even leaves a sickly tang in your mouth. Like a... like licking between the legs of a frog with an STD!"

Chris and Stander laughed at the crude analogy but their banter seemed strained. Turning from the deep chasm the wooden crate was pulled from, neither noticed the brief flash of eyeshine from a nearby, unlit corridor. Two floating orbs of green peering out from the darkness and observing the ongoing work. Instead, both men busied themselves with helping Lucas and the team document, measure and catalogue the discovery. Each unwilling to admit how uncomfortable they felt working in such close proximity to the new hole. Both rushing for the exit when the end of their workday finally came to a close.

CHAPTER TWENTY-ONE

THE CHANT WAS LOW and ominous. The melody a dark hymn you'd expect to hear echoing through a candlelit monastery made of stone. The repetitive *hum* so deep there could be no mistake in the masculinity of the singers. It had to be a chorus sung by a group of men.

"Seriously? Both of you?" Stander merely nodded in response before reaching over and turning the volume up. In the seat behind him, Chris played air-guitar while Stander kept time with the rap of his knuckles on the dashboard of Lucas's car. "Alright. Whatever. You know where you are going when the song is over. Just be sure to lock my car when you come inside. I'll get everything ready so we can show Chris what we've been working on these last couple months. Ciao!" Stander and Chris watched Lucas walk to the dig site entrance and disappear inside. Making his way back into the depths where the ancient monolith was being painstakingly uncovered by his team.

"You can't stop them. (God bless ya)
They're coming to get you
And then you'll get your
Balls to the wall"

"You know what this song always reminds me of, don't you?" In the background, the German heavy metal group *Accept* continued chanting from the car's speakers. Their decades old song, *"Balls to the Wall,"* one that had been a favorite of both Stander and Chris when they'd been much younger.

"No. Not really. I mean, the lyrics are not exactly touching..."

Chris snorted once and both men shared a smirk. "Really? Nothing comes to mind?" Stander managed to shake his head no while it still bobbed in time with the music. "Oh, come on! Remember when we were kids and my oldest cousin, Tim, took us to that little teen dance club over in Peoria, Illinois?" Chris paused briefly before adding, "Or was it Peru? Anyway, all those girls dancing to this song."

"I thought it was Pekin he took us to?" Stander grabbed for the keyring; the song ended. "I mostly remember being terrified riding in the back of his car. That guy drove like a fucking maniac! We kept looking for seatbelts but the buckles were all missing from the straps. We were laughing and pretending to tie ourselves up in the loose belts." Stander started laughing loudly. "As if that would have saved us."

Chris joined the laughter. "Pekin, Peru, Peoria, whatever... One of those 'P' towns had some short-lived teen club that Tim was always bragging about meeting girls at. I begged him to take me, and you were in town visiting your great aunt when he finally agreed." Chris exited the vehicle right behind Stander.

"Yeah. Seems like he'd just gotten a car of his own. Wasn't he like 16 or 17? And we... we must have been maybe what... 13 or 14?" The car alarm chirped as Stander hit the lock button on the key fob. "Didn't we have to pay his way into the club? Or buy his gas or something like that before he agreed to even take us with him?"

"Probably. I know he wasn't thrilled having us tag along. Thought we were still children even though he was only a few years older. I think that was why he dumped us once we finally arrived. He avoided the two of us the entire four or five hours we were there. Didn't want to be seen hanging out with little kids." Chris fell in step with Stander as they walked the gradual incline that led to the entrance Lucas had used minutes earlier.

"I don't really remember." Stander mostly recalled the white-knuckle ride as Chris' cousin had roared down a curvy, hilly two-lane highway at crazy speeds. "I know we were bitching about the lame music the club kept playing. Didn't they only do one or two rock or metal songs an hour?"

"Yes! That's what I was talking about. One of the only real metal songs the place played was *"Balls to the Wall"* and the dance floor was packed." Chis paused, his eyes unfocused. "And all those high school girls lining the wall..."

"Most of them a lot older than us. Sure. Yeah, I remember that now." Stander and Chris took slow steps together as they reminisced. "They'd dance and... What were they doing? Pretending to basically hump the wall, right?" Stander gave Chris a quizzical look. "Did we ever figure out how or why that started?"

"Doubt it. We were too busy enjoying the greatest night of our 13 or 14-year-old lives up to that point." Chris was smiling as he recalled his first-ever, albeit mini, road trip. "God bless whoever those older girls were swinging their hips in those tight blue jeans. Not sure I ever looked at girls the same way after that night. They helped turn me into a man." Chris felt his smile wane. "Most of the night I spent girl-watching while I drank one Mountain Dew after another."

"God, were we really that chickenshit that we never talked to any of them?" Stander paused as both men reached the doorway leading into the underground dig site where Lucas and the team labored. "I'm surprised I didn't at least try".

"You had Izzy," replied Chris, as he looked over at Stander. "Once she showed up, you were either dancing or making out with her. The last hour or so I just sat in a corner and waited until..."

"What?" Stander pierced Chris with a dumbfounded stare before his eyes drifted across the nearby meadows. Lost in thought. "I don't remember that at all. Are you sure?" Chris nodded confidently, sadness touching his eyes but not his smile. "How would she have even known where we were going? Or been able to find us? I don't think we even knew where we would end up that night."

"Beats me. I guess I never really gave it much thought. Figured maybe you called her or something. Back then, the place probably had a pay phone." Both men stood talking beside the unopened door that led deep underground. Neither in a rush to grab at the handle. "Good thing she did though. Otherwise, we would have been riding with Tim when he wrecked."

"Wrecked? Your cousin got in a car wreck the very same night?"

"Geez, you don't remember that either?" Chris had a strange expression on his face as he looked at his childhood best friend. "It was all we talked about the next couple days." Stander just shook his back and forth. "Tim fell asleep or something on the way back home. His car slipped out of his lane and he crashed it in a shallow gully. Totaled his car and broke his leg and some other bones. If we'd been riding with him in the backseat, we wouldn't have had seatbelts on since they'd been disassembled."

"We'd have been killed for sure. Probably catapulted right through the front windshield." Stander's complexion seemed to fade, replaced by a haunted pallor. "How... how did we get home then? That night, I mean. Izzy was our age. She couldn't have driven."

"Harold, your Great Aunt Madeleine's gardener, came and picked us up. He had a really cool Camaro. Like a '67 or '68 with big fat tires on the back. It was mostly Bondo and body putty, but the engine was..."

"I called Harold?" Stander blinked slowly.

"No. I think it was Izzy." Chris stopped momentarily, trying to recall. "I guess maybe she got a hold of him?" Chris shrugged.

"Izzy called Harold, who worked for my aunt in Almore almost two hours away, to drive over and pick us all up..." There was no question in the tone of Stander's voice. Or recollection. Just a man repeating a story he didn't recall. He stayed still and silent until Chris finally made a move for the doorhandle.

"Now, show me this gigantic monolithic statue Lucas is digging up. I'm dying to see what has you so tightlipped on the subject." Chris held the door as both he and Stander entered. The steep, winding black tunnel they descended cut deep into the earth. Behind them, the door to the outside world slammed shut with finality. Somewhere unseen in the dark abyss, water dripped incessantly.

The two men trailed after a single strand of electric lights that lit their way and led them down the chiseled passageway. The limp cord ensuring they stayed on the right path and making it easy to spurn the many shadowed doorways that beckoned inspection. Each unlit black corridor channeling into even more unknown passages and caverns. Deeper and deeper underground they went. A sickly smell reminiscent of a carnival dumpster on a muggy summer day growing gradually stronger the farther down they went. Neither man felt truly relaxed until the familiar voices of Lucas and the team reached their ears in the shadowy tunnel.

When Chris was finally shown the partially uncovered find, his look was one of unabashed shock. Though it was hard to tear his eyes from the ornate and deeply carved object, he peppered Lucas with questions. Stander appeared to be listening as he stood nearby, but had a distracted look in his eye. He'd been uncharacteristically reserved and quiet since entering the earthen cavity.

The rest of the team of archeologists working under Lucas toiled close by in near silence. Jack, Emma, and Helen were all surprised to learn no one had heard from Charles and Antoine for a second straight day. The two missing graduate students now officially under investigation after disappearing for over 24 hours. The mood of the team was somber as the reality of what that might mean began to set in. The young men's absence had not been a mistake, joke, or an explainable occurrence as they'd all expected. Had the two young men really vanished with whatever treasure they'd found in the buried crate? If not, had they fallen victim to foul play? Each query only led to more unsatisfying questions without answers.

"So, let me make sure I've got this. You two," Chris gestured at Lucas and Stander, "only became aware there was something massive buried deep underground here after finding the pit? The nearby quarry filled with all the dead?"

"Yes," replied Lucas. "We had commissioned a series of deep underground scans using some of the latest ground penetrating technology available. I did have a hunch there could be something nearby based on all the queer activity we were seeing, the local rumors, and all the old legends that seem to center around this area of France. But there was also a safety component. The ground all around us is riddled with voids, underground rivers, and partially collapsed tunnels, passages and caves. We turned over all that data to the university and government officials to ensure everyone's safety working at both sites. But what we found in this area," Lucas gestured at the area where the work was happening, "we kept to ourselves."

"At least for now." Stander making a rare comment that morning. His eyes roaming the features of the mammoth carving before him. Subconsciously, his hand drifted across the many inked images that colored his arms from top to bottom. His fingers finding and tracing the ridges and bumps of the birthmark he'd once been so embarrassed by that the first tattoo he ever had done was designed to hide the unusual symbol.

Chris followed the upturn of his gaze. Though Stander had seen weekly images as the human-like face had been slowly freed from its earthen tomb, and seen the visage in person on previous visits to the site, he was still awestruck by the amount of emotion revealed within the expression engraved on the stone face. Stander barely noticed when

Chris stepped to his side. Both men equally enraptured by the massive find.

The stoic face they stared into was intimidating to say the least. Some twelve feet across with very human-like positioning of its opened eyes, presumed nose, and mouth. The latter stretching across half of the features and likely 6 feet wide itself. When Lucas had first given Stander the dimensions of the head and face, he'd done so in meters. Too embarrassed to admit he'd never learned metrics, Stander had asked Lucas for a real-world comparison. Questioning (only partially in jest), if it was Greek statue size or Statue of Liberty size. The reply Lucas gave had stuck with him. The head and face nearly identical in all dimensions to the head and face of the Great Sphinx of Giza in Egypt.

On the forehead of the long-hidden monolith, a symbol of unknown meaning and origin had been carved deeply into the worked stone. It resembled a teardrop in shape; circular and rounded. Upon discovery, as Lucas later informed Stander, each of the archeologists working on the dig had commented about the symbol's similarity to the Egyptian Ankh. The only major difference being the strange markings that crowded the interior of the character itself. A series of lined script - like bent crosses seeming to mirror one another. One after the other, line after line. The duplicated symbol recognizable worldwide despite being corrupted across the history of mankind.

Swastikas.

Though in recent times the ignorant exalt the symbol as one of hatred and racism, it's true meaning, as Stander was already aware of, is vastly different. The swastika as ancient as any manmade mark ever discovered, and found in deep antiquity across the globe. Many scholars believing it originated as an ancient religious icon within the cultures of Eurasia before the continents drifted and separated. Its true meaning more akin to the divinity and spirituality the symbol still holds in the Indian religions of the far east. But what the crowded markings were meant to convey on the massive stone statues forehead was an unexplained mystery.

Much like the matching birthmark on Stander's shoulder.

Thus far, only the head, face, neck and wide shoulders had been revealed. The remainder of the gigantic stone figure still buried under tons of rock and debris. Though only the top of the troubling effigy showed, as if the rest of the huge statue were merely standing underwater, several unique and puzzling characteristics were easily identified. The two eyes had been etched into the rock with almost laser-like precision. Hallowed out and concave; one eye's pupil was blank and missing. The other filled with a near bowling ball sized shiny, smooth and reflective black stone. The shape and measurements identical to the obsidian rock Stander had recovered from the burial of an unknown Norseman discovered near his home in Michigan.

Under the chin of the stone face, markings meant to mimic a decorative necklace stretched across the statue's neckline. Like the empty pupil of the monolith's blank eye, many of the baseball and golf ball sized decorative stones were missing. Though Stander and Chris still stood side by side, neither commented. But both could tell the shape of the jewels – missing or not – all appeared to match the "lucky charm" (as Chris called it), they'd found as kids near Almore, Illinois. The small farming community where Chris had grown up and near where Stander's Great Aunt Madeleine had lived. The lucky charm – made from Iridium and likely having come from a meteorite they'd later learned – had saved them both from near certain death. Stander, at age 14, using his slingshot to fire the strange stone at a horrific creature who had savaged one of their boyhood friends.

"Chris," began Stander after long minutes of awed silence, "I know what you are thinking. If this huge statue has been buried this deep for thousands of years..."

"Likely tens of thousands of years based on the undisturbed soil." Lucas gently correcting Stander. "As ridiculous and incredible as that seems." His voice trailing off as if only talking with himself.

"A thousand years, ten thousand years, or just one long fucking time," replied Stander before turning back to Chris. "Whatever. Point being, I know what you are thinking. I just don't have an answer. At least yet..." Stander lowered his voice so only Chris could hear. "After what we learned from that lingering being who took out Brian and Denny, I'd say nothing is off the table."

"What if we are the ones on the table?" Chris, with something like fear or regret teasing the edge of his expression, turned away. Joining Jack, Helen, and Emma as they worked to uncover more of the mammoth monolith. Stander and Lucas soon joining, the entire team worked uneventfully for the remainder of the work day under the unrelenting gaze of the stone effigy.

CHAPTER TWENTY-TWO

ALONE IN THE VEHICLE, Stander sung loudly to himself. He watched Chris and the car's owner, Lucas, disappear inside the entrance that led down to the dig site where Jack, Helen, and Emma were already at work deep underground. Stander had never shied away from a full workday. But he couldn't deny he was dragging his feet. His unease within the winding, pitch black caverns they were working inside of had been climbing steadily ever since the two graduate students had unexplainably vanished.

Stander tried to lose himself in the loud music he blasted from the car's tiny speakers. *The Scorpions*, one of his all-time favorite bands, telling him over and over again that there was no one like him. Pulling his phone from his pocket, he decided to try calling Secrist one more time before heading inside the dig site. He'd kept forgetting about the time difference between the two countries, and now hadn't spoken with Secrist in several days. Stander made a mental note to do the math on the time change so he'd know the best time to call home going forward.

Predictably, the attempt to reach Secrist failed. Cell service practically non-existent in the surrounding French countryside. Stander nearly dropped the phone when he went to repocket it. Mistakenly snapping a picture when his thick fingers fumbled for the device. He glanced at the comically blurred image before impulsively texting it over to Secrist. A quick test. Thinking if the picture went through, he could at least send Secrist a few snapshots from their work.

Exiting the car, Stander inhaled and exhaled deeply before making his way to the entrance that led down into the subterranean passages. He pulled open the door, but paused. Casting his eyes upward, he let the warmth of the sun radiate briefly against his cheeks. Somewhere unseen, he heard the screech from a bird of prey. Likely a hawk, he thought, based on the call. When Stander finally closed the door, the darkness of the underground enveloped him completely. He made his way alone down the dank corridor. The fall of his footstep and *plop-plop-plop* of unseen water echoing around him.

Several hours after the team had broken for lunch, Lucas received word of trouble brewing over in the quarry. Workers removing debris had dislodged several boulders blocking a previously unknown void. Disturbing thousands of roosting bats that almost immediately began pouring out of the underground cavern they'd called home. Flooding the quarry with their winged flight. The ensuing melee emptying that side of the dig in record time.

"We are shutting down and calling it a day." A peer of Lucas, one of the lead archeologists conducting the recovery within the quarry, came over to notify Lucas of the emergency. And ask a favor. "Hopefully, over the weekend the bats will calm down or vacate. If not, we may have a more serious problem." The man was tall with sharply angled features and spiky blond hair. He spoke in clipped English with a strong German accent. He had a face you'd expect to see on a World War 2 Nazi scientist or maybe on a stoic keyboardist in a German metal band.

"Everyone is gone except the electrician. Just needs another hour or so to completely finish the contracted work for us. We'd hate to make them come back on Monday just to wrap up. Can I have her exit out through this way when done? The guard service wants to pull down the gate, leave, and completely shut the main entrance down. They're worried if the bats start going in and out through that entrance it will become habit." The man shrugged.

"Sure, that's fine. Just have them pound on the metal doorframe when ready to leave. We can all walk out at the same time." Lucas gestured at the five members of his team who had gathered to hear what happened. "With only the one passage between our dig and the quarry, we should be able to keep the little vermin sequestered over on your side. I think we'll be safe in here until she's done."

Lucas walked his peer out. Returning minutes later as Jack, Helen, and Emma continued with their work. Each periodically directing Chris and Stander as the team focused once more on their individual tasks. Work continuing uneventfully for some thirty minutes.

Then everything went pitch black.

Once the initial exclamations and shock faded, the group quickly huddled around Lucas. Each person using the light on their phone to make it safely over to where he stood. Undisguised concern and worry etched in the lines on Chris's face.

"As unpleasant and unnerving as being plunged in total darkness is," Lucas began, "we all know it has, unfortunately, not been uncommon during this dig. We certainly have had our fair share of equipment failures and strange occurrences over these last few months. Please just remember that if you get uncomfortable or worried," Lucas turned and shined his light toward the bored tunnel they all used each day to enter and exit the area, "it is a straight shot back up to the surface. If anyone needs some fresh air or something, just let me know."

Stander appreciated the reminder. The rocketing of his pulse slowed as he noted the calmness of the gathered archeologists. Though his chest was still thumping, he fed off their relaxed demeanor. He also knew he needed to stay calm for Chris. Stander glanced back and gave the redhead an easy smile as he shrugged in what he hoped looked like a relaxed manner. Chris's face an unreadable mask.

When the power and lights still hadn't been restored some five minutes later, Lucas called an end to the workday. "The electrician must have run into a problem. I'll run over to the other side and see what's going on." Lucas and the other archeologists working with him seemed unfazed. Delays and troubles of varying degrees typical on sites often far away from modern conveniences.

"Wait a minute." Stander put one hand out to stop Lucas. "You are the only one with the key that can lock and unlock the door between the two dig sites. I know you can't just hand over that responsibility. Why don't you let me go see instead?"

"Wherever you go, I go." Chris stood at Stander's elbow, his face contorted in concern. Or fear.

"No way," replied Lucas. "You don't know your way around the passages like I do. Or where the electrician has been working all week. You'll get lost trying to locate the right tunnel."

"I'll go with them." Jack spoke with confidence. "I know where the work was happening. You," he pointed to Lucas, "stay here with Emma and Helen in case the electrician shows up while we're out looking. Give us maybe fifteen minutes and then we can all leave together."

The group walked to the metal doorway that separated the work they were doing from the ongoing excavations within the quarry. Lucas unlocked the steel door and let Jack, Chris, and Stander pass through. "Watch your step. I'll wait for you here outside the door. If you get turned around or anything, just follow the hanging strands of lights. Even if they aren't lit, they still connect the main channels and both work sites." Lucas waved, Helen and Emma just behind him nodded encouragingly. As the three men turned to leave, Lucas called out once again. "If something unexpected happens just holler for me. Sound travels far down these hollow passageways."

With Jack in the lead, the three men headed down the black corridor. The lights from their phones swinging wildly and throwing strange shadows up at the rock-lined walls. They carefully sidestepped the large hole the crate had been pulled from just days before. The dirt encrusted wooden box still opened and empty beside the manmade crater. It was a short and uneventful hike. Jack quickly located where the electrician had been working. Spools of cabling and electric wiring found beside an open toolbox and laptop.

They called out without reply. The ensuing silence like a lack of breath. No sign of the electrician. Chris cried out into the darkness a second and third time before Jack stopped him. "Please don't keep hollering like that. If the electrician was near, she'd have come by now. All the yelling will only make it harder to pinpoint the reply. These long tunnels are echo chambers that keeps sound bouncing back and forth. We'll still be hearing your calls reverberating for a while."

"Sorry. Guess this was a waste of time, huh? Let's head back." The tone of Chris's voice and wide-eyed expression making it clear he now regretted tagging along. "Probably just walked a different route and is shooting the shit with Lucas while they wait for us to get back."

"I hope you are right." Jack turned and shined his light down a different passage. "Let's go back using this tunnel. It comes out where the empty crate is. Maybe you're right and the electrician walked this channel instead of the more main one." He shrugged before adding, "Worth a shot."

The tunnel they traversed this time was more constrictive and with tighter turns than the previous one. But the same chipped, rounded walls encircled them. Each underground passage colorless and numbing in its uniformity. They'd nearly reached the connecting passage where the recently discovered crate had been found when Jack abruptly halted.

"Ugh! There is that awful smell again." In unison, all three men clamped a hand over their nose and mouth. They made it four more steps before Jack stopped once more. He said nothing this time. He didn't need to. The two ravaged bodies screamed for all of their attention without a word. Each had clearly been dragged down the adjacent passage before being tucked away and partially hidden behind a cracked, squarish boulder that had likely been sitting in the same spot for a thousand years. It was Charles and Antoine. The two missing graduate students.

They'd been savaged.

Stander had only been briefly introduced to the two men the day before they'd gone missing. He couldn't remember which of the dead was Antoine and which was Charles. Not that it really mattered any longer. Their ashen faces twins of agonized terror. Stander squatted beside the corpses as Jack stumbled a few steps and turned away from the scene. Behind him, Stander heard a sickening retch followed by a wet splash.

One of the bodies was missing nearly all of its throat. The young man all but decapitated by the grisly wound. The ravaged neck like the exposed half of a partially devoured apple. One huge bite all the way down to the core taken out of it. The missing flesh exposing flaps of torn cartilage. The bits of meat left only a few sinewy lines threaded through bone barely tethered to the skull. The exposed vertebrae of the neck and the spine starkly white against the carnage. It appeared the young man had been bitten just once, but the single wound had clearly been fatal. The only question was where all the blood had gone. Though his shirt was splattered and wrung red around the collar, the viciousness of the attack should have left him drowning in arterial spray.

The second man, Stander noted, was as bone white as the first. A quick inspection of his body revealed a series of wounds on his neck, shoulders, and chest. Chunks of flesh missing and leaving behind half-moon shaped gashes that looked like the leftover rinds of pink watermelon. Awful bites taken by a malicious mouth of dreadful teeth. He'd obviously been milked much slower than the other student. However, the end result had been the same. Both men dispatched with cruelty and bled dry. When Stander looked up, Jack was still turned the other way and heaving. Beside him, Chris was noticeably trembling. Glassy eyed.

Stander stood and cocked his head. A dull roar like the approach of an underground subway building in his ear. A rustling like batwings in a deserted barn or... or a cave. Stander screamed "Bats!" as he leapt for Chris. Dragging him to the ground just before the thunderous flapping exploded over their heads. Thousands of bats filling the narrow tunnel as the leathery winged creatures rushed down the opening in a clustered swarm. When the fluttering of wings finally abated, Stander pulled both Chris and Jack to their feet. Pushing them out of the earthen channel. All three of them running past the wooden crate and the black chasm where it had long laid buried before being opened by the unfortunate graduate students.

"Come on! Lucas and the door out of here is just ahead." The three men rushed forward in the scrambled lights of their phones. Their panicked footfalls kicking up the loose dirt and dust as they ran. But when they reached the doorway, Lucas was nowhere to be found. Chris pushed past Stander and began banging on the door. Though merely seconds, it felt like an eternity before it swung open.

"Where is Lucas?" Helen and Stander spoke in stereo, each asking the same question of the other. Neither Helen or Emma had any idea that he had disappeared. Or exactly when or why. After quickly recapping the gruesome discovery of the grad student's bodies – and the missing electrician – Stander tried to convince the others to drive back to civilization to report everything. But no one would budge. Each member of the team refusing to leave without first trying to find Lucas.

"Fine," Stander finally relented. "But we are not splitting up anymore. We can do a quick sweep of the nearest tunnels just to be sure he didn't... didn't fall down and... and twist an ankle or something." Stander heard the emotion cracking in his voice but he beat it back down. "I know we don't really have any weapons. But why don't we grab a couple shovels and that pickax? Each of us should carry one and..."

"Here," it was Chris. He'd pulled the sword found inside the crate from out of the protective covering it had been sheathed inside. "You take this", he said as he handed the shiny blade over.

Jack sputtered a few times, his eyes beseeching Helen and Emma. "You can't just commandeer a priceless..."

"I'm taking it," the tone in Stander's voice rung with finality. "What about you?" He nodded at Chris. "Can you swing that pickax?"

"I don't need it." Chris pulled something free from the pocket of his jeans. "I have this." He held up one of the iridescent decorative stones that had been recovered earlier from the carved necklace of the ancient effigy. Both Helen and Emma gasped. The value of a golf ball sized piece of iridium - priceless. "It's just like my good luck charm back home. Saved our ass last time." A moment and look passed between Chris and Stander. Chris surprised them both when he suddenly reached out and hugged him. "Spit and sweat, brother."

"Spit and sweat...brother," replied Stander. His voice suddenly hoarse.

"When did you pocket that?" Emma pointed an accusatory finger at Chris and stabbed him with her narrowing eyes. "Thief!"

"Geez, lady. Don't worry. Once we are safely out of here you can have it back. But until that happens, it is staying with me." Stander appraised Chris with a look of slight reproach as the two men separated. "What?" Chris answering the unasked question. "You think I was above swiping shit to feed my drug habit? I got pretty good at sliding things in my pocket without being noticed."

The three men and two women, each now clutching something they thought protected them, passed through the doorway and out into the quarry. Jack in the lead and Chris bringing up the rear.

"Be sure that door handle isn't locked before you..." Jack began as Chris slammed the door behind him, "close the door." His hand still on the handle, Chris jiggled it once. The handle didn't turn.

"Whoops." Chris could think of nothing else to say.

Jack, a pained expression on his face began to open his mouth but Stander beat him to the punch. "Forget about it. It won't make any difference as long as we find Lucas. Let's get moving. Jack, you know these underground passageways better than any of us. Lead the way." Jack nodded curtly once. He turned and exhaled deeply once before starting forward. Directly behind him, Helen was followed closely by Emma. The combined light of everyone's phone chasing the shadows back into the cracks and crevices of the quarry tunnel. Stander and Chris, just a step behind the other three with their heads on a swivel.

Lucas, the light from his phone bobbing with each step, followed the whispering voices that tickled his ear. They'd begun almost as soon as Jack, Stander, and Chris had started their search for the missing electrician. Coming somewhere out of the earthen channel cut into the rock behind him, Lucas understood the noises he tracked couldn't have been coming from the three searchers. The men had walked the opposite way. Though he hesitated to call out very loudly knowing the echo of his own voice would muddle the noise he chased, Lucas began to repeat a low murmured "hello" at every junction he passed. His ears straining to capture the sounds he chased. After five minutes of uneventful searching, Lucas gave up hunting the ethereal whispers and turned on his heel. Following his own trail back to his post at the steel-door entrance.

Rounding one corner that split the rock passage he traversed in two, the roar of what sounded like a moving train began to grow. Lucas turned towards the sound puzzled. A moment passed before he understood what he was hearing, but even that quick identification didn't save him from being engulfed in a flurry of beating wings. Squeezing his eyes shut, Lucas threw himself to the ground and wrapped his head with both arms. Unseeing as the fury of the displaced bats slowly waned, Lucas had no idea the screen and light on his phone had shattered. The fragile electronics going dark as it struck one of the many rocks that littered the floor of the quarry. When at least Lucas felt safe enough to lift his eyes, he found himself swimming in utter darkness. He couldn't see even an inch in front of his face. Lost in the labyrinth that was the quarry.

Blind as a bat...

CHAPTER TWENTY-THREE

"I can find the way and lead us out of here." The *here-ere-ere* echoing so much it was hard to tell where it originated from. "Follow my voice until you see my light."

"Great!" Jack yelled back blindly, a wide smile on his face. Miraculously, the electrician had called out to the team from somewhere in the underground maze. Though yet to find Lucas, the brief back and forth elicited grins and sighs of relief from the searchers. Helen, Emma, and Chris, joining Jack in his audible relief. The group moving together toward where the voice called out from the black of the quarry.

"How do you know that is the electrician?" Stander kept his voice low as he questioned Jack. The hastened shuffle of feet kicking up dust that obscured the ground they walked on.

"Who else would it be?" Jack scoffed at Stander's paranoia. "Lucas is the only other one in here with us."

"I kind of doubt..."

"Look! There it is!" Emma exclaiming loudly as she pointed to the end of the subterranean channel they'd been walking. "The light!" She paused before calling out loudly, "Hello!" The three archeologists rushed to the flickering beam, Stander and Chris trailing behind.

Unseen, silently the thing dropped from the carved ceiling. Stander caught the reflective glint of both its narrow eyes just before being flung to the ground. The pounce of the monster falling from above knocking him sideways and sending him face first into the dirt.

Hairless and sickly, the attacker's pallor appeared more fungal than it did human. No pigment coloring the deathly white flesh. Though it may have been the panicked swinging of the handheld lights, its garment clung to its side like a living shadow. Flowing and rolling like waves across the horrid thing that landed atop Chris. But it was the gruesome fanged bite of that fearsome mouth that imprisoned the shocked onlooker's focus. Each of the group frozen as the barbed teeth vanished into the meager meat of Chris's neck and shoulder. His desperate shrieks reverberating and filling the cavern of darkness.

Stander roared incoherently as he scrambled to his feet. Lowering his shoulder, he propelled himself at the feeding wraith astride Chris. Like a linebacker starved of contact, he creamed the pasty white vampire with a bone breaking shot. Driving the thing to the far wall of the underground tunnel with the ferocity of his blow. The monster righted itself after bouncing off the rock wall. Its blazing green eyes affixing Stander with a heated glare that would make most wither and run.

The creature, angular and gaunt to the point of emaciation, suddenly teetered as if struck by weakness. Turning its head, it spewed whatever sustenance it had drained from Chris. The sound, sight, and smell a mini horror all in itself. When the fiend looked up, gasping, Emma pulled a gold necklace out from under the neck of her shirt. A small cross dangling from the thin chain of gold. Incredibly, the brave young woman advanced on the blood sucker. Holding the cross out in front of her as if the heroine in some cheesy vampire film made in the 1970s. Moments later, with a confused and pained look dominating the monster's expression, it dove for the surrounding darkness. Slinking from the lumination provided by the groups phones and vanishing somewhere among the endless corridors and caverns.

Stander ignored the retreat. Rushing to the side of Chris where Jack and Helen had begun to tend his gaping wound. Chris was unconscious.

Groaning and writhing on the dirt floor of the underground passage. A crimson stream flowing from the bite at his neck and shoulder.

The gathered group pooled what they had on their person to staunch the flow of blood. The blue handkerchief Helen had tied over her hair, the light scarf wound around Emma's neck, and the sleeves Stander tore from his and Jack's shirt. The various pieces of cloth used in layers to dress the wound.

"What was that thing!" Jack kept turning in circles where he stood. Holding his phone at the end of his outstretched hand trying to locate where the attacker had run. "Is there some crazy guy living in these tunnels?"

"Looked like Nos-fucking-feratu to me." Stander didn't look up, his hands still working to stem the flow of blood at Chris's neck. "Didn't you see the teeth on that pasty motherfucker?"

"Jesus saved us..." Emma had a hand over her chest as she fingered the gold cross around her neck. "It was the cross. Vampires are real!" The expression on her face one of pleasant surprise.

"Maybe." Helen looked on doubtfully, her eyes going from Chris to the pool of blood the fiend had vomited after biting him. Stander caught her look and understood her questioning.

"I hit that thing with all my body weight. Felt like I ran down some eighty pound kid." Stander was shaking his head. "If I saw a man walking the street looking as sickly as that thing, I'd think the cancer already got him and he was days from dying. No way would I fear fighting that." Stander pointed the way it had fled. "Even blind."

"Yeah. Some monster." Jack pointed at Stander. His voice said, "If he comes back, we can take him." But his eyes didn't back the boast up.

"You... you don't understand. Didn't you see it's expression after it was thrown from Chris? That wasn't fear in its eyes. That was fight." Stander paused, frowning. What else was it about those eyes? Something he couldn't put his finger on.

He exhaled and looked at Helen. "I think it was just the blood," he began. "Bad blood."

"What do you mean by bad blood? Is Chris sick or something?" Helen kneeled and gently pulled Stander's gore-soaked hands from Chris. She checked the wound before reapplying pressure. Taking Stander's place beside Chris.

"In a way. He'll always be an addict. Isn't that what they say?" Stander rubbed the croak of his arm across his damp eyes. "But as far as I know, Chris hasn't ingested any of that poison for a couple months now. On the road to recovery." Stander smiled briefly, "I'm real proud of him. But doctors have him on a host of medications to help. I know he takes methadone and a couple others that I can't pronounce. As desperate and malnourished as that thing looked, I bet it made for a cocktail that didn't exactly agree with the toothy bloodsucker."

"Why do you think it went for Chris?" Jack moved in closer but kept sweeping his eyes around the dark cavern. Watching for the things return. "You'd think that maybe it could smell the toxins. Or would have attacked Helen or Emma before trying for..."

"My faith saved me." Emma spoke with a beaming face despite the horror they'd all just faced. "It knew it could never harm one of God's children." Stander opened his mouth to reply but shut it again soundlessly.

"Well," Helen briefly pulled the saturated cloth from Chris, "I think the blood flow is beginning to slow down. But we need to get Chris to a doctor as soon as possible."

"Do you think that thing already got to Lucas?" Jack's voice was low. "We're trapped and can't go anywhere until we find him."

Lucas, though unable to see a thing, felt the weariness in his useless stare. His tired eyes straining for any hint of light. Something he could use to guide him. Knowing he was well over a hundred feet below the surface, Lucas knew better than to expect any natural light to lead him anywhere. The only question is if he should wait for the missing electrician to restore power or if he should try to locate his team. By now, he suspected, his disappearance from the doorway would be noticed. Are they looking for him already?

The voices came again. The words indistinguishable but somehow the vague mutterings chilled him. At times, the whispers seemed to be at his ear. Yet when he would turn towards the sounds they'd vanish. "Hello?" Though he barely breathed the word out, the question seemed like a scream in the otherwise soundless chamber. The *o-o-o-o-o* echoing down the passage he'd stay rooted in since the bats had driven him to the ground and left him disoriented within the maze of rock-lined tunnels.

Sighing, Lucas blindly put both hands out in front of him. He shuffled a few steps. Fearful of even lifting his feet off the solid ground since he couldn't see where the fall of his step would land. His hands brushed something cold and he quickly pulled them back. Seconds later reextending them and sightlessly groping until he understood he faced one of the earthen walls. He turned slightly and shuffled to his right. Back down the way he hoped he'd first come. When he tripped over what felt like a softball sized rock, he exclaimed loudly. His every movement potentially held an unpleasant surprise. One misstep could send him tumbling to the ground or careening into a hole.

There! The sound came again! "Hello?" Lucas strained to hear. The barely audible voice held a familiarity. "Anyone? I broke my light…" A thick and putrid smell grew stronger as he gradually inched his way down the pitch-black passageway. The murmured words came again and Lucas froze. He thought he felt a presence very near. "Are… is someone there?"

"Always," came the unseen reply.

Lucas screamed. His legs, no longer under his command, bolted out from under him. Panicked and blind, he ran without thought. Careening and pinballing down, unbeknownst to Lucas, a dead-end tunnel. Stopping only when he'd ran face first into the hard-packed wall at its end. His glasses shattering upon contact. An unseen gash near his eye dripped blood as he collapsed in terrified sobs. His arms waving blindly in the black of the lightless cavern.

"Please... please don't hurt me. Please..."

"Did you hear something?" Stander turned once and looked behind him. But only the baleful black of the underground followed. "Uh... never mind. It was nothing."

He was carrying the still unconscious Chris in his arms. The group had abandoned their effort to reach the light or communicate with the voice they'd first thought was the missing electrician. Fearful they'd been tricked and ripe for a second ambush. Desperate to get Chris back to the relative safety of the locked doorway so he could be rushed out to a car once they'd located Lucas.

Reaching the steel door, they found it unchanged. Lucas, who had the only key, still missing. Stander carefully laid Chris on the ground. Helen and Emma doing their best to make him comfortable. Stander turned off the light on his phone to save battery life. When he did, he was surprised to see a new text message from Secrist. He opened it and read the response to the comically blurred picture of himself he'd sent Secrist that morning. The timestamp showed the image had only been successfully delivered an hour or so previous. Why the phone had somehow found a signal hours after he'd sent the text unknown.

"Did you mean to send this? Or was it a butt dial? Too blurry to make it out. Resend if important. Later." Though his phone still didn't have a signal and showed zero bars — same as the others trapped with him — he texted Secrist back. Hoping the same miracle that randomly delivered the blurred photo hours after it had been sent would bless them again.

After sending a brief synopsis of the horrifying events unfolding over a couple short bursts of text, using the flash feature on his phone, he snapped a picture of the sword and forwarded it. Stander knew Secrist would recognize the aged weapon was a duplicate of the two already in his possession back in Michigan. He hoped that coincidence might mean something to the retired detective. Stander paused before impulsively sending one final message. Typing, "There's something down here with us." He hit send without feeling much hope. Like the rest of the team who had been unsuccessfully trying to call and text local authorities and loved ones for hours, he doubted his efforts would prove to be successful. But he had to try.

The hushed voice was at his ear again. The tone somehow comforting and familiar. He cupped a hand behind one ear and turned towards the sound. Had it been a woman's voice calling out to him? The ethereal whispers were somehow soothing after all the awfulness they'd stumbled upon. Stander quickly dismissed the notion as soon as it popped in his head. But the voice calling to him from out of the darkness sure sounded like Liz. When he looked up once again to question if anyone else was hearing what he was, Helen had a strange gleam in her eye.

"Are you hearing a voice?" Stander kept one eye on Helen as he questioned the team. "I know it is ridiculous, but I swear I keep hearing someone calling out to me. Even reminds me of a woman I know. Or knew..." Stander recalling the days and passion filled night he'd spent with Liz months earlier. How easily he'd fallen under her charms. A spell somehow, it seemed, still unbroken. After all, here he was, imagining it was her voice calling out to him half a world away. He could still feel her warmth of her body at his fingertips, the smell of her hair and the taste of her lips. How her dazzling green eyes had melted his usual defenses. Those amazing eyes...

"I thought it was just me," said Helen. She was the only one in the group who didn't respond with a simple shake of her head. "But I hear someone calling out as well. I didn't think it was a woman's voice or in distress." Helen paused as if unsure what she should share. "I actually thought it was boy. A boy calling out."

Stander merely nodded. He was glad someone else was hearing the same strange sounds he was. At least it wasn't all just in his head. Stander didn't question that Helen interpreted the voice as being a child. He knew after all the bar bands he'd listened to, and all the rock concerts and music festivals he'd attended over his lifetime, that his hearing was suspect. But he'd have sworn it was Liz calling out. Beckoning him deeper into the black of the quarry.

"We have to find Lucas." Jack squatted beside the still unconscious Chris. Taking Helen's place as she stood and stretched. "You heard what that German archeologist told him. The main entrance is shut down and will be locked tight all weekend. No one will come looking for us until one of our family's starts getting worried. But even then, they'd have to contact the university first. Convince them to start a search, get the..."

"I'm not confident Chris will make it much longer without medical attention." Emma wiped the beaded sweat from the wounded man's forehead. Her face hooded in concern.

"And I'm not confident we can last much longer trapped down here with whatever thing savaged Chris." Stander held up his phone. Except for Chris, his was the only one without its light lit. "How much juice do your phones still have? Once they go out, we all will be blind."

"Where did Helen go?" Jack turned just in time to see a light vanish down a nearby corridor. "Is that her? Was that her light?" Jack took a couple steps towards where the light had disappeared. "Helen! Helen!

What are you doing!" His voice echoing and reverberating down the earthen tunnels. The sound returning unaccompanied by any sort of reply.

"Fuck!" Stander stood and reached for the sword he'd stuck in the dirt at his side. "I'll run after her and drag..."

"I'm coming as well." Emma stood, the tiny gold cross of her necklace clutched in both hands. "That sword won't do you any good. The cross and my faith are our only chance." Before Stander could object, Emma took off in the same direction Helen had.

"Jesus Fucking Christ!" Stander tore down the channel after her. He called to Jack over his shoulder. "Don't you fucking move until I get back! Do not leave Chris alone!"

***

"Edward, honey. I'm here..." Helen held her phone out in front her with a trembling hand, the light quivering. "Grandma is here. Come to me." She strained to hear her grandson's reply. His tenuous call had been so soft she'd barely been able to hear. "Quit trying to scare me! Where are you?"

The whisper came again. This time from the passage to her left. Helen went down it blindly, unhearing and unaware of the panicked rush behind her. Both Stander and Emma jogging past the tunnel she'd just turned down. Helen slowed her pace, confidence slipping as she descended the passage. The mummering came again and steeled her resolve. Rounding a slow turn in the underground channel, the hushed tones became clearer.

"Grandma Helen is..." Helen paused; the words no longer sounded like they were Edward's. The voice like two stones scrapping together. Too late she saw the flash of the bone white, hairless thing that rushed out of the darkness towards her. The blur of a hungry mouth rimmed red and loaded with fangs. On either side of the gnashing teeth, hands tipped with daggers of yellowing fingernails. The aborted scream choked from her throat as it was ripped open. Her phone, the light from it illuminating her last breaths, thrown several feet in the fray.

The bone thin wraith seemed to grow and swell with each shudder of her lifeless body. When it was done feeding, the new corpse drained of all it wanted, the thing scuttled away. Secreting itself behind one of the chipped and broken blocks that those who raped the quarry in the distant past had discarded. Lying in wait as two lights bobbed and grew brighter. Stander and Emma running for the lit phone on the floor of the passageway. The vampire's green eyes animated with heated anticipation.

CHAPTER TWENTY-FOUR

"THERE IS NOTHING WE can do for Helen." Stander gently helped Emma regain her feet. They'd discovered the older archeologist lying broken and discarded on the ground. Her lifeless stare illuminated by the light of her nearby phone. "We need to head back to where Jack and Chris are. Decide what our next move should be."

"I tried to tell her. Warn her she needs to get right with God." Emma twirled the gold cross hanging from the necklace that circled her neck. "If she'd heard and opened her heart, Helen would be alive. Saved like..."

"Time to go." Stander turned and beckoned Emma to follow. It pained him to abandon Helen's marred body. But it seemed likely the creature who'd taken her life was still near. The older woman's shredded throat uncoagulated and dripping wet gore. "Once we are safe, we'll come back for her... her remains."

Stander started for Helen's lit phone, heading back the way they'd come. The little side passage where they'd discovered her corpse so narrow that both Stander and Emma walked it single file. Stander barely broke stride as he bent down and scooped Helen's phone off the ground. "If nothing else," he spoke to Emma in a hushed tone, "this gives us more of a chance. It is only a matter of time before all of our batteries go dead."

"I'm praying that Lucas has already returned. I bet he and Jack are waiting for us." Stander grunted noncommittally in reply, his concentration focused on the newly acquired device in his hand.

"Fuck! We need Helen's password to shut her light off." Stander hurried to where they'd left Jack and Chris back at the locked doorway. "I don't suppose you know that, do you? Otherwise," Stander turned with Helen's phone in hand, "her phone will die before…" But Stander found he was talking to himself. Though only a few feet behind him mere moments earlier, the tunnel behind him was now empty and dark.

Emma had vanished.

Long and unnaturally thin, the bony fingers smelled of death and rot. They closed across her features and clamped down on her mouth and nose. Soundlessly, Emma was dragged backwards into blindness. Her eyes wide and white as she watched Stander, eerily illuminated in the skinny passage, grow dimmer and smaller. The tiny light from her own phone buried in the folds of her clothing and barely visible. Unable to scream, the black of the quarry swallowed Emma whole.

Desperate for a breath, she fought for footing and struggled against her captor. Unseeing, she could feel herself being whisked down long tunnels. The backs of her heels, at times, banging painfully against the sharp rocks that littered the floor of the subterranean passages. Her arms pinched awkwardly at her sides by the rail thin arm wrapped tightly around her, Emma was half dragged and half carried deeper into the quarry. She lost track of the many twists and turns she could feel herself being taken down until finally arriving at their destination.

Tossed to the ground, it took long minutes to catch the breath the blind journey had kept from her. Blood roared in her ears as she sucked in the rank and damp air of the cavern where she'd been brought. Emma had just begun to lift her eyes and raise the phone in her hand when she heard the voice. Raspy, strained, and panting between words, what had grabbed her now spoke.

"I hope you can forgive the meager accommodations provided. I promise you won't be uncomfortable for long." Devoid of accent, the fiend slowly emerged out of the darkness. Emma raised the phone higher and bathed her captor in the light it provided. Skeletally thin and clothed all in black, its green eyes blazed with life. "I have such plans for you."

Stopping, it loomed over Emma as if savoring the tremble of her lips. Drinking in the curvature of her body, its eyes blazed with undisguised lust. Hand flying to her neck, Emma grasped the tiny gold cross lying hidden across her breasts. In the same instant, the fiend's claw-like hands snaked out and grabbed her by the shoulders. Effortlessly, the vampire lifted the young woman before turning and tossing her. Emma's phone flew from her hand midflight, landing on the dirt floor of the underground cavern, the meager light it put out dully illuminated a portion of the carved room.

Emma recognized the wooden box where she landed, but was unable to move or speak. The breath knocked out of her when she'd hit the unforgiving wood. Even the painful bite of the splintered bottom gashing her shoulder barely elicited a gasp. Mutely, she watched as the monster slammed the lid over the top. Sealing her inside with successive blows that drove the rusted old nails back into the holes made over one hundred years prior. The vampire imprisoning Emma inside the crate she'd help unearth just days earlier.

"Now," the vampire spoke briefly, "let me just go slip into something more comfortable." Despite the horrid smell of the crate, Emma pressed her face to it. The cracks between the planks that made up the wooden box giving her an aborted view of the cavern. The dim light from her phone showing she was now alone.

Emma screamed, and screamed, and screamed...

Jack watched the circle of light grow brighter and wider. Though he'd never admit it, until Stander had called out from the expanding halo, Jack had nearly abandoned Chris. Unsure if he should hide until he was certain who was advancing on them. But the familiar sound of Stander's voice soon put a smile on his face.

Temporarily.

After quickly checking on the still unconscious and unchanged Chris, Stander stole the relief he'd just bestowed on the bald archeologist. Updating Jack on how they'd found Helen and how he'd lost Emma. Their team of six now reduced to just three with one of them, Chris, prostrate and helpless. Jack's face grew darker the more Stander filled him in. Jack, in turn, informing Stander that Chris had remained largely unchanged and that Lucas remained lost. Or worse. Just like Helen and Emma.

"What do we do now?" Stander had taken Jack's place beside Chris. Though Chris muttered a few incoherent words occasionally, he appeared all but lifeless. Stander carefully inspecting the bite wound at his shoulder as he answered Jack.

"Lucas is key. Literally. No matter what has happened to him, we have to locate the key to this door." Stander leaned slightly and rapped a fist lightly against the steel door. "Inside are all the battery powered lights, a first aid kit, underground GPS units, and walkie talkies we should have grabbed earlier." Stander sighed. How could they have been so foolish? "Not to mention our way back to the surface. We have to get that key if we want to help Chris and find Emma."

"What about the missing electrician? Do you think power might still be restored?" Jack was pacing nearby. His hands absentmindedly rubbing back and forth over his shaved head with an expression twisted in worry. "What are we going to do when the batteries in our phones die?"

The cadence in Jack's speech was quickening and his voice was an octave or two higher than it had been previously. Stander understood Jack was nearing a breaking point. He changed the subject in hopes it would take Jack's mind off the rising panic he was beginning to show. "You keep rubbing your head that much and your hair will never grow back." Stander flashed the younger man a casual smirk.

"Sorry, just a nervous habit," Jack smiled and laughed but it sounded forced. "Besides, my hair growing days are all behind me." Though Stander doubted he even realized it, Jack wiped the top of his head with one hand again. "By the time I graduated high school, my hair was already thinning. It was like Moses from the Old Testament was up there parting things left and right like the Red Sea..."

Thwack!

Jack stopped speaking midsentence. Confused, Stander looked up just in time to see Jack blink slowly once before both eyes rolled up in his head. The blank white stare unnerving but failing to capture all of Stander's attention. A wide swath of blood like a crimson river began pouring down his face. Jack's chin dropped haltingly to his chest as gore began dripping to the ground. He'd been struck from behind, the blow to his head likely fatal. Though his legs gave out, Jack never hit the dirt. Before Stander could even stagger to his feet, Jack was gone. Pulled backwards into the darkness by something unseen and disappearing completely.

Stander now left all alone in the bowels of the ancient Roman quarry. An unconscious Chris muttering from the ground beside the locked steel door.

Lucas sat with his back to the cold stone wall behind him. Despite remaining utterly sightless in the black of the underground, he'd managed to slowly pull himself back together. The tremble in his hands had ended, and he'd been able to calm the soaring of his pulse. Both the cloying rot and muttered words had left him.

Left him all alone.

Lucas tried to puzzle out where he'd run. Generally, he still knew where he was within the quarry. But there were far too many dead-end passages to know for sure which one his desperate, blind flight had taken him down. Or how far he now was from the doorway he'd been stationed.

Cautiously, he staggered to his feet. His head swam for long seconds, and Lucas gingerly fingered what felt like a gash splitting the corner of one eyebrow as he waited for his equilibrium to rebalance. Unable to see how badly he was bleeding, he tentatively poked the end of one exploring finger in his mouth. The coppery taste of blood spilling along the top of his tongue. Focusing on the new wound, he soon recognized the steady drip from the gash splattering on his cheek. Though it seemed likely he'd need medical attention for the injury, Lucas thought he'd survive his crash into the earthen wall. He might need stitches and the cut would likely scar, but it would take more than that to keep him down.

Staying as silent as possible, his fear bubbling just below the surface, Lucas slid slowly along the rocky wall at his back. Creeping quietly, he inched forward step by step. He needed to free himself from the dead-end tunnel. Move into one of the main arteries of the quarry and give himself a chance to figure out where exactly he was. He didn't like the idea of staying trapped at the end of a blocked tunnel with no options to escape should his smelly visitor return.

Lucas kept the wall at his back. Gradually making his way back down the passage he'd fled.

CHAPTER TWENTY-FIVE

"Hel... hello?" The voice was masculine but timid. Likely, Emma thought to herself, coming from a nearby earthen chamber or from down one of the long passages. "Is anyone there?" A pause. "I'm hurt and bleeding. I was hit from behind. Woke up alone and I don't know how I got here or where I'm at. But I can see a sliver of light." A longer pause. "Hello! Do you have a flashlight? I can... I can see..." Despite the distortions of the echoes that followed it, the voice sounded familiar. Perhaps Jack? Emma bit down on her lip and stayed silent. Cowering inside the wretched crate she'd been locked inside. Too terrified to reply, but equally fearful of remaining mute.

"Oh, forget it." The voice was much softer now. As if only speaking to himself. "Must just be a light that got dropped. Maybe Helen's phone..." The voice faded. The ensuing silence reminding Emma how utterly alone she was without it.

"Here!" Emma screamed out. Her throat and voice raw. "I'm here! Please! Please don't leave me!" She began to sob, her cries reverberating within her wooden prison. "Follow the light! You must be seeing my phone. I'm down here!!!" Emma screeched in desperation. Now that she'd begun to call out, the thought of being unheard terrified her. Surely this must be God answering her prayers and giving her a chance to escape. Must be! "Help!"

"Emma?" The voice was nearer. It was Jack! Emma pounded on the wooden lid of the crate with all the strength she had.

"I'm here! Here!" She pressed her face to the wood and watched through the cracks as a dark shape stumbled into the same subterranean cavern she was being held in.

"Emma? Is that you?" The form lumbered towards the crate. "I'll get you out of there. Just give me a bit." Though it took several tries, the top of the crate was cracked open and then wrenched free. Emma practically flew out of the wooden container. Her arms encircling Jack's neck as he helped pull her from the crate. When they separated, Emma's hands came back dripping blood.

"You're hurt!" Emma quickly wiped her hands free of the gore. "We need to dress the wound!" With Jack's shirt already soaked and dripping in blood, Emma pulled off her own top. The Cami she wore underneath was modest, but she caught the sharp intake of Jack's breath as she swaddled his head. Wrapping her shirt around him and tying it sharply to stop the flow of blood. Jack's head buried between the ample mounds of her chest as she worked. The gold cross hanging from her necklace pressed hard against his forehead.

"Thank you," Jack raised his head. His eyes meeting Emma's. "I always knew you were kind..." Emma took half a step backwards. His stare causing a flutter between her legs as her nipples hardened in the cool air of the underground cavern. She felt her face flush as she wrapped bare arms across her chest. Jack reclaimed the step, pressing close to her. "...kind of sexy underneath all those layers of clothes you always wear."

Emma was disgusted by the inappropriate comment. Especially at such a grave time. Looking directly into Jack's eyes, she angerly opened her mouth but no sound escaped. She felt all the willpower suddenly drain from her in a rush. Jack's sparkling green eyes locked on her own. Holding her stare as his mouth covered hers. She melted into the kiss, her only thought of surrendering.

The couple entwined themselves in the glow of the light from Emma's phone. Still standing, Emma felt Jack's sure hands roam freely over her body. Touching, feeling, and squeezing parts of her she'd never allowed another. Saving herself for marriage, Emma had remained a virgin despite having been engaged twice in her twenties. But now her body longed to be explored. She pushed hard against Jack's coppery tasting kiss. Her hands pulling him to her. Clutching at his head, his ears, and the thick beard at his neck. Her fingers tugging and twirling as the urgency and passion of their kisses grew in intensity.

Emma paid no mind when Jack bent slightly and flipped the crate she'd been imprisoned in over. Distracted and wanting only to give herself, she gave no thought to the ease at which the heavy wooden crate had been turned. She pulled down the straps from her shoulders and let her Cami fall to the dirt floor of the cavern. Then let herself be lowered to the filthy, dirt encrusted box as Jack nuzzled her bare breasts.

Though she could hardly remember how, Emma soon writhed nude across the top of the crate. Pink panties left twirling around one ankle, and her long brown hair spread around her like mud in still water. She groped at Jack, an intense longing to feel him inside her driving her to near desperation. Emma peeled off his bloody shirt and fumbled awkwardly at the fasteners of his pants. With eyes closed, she stripped him. Pulling at every loose strand she felt. The unbuckled belt, his pants and underwear, socks, shoes, and... and shirt?

Again?

Emma had it pulled completely off before re-opening her eyes. She glanced at what she held with confusion. Jack's shiny bald head, face, thick beard, and bloody chest. She let the empty shell of wet flesh fall to the hard-packed dirt floor. The sound like the wet slop of a butcher's hammer striking meat.

Uncomprehending, she looked up as she was mounted. Her virginity lost as something hard and hot seared the tenderness between her thighs.

Intermingling, her cry of pain blended with her scream. Her virginity taken by something hardly of this world. The vampire splitting her thighs.

The sharp pain cleared Emma's mind. Confused at how she'd ended up on her back and given away her most prized possession, she looked up at what rode her with such gleeful ferocity. Pale, smooth, and all but hairless, what rutted inside her spread legs was a living nightmare. Shockingly spindly, it was the creature that had felled Chris and, likely, Helen. Bright red gore fell from it in small drips and large gobs as it shed the last of its disguise. Only the slit of its awful mouth was free of the splatter. The long canines held within appearing brilliantly white against the crimson backdrop as it grunted gutturally with every stroke. Unheeded, the gold cross at her neck bouncing up and down as the vampire groaned in ecstasy and sneered grotesquely.

Emma's shriek dying in her throat when the vampire opened its eyes. The two bright green orbs sapping her strength and the last of her resistance.

Lucas crept steadily forward in the black abyss. He had no idea how long it had taken him, but he'd reached the junction where the dead-end tunnel intersected with one of the larger subterranean passageways. Making it back, he hoped, to the same spot he'd been before panicking and crashing into the wall behind him.

Now what?

Still utterly sightless, it was the accompanying tomb-like silence that began to haunt his imagination. Every drip of water, groan of rotted wood, or distant flap of leathery wings clawing its way into his head and filling it with fear. He began to hum an old *Shania Twain* song if only to hear the sound of his own voice. Soon, timidly singing the chorus.

"Men's shirts, short skirts

Oh, oh, oh, really go wild, yeah, doin' it in style

Oh, oh, oh, get in the action, feel the attraction

Color my hair, do what I dare

Oh, oh, oh, I wanna be free, yeah, to feel the way I feel

Man, I feel like a woman"

With no light and nothing to see or focus on, Lucas conjured to mind the accompanying music video. He'd been enamored with the country music star while in college, and still listened to her albums from time to time. Humming and singing to himself as he tried to determine what his next move should be. Solely focused on his plight, he didn't notice the song in his head had changed until he'd begun to sing along in French.

Frère Jacques, Frère Jacques,

Dormez-vous? Dormez-vous?

Sonnez les matines, sonnez les matines

Ding dang dong, ding dang dong.

The nursery rhyme, an old one that had been translated into many languages. Lucas's own mother had been fluent in many of the world's dialects. He recalled her soft voice singing the tune to him as a child and changing the language at every verse. "Always remember," she would often say, "music is the only thing that soothes the savage beast."

Lucas shook his head wryly in the dark. Thinking to himself, I must really be scared to suddenly be thinking of my mommy. His thoughts of her coalescing with memories of growing up in his childhood home. A picturesque French chateau that sat on the border of France and Germany. The home and surrounding acres had been in his family for generations. Though the family had been forced to sell much of the land in the far distant past – some family scandal in the 1700's ruining their once proud name according to family lore – the chateau still remained in the Chanet family. Lucas supposed the home had come to mind because of its own underground passages. The chateau had originally been only one part in a network of ancient French strongholds. Though he'd only been briefly allowed inside the catacombs that ran under the property, the similarity to the passages of the quarry was undeniable. The tools and skills needed to work deep underground unchanged for much of man's history.

Are you sleeping, are you sleeping?
Brother John, Brother John?
Morning bells are ringing, morning bells are ringing
Ding dang dong, ding dang dong.

The melody in his head seemed to grow in strength. Then ebb and flow over and over again. The fade leaving an echo he longed to hear more of. Without realizing it, all alone in the dark chasm he was lost inside of, Lucas began to shuffle after the dwindling music. Stopping his feet only when the repetitive lullaby grew louder. Step by tentative step, Lucas chased the sound.

Stander, with his back to the locked steel door, held Chris in his arms like a child. Though he remained unconscious, the bleeding from the bite had been stemmed. Chris had groaned and murmured a few unintelligible words when Stander inspected the wound. But otherwise, he remained mostly catatonic. Despite the coolness of the underground cavern, a sheen of sweat still dampened his forehead and upper lip. Stander dabbed at it periodically if only to briefly relieve his mind of the choices he knew he needed to make.

He'd heard and seen nothing since Jack had been ambushed and dragged away. According to the lighted phone in his hand, that had been over an hour ago. Stander knew the two graduate students were long dead. He'd also seen how Helen's corpse had been drained and the cascade of blood that had poured down Jack's face as he was attacked. With those four members of the team all dead, Stander had to assume the missing electrician, Lucas, and Emma had all suffered the same fate.

Had he led them all to their slaughter?

He felt certain the vampire was only getting stronger with each victim it consumed. It stood to reason Stander's best chance against it would be sooner rather than later. He might be able to sustain himself over the weekend by sourcing some of the dripping water in the quarry, but without food, Stander knew he would only gradually weaken. He shifted and gently lowered Chris to the ground. Regaining his feet, he turned and picked up the sword from where it rested against a broken boulder. Looking down at the long glinting blade, Stander admitted to himself how good the sword felt in his grip. The weapon's handle seemed tailor made for his hand. If he had any chance of getting Chris out of here and saving him, it would have to happen now.

Waiting was suicide. Fighting the fiend likely the same. But he would make his stand here.

Stander swung the blade back and forth by the dim light of his phone. Envisioning how he could attack and parry with the sword, and searching for any tactical advantage his surroundings might offer. But in the distance, somewhere down one of the black connecting passages, a new sound began to emerge. A grating or dragging of something heavy along the ground. Haunting and eerie. The noise gradually getting louder as it drew near. The growl of disturbed gravel as it was split.

From out of the darkness that was the quarry came a voice layered in sarcasm. "Bravo," it intoned, followed immediately by a slow clap meant to mock the exclamation. "You? Really?" The voice seemed to surround Stander, coming from everywhere and nowhere at the same time. "You are the reason Mithras called me here?" The fetid stench of death fouling the air. "Imprisoned and starved for a hundred years to ensure my rage would be unabated... for... for you." The chuckle that followed low and ominous. "Our play will leave you with no bone unbroken."

Stander barely glanced what struck him before being slammed into the cavern wall at his back. But he knew it was the same creature that had felled Chris and likely all the others. A wretched ghoul composed of horribly bony angles and famished features that stood out sharply like the bite of a razor. Stander pushed himself off the wall, sword in hand and embarrassment stamped on his face. He faced the darkness his adversary taunted him from. Straining to see which tunnel the wraith hid inside and readying himself.

The next blow he never saw coming. Unaware he'd been struck until he felt the ground under his back and the blood trickling from his ear. Head spinning, he scrambled to his feet only to be flung backwards once more. Whatever struck, leaving him with a mouthful of his own blood.

"I do see the wisdom of Mithras, though. I cried and begged for release all those long years. Caged in that wooden box and hidden away. But he refused. I didn't understand then, and hated what I thought was a betrayal." Stander struggled to gain his feet, the blood he spat thick in his mouth. "But now I see Mithras never truly abandoned me. Ensuring the boy kept watch over me. Through the years bringing me just enough sustenance to live. Hunting my quarry for me and caring for my physical wellbeing. As a son does his father. The boy Gunther, as he grew into a man, never straying far from my side."

Stander, wobbly on his feet and unable to track the voice that taunted him, paused. Gunther? Why was that name familiar? His confusion must have been plain on his face, the vampire answering the unspoken question.

"You know of Gunther, yes? Your very own grandfather?" Stander was startled by the revelation, but did his best to remain impassive at the reveal. It didn't work. "Well, tsk, tsk, tsk...," the mocking voice grating in its arrogance, "I imagine your mommy could tell you a few stories about him. Her daddy, that is. They really... hmmm... really bonded down here together." The ensuing laughter filling the hollow passages of the quarry with menace.

Stander lunged down one black tunnel but the sword sliced nothing but the air in front of him. He stopped his advance and peered into the darkness. He was certain the voice had come that way.

"But you and that blonde bitch took all of Mithras's toys away, didn't you?" Stander spun on his heel, the mocking tone seeming to echo out of a different passageway. "That's why you're here, you know. To take their place as his new play thing."

"Blonde...?" Between the revelations and blows, Stander's head was spinning. He was having a hard time focusing on where the voice came from and what it was saying. "You mean my mom? Jeanne?" More laughter.

"No. I mean your little watcher and protector, Elizabeth. She's here now, you know. Trying to be so clever and determined to help you pass another little test. But neither of you will ever leave this place. Mithras would never let such delectable treats as you two fall from his lips." Stander suddenly felt a hand at his throat. The limb, withered awfully and smelling like rotten honeycomb, shooting out from the black at Stander's side. "Does your forest of questions yet grow? Wish you could breach the thicket of the past?" Stander scrabbled at the fingers around his throat, the sword dropped to the ground in his desperation to free himself.

Just beyond the outstretched arm, the head and face of what held him slowly emerged out of the surrounding darkness. A horrid face with a graveyard tan. A thick vein pulsed near one temple and its mouth grinned obscenely as it pulled nearer. A tongue of black lapping the crimson stream flowing from Stander's ear as it whispered inside. "Don't worry, you won't be ravened just yet. Daily I will splinter and grind your bones to make my bread. Your creamy insides a delicacy I'll use to butter both sides."

Effortlessly, the vampire carried Stander by his neck with one arm. Walking him to the unsettled soil the crate had first been pulled from. The wooden box, now moist and stained reddish brown in places, had been dragged over and lowered inside the hole in the ground of the quarry. Stander was unconscious when the fiend let him fall into the wood encased void. He never heard the cover being put back over the opening, nor the dirt pattering the lid as he was buried alive.

"Let's see how you like spending a hundred years in a box..."

When the vampire finished, Stander and the crate covered with a layer of dirt at the bottom of the hole, it advanced on Chris. A desperation in the search as it rummaged through the clothes he wore. Stopping only when it plucked the iridescent stone from the pocket Chris had stashed the "good luck" charm in. A soft moan bordering on ecstasy slipping from it's mouth of barbs as it mindlessly dropped the unconscious Chris back to the ground in a huff. The stone in hand pulsing with blueish light and throbbing. The vampire raised it's chin and roared. Not a cry of pain, but one of victory. A triumphant announcement of the fiends full return to power.

"Mithras is good! I am reborn anew! Glory to Mithras!" Entranced by the glowing object and sporting an evil grin, the vampire turned. Walking the same dark passage it had dragged the crate down earlier. Retracing it's steps along the shallow trench. "I am oh so hungry," it breathlessly whispered.

CHAPTER TWENTY-SIX

Lucas weaved his way carefully down the blind passage. Following the ethereal singing of the nursery rhyme he most associated with his mother. The tone soothing and, Lucas thought to himself with some trepidation, likely the only thing that could have gotten his feet moving again.

With no way to track time or distance, Lucas was uncertain how far his cautious steps took him. But soon, from out of the black of the tunnel, a small light emerged. Lucas rubbed at his eyes in shock. Terrified his mind was playing tricks on him, he blinked profusely until he was sure the lumination was real. Silently, he inched forward until he was able to see inside the chamber the glow originated from. The light coming from a phone lying unattended on the ground. Beside it, something stirred. The sight one that Lucas will never forget.

Stifling the scream that climbed his throat, Lucas watched horrified as the thing worked in the dim light. The creature almost completely bald and dressed all in black. It sat cross-legged on the dirt floor of the room gnawing contently on what it held in its grip.

A human forearm.

Lucas couldn't stop his eyes from seeing the arm remained attached to the body it had grown from. Emma, nude, deathly white, and torn asunder, looked sightlessly across the room at him. If the monster consuming her was aware it was being watched, it showed no sign of caring. It pulled long strips of flesh from the bone and slurped up the dripping gore that fell. The awful mouth of the thing smeared in what looked like raw batter from a red velvet cake. Licking more of the same off the bone with the glee of a small child handed a dripping mixer or beater.

Lucas screwed his eyes shut and backed away. Retreating until he felt it was safe to open them again without having to witness the desecration of Emma's corpse. His eyes slowly adjusted once more, only a dim glow coming from the chamber of horror he'd abandoned. He turned from the light, only to find a second glimmer twinkling at him from a nearby tunnel. Again, he blinked, disbelieving his own eyes, but the wave of the small light seemed to beckon him. Focusing more closely, he recognized it was the electrician, Beth, soundlessly flagging him down. Lucas quickly checked behind him to ensure the wretched cannibal hadn't seen him before trailing after the light. Silently following after his savior.

He tracked the pinprick of light. Desperate to call out but terrified they'd be heard by the monster looming in the darkness behind them, silently he followed. Moving down several long passages but never getting close enough to catch a second glimpse of the electrician. Soon, Lucas recognized the tunnel he was in and his heart raced with hope. Another fifteen feet and the saving light seemed to dissolve, but Lucas paid no mind. At his feet, the hole they'd originally pulled the crate from. Coming out of it, a voice of madness.

Secrist yanked open his backdoor. Running as fast as he could towards the chilling howl. Frazier was in the corner of the backyard, digging frantically with his front paws and periodically yowling. Breathing hard, Secrist hollered at the dog, calling him to his side. Corralling the now dirty dog with muddy paws, he approached the new hole in his yard and peered inside.

It was deep. And empty.

Secrist raised his head and spotted two more fresh holes marring his normally well-manicured lawn. He scowled down at Frazier. The dog bowed his head with an unmistakable look of shame. "What possessed you to start digging like crazy? You trying to tunnel all the way to the other side of the world?" Frazier looked up at him panting before suddenly bolting across the yard. Seconds later, howling once again as he began digging another new hole. "Frazier! Leave those damn moles alone! Find some quarry above ground, for the love of God."

He walked to the fresh dig and shooed Frazier away. Following behind the dog until they both were back inside the house. Secrist spent the next thirty minutes giving Frazier a quick bath and a stern lecture. Neither development well received by the remorseful looking canine.

Finished with the impromptu doggie bath, Secrist sat at his kitchen table. Scrolling through each text he'd received from Stander, bothered by the sudden flurry of messages and pictures. He flipped to a new page on his pad of paper and began carefully copying each of the disjointed messages. When he once more came to the picture of the weapon, he enlarged the image of the sword. Moments later recognizing it as a match for the other two swords in Stander's possession.

"What is this? Why would he send me a picture of that?" Secrist dove back into his scrawled notes looking for clues.

When Lucas was finally able to pry the lid of the crate off, Stander all but vaulted from the hole he'd been buried inside of. Scrambling up the side with the help of his rescuer. The dirt that had fallen through the cracks of the slatted wood crate coated Stander's face in a chalky dust. The blood from his mouth making a muddy smear under his bushy moustache. As both men tended Chris, his unconscious form laying crumbled on the ground, they filled each other in.

"I have a hard time believing the electrician was able to avoid that thing. Much less that she was able to successfully navigate this underground labyrinth." Stander searched Chris fruitlessly, the "good luck" totem he'd pocketed missing and presumably taken by the fiend.

"I also can't explain all the sounds we both have been hearing at different times. Some of it may just be the echoes or returns of our own voices, but I swear I heard music." Lucas bent to retrieve the sword before handing it over to Stander. "But we can figure all that out later. Right now, we need to get Chris to a doctor." Lucas walked to the steel door and unlocked it, holding it open until Stander carried Chris inside before relocking it behind them.

"Grab those battery powered lanterns," Stander motioned to the rack of supplies, "and the first aid kit. I want to get a good look at the wound and rebandage everything before we go." He laid Chris across one of the work tables and went to work. As he finished, tying off the fresh gauze he'd wrapped the wound in, Chris slowly regained consciousness. Groggily asking what had happened and given a quick synopsis, the most gruesome details left out.

"I was... was kind of aware when it had a hold of me." Chris was sitting up and passing a bottle of water back and forth with Stander. Lucas, chugging one of his own, paced anxiously as he listened. He'd been advocating for a quick departure but Chris kept waving him off. "I could feel, like really feel the thing's excitement when it found that decorative piece from our ancient rock God or whatever that huge statue is supposed to represent." Chris waved a weak hand towards the monolith. "It was like it smelled it on me."

"Like you said, that was our good luck charm. If that bloodsucker hadn't found it and been so enthralled, I'm not sure we'd still be alive. We were lucky. Now," Stander stood and reached for Chris, "let's get you to a hospital." But Chris ignored the offered hand.

"We can't leave." Chris looked up at Stander as Lucas began objecting from across the room. "Don't ask me how I know. But we can't let that thing keep what it stole from me."

"What the fuck are you talking about. That thing out there," Stander poked an angry finger at the steel door, "can keep every stone in this hellhole for all I care."

"Are you just worried about the electrician?" Lucas, an exasperated look on his face and holding a wad of bandages to the cut above his eye, stood beside Stander. "As soon as we get a cell signal, I'll be notifying the authorities. The police can find her and deal with the cannibal corpse roaming these dark tunnels a whole lot easier than we ever could." But Chris was already shaking his head no before Lucas had stopped talking.

"You don't understand." Chris turned his pleading eyes to Stander. "Those stones. These pieces of meteorite, or wherever the bits of iridium and obsidian came from that adorn our big friend over there," Chris gesturing once again to the partially unearthed statue, "are powerful. Even that little golf ball sized chunk gave that monster a surge. I could feel it."

Stander sighed heavily. He flashed back to the power he'd felt when first holding a decorative piece recovered out of a 1,000-year-old burial cave in Michigan. The eerie obsidian stone now secreted away in his safe back at home. The strange rock had turned out to be an exact match to the shiny black stone of the same material still adorning the pupil of the massive statue next door. He recalled how both he and Secrist had watched Liz vanish using the power it somehow held within. As incredible as it sounded, deep down he had no doubt what Chris said was the truth.

"There are minerals and rocks that retain magnetization and have been proven to hold a charge. Even in our oceans, miles below the surface, there are fields of rocks called polymetallic nodules. They contain nickel, copper, cobalt, and manganese. Same stuff many batteries are made out of. But the effect is weak and unstable." Though he was agreeing in principle with what Chris said he felt, Lucas looked doubtful.

"See! Exactly what I was saying!" Chris turned to Stander with pleading eyes. "What if that thing gets a hold of more pieces? Or that big black one inside the eye? If what Lucas and I are saying is correct, who knows how powerful it could become?" Chris paused briefly in thought before continuing. "What if it escapes the quarry? We'd be responsible for what happened."

"Correlation is not causation." Lucas, unconvinced, stepped towards the exit that led back to the surface, car keys in hand.

"I can't explain why or how I know. But I think these special stones, whether first rained down as meteorites or somehow shaped and blessed or cursed, affect people differently." Chris's eyes were unfocused as he spoke, his stare unseeing. "Maybe some of us can use them for protection or defense. But I think maybe the worst of us are drawn to them as well. But, almost like radiation leaking from a nuclear missile, the awesome power held within can contaminate and corrupt." Chris met Stander's eyes. "Maybe turn someone predisposed to violence into a monster. For real!"

"But only massive sulphides and graphite-bearing rocks are truly conductive. That is not what the ornaments on our big friend next door are made from." Lucas looked from Chris to Stander. "There is no scientific proof of anything Chris is theorizing."

"A hundred years ago was there proof of anything you just said?" Stander pinning Lucas with his eyes.

Lucas snorted once but shook his head wryly. "No. It would have sounded crazy."

"Exactly. So, we can 'humor' Chris then, right?" Stander did air quotes and winked at Chris when he'd said humor. "Put science to the test."

"You are both certifiable." Lucas exhaled, "Fine! Go grab one of the... Putain! Fuck! Not that one!"

Stander ignored the protest. Using the tip of the sword to pry the jet-black pupil from the eye of the primordial statue. Owning the carved jewel's twin back in Michigan, he'd known right where to apply a bit of leverage. "This is the best bait we've got." Stander turned to face them, the cantaloupe-sized carved stone in his hand. "See if we can lead the wolf right to our offer."

CHAPTER TWENTY-SEVEN

Stander laid the black stone on the ground two yards outside the steel door. He stepped back one yard to join Chris and Lucas just outside the opened doorway. He thought he felt his phone alert him that he'd received a text, then another two in quick succession but he ignored them. Long seconds ticked past. Now nine, now ten when, "Ssshhhh!" Chris, weak and unsteady from his earlier attack, swung his finger clumsily and coated it with his spit. "What is that…"

"Relax," Stander exhaled. "That is the swarming colony of bats again. Quick," he waved his arm at the entrance, "we'll step back inside until they…"

"That's no bat!" For a split-second Lucas, both pupils blown in fright, locked his eyes on Stander before they beseeched him to look elsewhere. All three men turning towards the growing rumble from out of the bowels of the quarry. The site forever seared into their minds. Like the childhood jolt of innocently exposing your naked eye to the backlit opening of a tube and seeing a long-limbed spider scurrying to touch your face.

Such was their fright.

Like a luminescent behemoth rising out of the deepest depths of our oceans, the squirming mass accelerated towards them through the tunnel lit by a throbbing, blue-tinted glow. Propelled forward by a mass of writhing tentacles that slid and twisted along the ribbed walls and carved ceiling with ease. Each arm slick with a drool-like ooze that dripped from the clacking mouths at the center of each sucker. The sharp beaks ripping huge chunks of rock and soil as each limb crawled forward.

Ever closer.

The head was a mass so bloated by gluttony it was nearly unrecognizable. Nearly. Gore dripped from the vampire's gnashing teeth. Sinewy strands of red meat mixed with gristle and bone. A human hand, tethered only by cartilage, flopped ridiculously near one ear. The head was hairless and the face without expression. The features and lines that give the wretched face character all bulging and straining the flesh. The creature had become featureless.

A faceless disciple of Mithras.

Stander dove for the shiny black stone and felt it pulse once as he pulled it to his chest. He scrambled through the doorway and nearly bowled Chris over as Lucas slammed the steel door shut. The door locking automatically upon closing. Stander tossing the stone onto a padded office chair as his phone received another unheeded text.

BOOM!

The steel door and jam thundered and shook. Dirt and rocks skidding down the side of the cavern. Dust fouling the air.

BOOM!

Repeatedly ramming the door, the metal doorframe – bolted directly into the rock wall – began to bow inward slightly.

"Little pig, little pig. Let me in! Or I'll..."

"Blow me!" Stander retorted, his voice confident but his eyes unsure. More quietly he yelled to Lucas, "We need to run! Get to the surface and regroup or..." Stander pulled his phone. He'd felt the text alerts, could he make a call? But although he now showed a series of unread text messages from Secrist had arrived, there was no signal. He quickly opened the first message. It was a picture of a handwritten note. Or, as Stander quickly skimmed the words, maybe a letter. Confused, but trusting in Secrist, he read the photographed page.

In desperation, I threw the fleshless head at the monster. But the errant, off-balance heave sent the skull sailing harmlessly past both the vampire and the bleeding boy. Landing just beyond them, near the throbbing stone before rolling back down the mound of the dead. The slow roll ending when it connected with the oddly etched sword. Bone barely kissing the steel blade.

The vampire lurched half a step before again toppling. A seizure grabbing him firmly in its grasp once more. Imprisoning the monster inside itself as, on the outside, the body of the fiend seized and locked up. Struggling to my feet amid the rounded bones underfoot, I ignored my rifle this time and ran for the sword. I pulled the blade from its last victim. The odd hum of the steel increasing as it clanged against the hard bone from which I withdrew it. Returning to the side of the prostrate vampire, a shiver slipped down my neck as I ran the wretched thing through from behind. My desperate gamble either ending the undead life that animated this thing or my own...

Neither happened.

The screech that came out of the vampire's mouth was horrifically anguished and tortured. The agonized sound sweeter than any I'd ever heard before. The sound of real pain. No blood came from the bite of the blade, but obscenities soon began to pour from the fanged mouth. The fiend spewing them in various unrecognizable languages of which I could only guess their origin.

BOOM!

Stander watched the door shudder. He glanced back at the words he'd read. Obviously, this somehow referred to the monster at the door. But what was Secrist trying to tell him?

"What are you doing?" Lucas was screaming over the thundering noise as he helped Chris hurry to the exit. "That won't hold!" Chris suddenly pulled himself away and darted back to Stander's side. Stander opened the second text he'd received and then third. Reading each in quick succession.

"Use the sword!"

"Hit it!"

No shit, Tommy, Stander thought to himself. He'd sent Secrist a picture of the sword and his best advice is to use the blade?

BOOM!

One corner of the doorframe gave. An opening at the top the size of a man's fist that was instantly filled with a snake-like tentacle. The tip of it wrapping around Chris's bare arm and pulling him towards the doorway. Stander screamed in desperation for Lucas to help. Dropping his phone, the last text message from Secrist was opened by the brush of his thumb. The phone came to life as it tumbled to the ground. The iconic tune blaring from the phone's speaker.

"Well, you're slim and you're weak

You've got the teeth of the hydra upon you

You're dirty, sweet and you're my girl

Get it on, bang a gong, get it on

Get it on, bang a gong, get it on"

In an instant, Stander understood the meaning of Secrist's messages. He spun from Chris just as Lucas scrambled to his side. Sword in hand, Stander raised it above his head. Bringing it down with a grunt and slamming it against the steel door, hitting it dead center. The ensuing hum a resonance felt as much as heard. Felt deep down in your soul.

Such was the power of the tone.

The brief screech that followed from the far side of the door was equal in passion but not power. The tentacle grappling with Chris froze in an instant before beginning to waver like the mirage of a desert oasis. Seconds later splitting from the inside with enough force to coat much of the doorway in viscous white matter. The consistency and stench not unlike the rot found at the bottom of a seafood restaurant's alleyway dumpster.

The beautiful and harmonic pitch and timbre reverberating from the sword lasted long minutes. Even as it faded, you sensed the acoustics still working. Despite the horror they'd faced, smiles filled the faces of the three men. Stander, Chris, and Lucas nearly overwhelmed by emotion.

Then the rumble began.

Somewhere down the desolate passages of the quarry, walls began to give. Tunnels and passageways shuddering and collapsing. Much like an earthquake, the ground underfoot began to shake. Lucas, understanding the potential danger the honeycombed earth poised, moved quickly to lead Stander and Chris to safety. All three racing up the passage that led to the surface. Bursting from the door and spilling out into the early evening air of the French countryside as the rumbles slowly subsided.

Panting, Lucas spoke first. "Thank God we made it out!"

"Thank Marc-fucking-Bolan, you mean." Stander, his face puffy from the beating he'd taken, smiled wanly. "It actually makes a weird kind of sense to me. Glam rockers were some of my first heroes..."

Stander's phone rang. Incredulous, he answered the previously near useless device. It was Secrist shouting a series of questions and babbling something about his grandfather and a diary. Frazier barking in the background. When the verbal tirade finally slowed, Stander spoke.

"Tommy," he said, "start packing. You're coming over on the next plane to France..."

EPILOGUE
AMERICA, 1929

IT HAS BEEN DIFFICULT to reread this after so much time. The lone diary I kept during my last days as a soldier was written when I was barely out of my teens. A child even. For it's hard to think of myself as a man before I'd returned to the states after being discharged. The experiences I'd faced on the battlefields of the First World War maturing me far beyond my years. To say I came back a changed man belies the fact I'd left as a mere boy.

I remember very little after leaving the dark tunnels and caverns of the quarry. There are no memories I can call to mind from the time I'd left that black hole until waking in a make-shift infirmary far away from the frontlines. The cot at my side occupied by one of the soldiers I'd rescued.

He'd gone mad.

When calm, I questioned the man about what he'd seen, and how he found his way out of those dark passageways. Asking if the second soldier, H.P., had also managed to find his way out of that maze. But I got very little that made any sense from the skittish and damaged shell-of-a-man. His gibberish filled with denials and lies. Refuting what we'd experienced together and denying being held captive alongside a soldier named Howard Phillips.

Unfortunately, the meager medical staff offered me no further explanations. Saying only that I'd been exposed to poisonous gas and found wandering near the small French town of Vieux far from the frontlines. None of the nurses or frazzled doctors aware of any other men found with me. Or of the quarry that haunted my dreams. All my nights, terror filled unless I'd been given my medicine. Unsettled, discouraged, and every breath wracked with pain, I took comfort only in the elixir of opium they prescribed. Drifting away until I was troubled no more.

Though it has taken me years to come to grips with, I now believe it had been the robed men's chants, sacrifices, and devotions that brought me to the quarry. Commandeered even. Like a prayer miraculously answered, I'd delivered the ghastly cargo Mithras had demanded of his followers. For even if I'd driven that horse and cart night and day it seems unlikely I could have made such a distance. There had to have been some infernal intervention. And if I believe that to be true, how could I possibly destroy this account of my time? I hope by saving this journal and passing it on, my words may one day help another.

After initially waking in that field hospital, and coming back home once formally discharged weeks later, I lost the next ten years of my life. Crawling inside a bottle and doing my best to stay there until I had drowned. My newborn daughter was the only thing able to finally pull me from that pit of despair. But her mother, suffering and struggling to stay sober during the pregnancy same as I, left us once my little angel was born. And I know that even if I could find work here, I couldn't properly care for her. I'm only now beginning to take care of myself once more.

I have made arrangements with a small group of nuns and sisters that follow the teachings of St. Francis of Assisi. Their kindness and generosity all that kept me going this last year as I warred with myself and sobriety. They understand why I must leave my swaddled baby girl behind. Sister Judy, one of the kindest and most sincere people I've ever met, promising my daughter will be well cared for. Also swearing to me that this diary, along with a letter meant for only my daughter's eye, will be passed to her when she reaches maturity. I only hope she can one day forgive me for abandoning her, and achieves the wisdom needed to ensure this dark tome reaches eyes that can puzzle out the content. Someone who will benefit from my horror and pain.

In the morning, I head west. One of my mom's many older brothers – a mixed Native American like me that rode the rails for years before finally settling in Utah – has promised me a paying job. Saying the ranch he works on is expanding, and needs someone with both the skills of a ranch hand and a carpenter. The homestead, located in a basin bordering the Uintah and Ouray Indian Reservation, is supposedly cursed by the local tribes. But, after surviving years in the middle of a world of war, what could one tribe's hateful words mean to me?

It's not like the ranch out in Utah has Skinwalkers...

ALSO BY DM GRITZMACHER

The Relict

Skulldiggery Book 1

The Quarry

Skulldiggery Book 2

The Lingering

Skulldiggery Book 3

The Shroud

Skulldiggery Book 4

The Trench

Skulldiggery Book 5

Coming Soon!

The Shrine-Skulldiggery Book 6